STACY M. JONES

The Witches Code

First edition

ISBN: 9798748179171

This book was professionally typeset on Reedsy.
Find out more at reedsy.com

For Maria P. for teaching me all things tarot

Acknowledgement

The Witches Code would not have been created without a wonderful creative team working with me. A special thanks to 17 Studio Book Design for the great cover, and Dj Hendrickson for her invaluable editing and suggestions. Thanks to Liza Wood for proofreading and revisions. A special thanks to all of the magical women who have shared their knowledge with me about tarots, crystals, ghosts, and spells.

Chapter One

Hattie Beauregard-Ryan yawned in the backseat of the SUV. Retired Army Colonel Jackson Morris, Hattie's neighbor and friend, had driven her and her niece, Harper Ryan, back from a trip to New Orleans. It was nearing ten in the evening and exhaustion had dulled Hattie's senses hours ago.

As they drove up the road and neared the house, Hattie thought she was seeing things. She blinked three times and adjusted her eyes. A hunched-over woman sat on Jackson's stoop.

"Who is that sitting on your front stoop, Jackson?" she asked, stifling another yawn.

"I saw her," was his only response. He pulled into Hattie's driveway and shut off the car.

Harper, who was also Jackson's girlfriend, reached over and placed her hand on his thigh. "Is it Cora?"

Jackson sighed loudly. "I swear I have no idea why my ex-wife is sitting on my stoop. I haven't returned a call or text in months, especially since she told me she arrived in Little Rock."

"I'm not worried about that," Harper reassured. "I'm worried about you dealing with her alone. I know she's a handful. If you want Hattie and me to go over to your house with you, all you have to do is ask. If it's better we leave you to it, we can do that, too."

Jackson sat back in the driver's seat and rubbed his eyes. "I don't want you to have to deal with my drama."

Hattie reached her hand up through the space between the two front seats and rubbed his shoulder. "You went to New Orleans with us. We made you fight demons and deal with that crazy exorcist priest all to help my friend. I think we owe you one."

Jackson let out a soft chuckle. "Can we never mention demons or the exorcist priest again?"

Harper turned and caught Hattie's eye. "I told you it was going to be too much for him."

Jackson opened the car door and put his feet on the pavement. "Come with me, and let's get this over with." He went around to the back of the SUV and pulled out his luggage.

Harper and Hattie both got out and came around to help him. "Let's leave our bags right here. We can go with you and then we'll take our things into the house later," Hattie said.

Jackson agreed and he carried his bag across the street and up his driveway toward the front of his house. As he got close to the front porch, he grumbled, "Cora, what are you doing here?"

The woman stood and threw her arms around him, attempting to kiss him on the lips. "Oh baby, I've missed you."

Harper and Hattie stepped back and shared a look. Jackson dropped his bag and put his hands on Cora's shoulders to move her back from him. He did so gently, but it was clear to Hattie he wasn't having any of it.

"Enough, Cora," he said firmly.

The woman stood defiant and peered around him. She sneered at them. "Who are they?"

Jackson reached out for Harper's hand. "This is my girlfriend, Harper, and her Aunt Hattie, who lives across the street. Hattie has been one of my best friends since moving to Little Rock. You'll be respectful of them."

Hattie had never heard the tone that Jackson spoke with now. He was always so easygoing with both her and Harper. Jackson could be a pushover at times when it came to them both. She liked this new tougher side to him but was glad he'd never had to use it with them.

Cora didn't say anything. She peered around Jackson and looked Harper over from head to toe, sneering at her the entire time. The two women couldn't have looked more different. Harper had a trim figure, honey-blonde hair, and looked younger than her forty-one years. She was nearly as tall as Jackson who stood about five-foot-nine.

Hattie had no idea how old Cora was, but if she met her on the street, she would have thought well over fifty. Her long black witchy hair went to the middle of her back and had no style or shine. It didn't do her any favors. Neither did the deep-set lines on her face. From the few stories Jackson had told her about how Cora treated him during their marriage, Hattie knew the saying was true – evil ages you.

Jackson picked up his bag and headed for the door. "Let's go inside and the four of us can talk."

Cora stood still with her arms folded over her chest. "I don't want them here. Send them home."

Jackson's only response was to step up onto the porch and unlock the front door. He pushed it open and reached inside and flicked on the front light. That's when Hattie saw it and so did Harper, who gasped at the sight. Streaks of blood covered the woman's pant legs and the lower half of her shirt.

"Cora, are you hurt?" Hattie asked, alarmed.

"I'm not talking about this in front of you," she snipped.

"Stop it or you can leave," Jackson warned. "Get in the house."

The four of them walked into Jackson's living room. It was only then that he saw the blood.

"What happened?" Cora refused to respond. "Fine, then you can leave." Jackson walked back toward the door and held it open for her.

He glanced back when she didn't move. "Cora, I'm done playing around with you. We are divorced. You don't have a right to be here. If you want something, you're going to have to tell me or you can go. Those are your only options."

Cora locked eyes with him, but Jackson didn't relent. She glanced over at Hattie and Harper who weren't budging either. Hattie wasn't leaving this woman alone with Jackson. That wasn't going to happen on her watch. Hattie didn't like to judge anyone, but even if she hadn't heard stories from Jackson, she didn't like Cora's vibe.

Finally, Cora relented and let her arms fall to her side. Tears rolled down her face. "There was a man who attacked me at the hotel where I'm staying. He barged into my room and attacked me."

"Whose blood is that?" Jackson asked.

"It's his. I fought with him and stabbed him with a letter opener."

Jackson shook his head like he wasn't hearing the story right. "You did what?"

"That's why I'm here. I need your help. I think I killed the man."

Harper let out a gasp. "We have to call Det. Tyson Granger."

"No, Jackson. No police. I figured you'd help me." She went over to him and reached for his hand, which he refused to allow.

Jackson's eyes got wide. "Help you do what, Cora? Hide a body? Help you get away with killing someone? I've helped you out of a lot of jams in the time we've known each other, but this goes beyond anything I can help you with."

"Fine. I'm leaving then," she said and headed for the door. "I'll get someone else to help me."

Harper stepped in front of her and blocked the doorway. "You're not leaving. You can't come here and say you might have killed a man and then walk out. That's not how this is going to work."

Cora's temper flared and Hattie worried the woman might attack Harper, who stood her ground. Cora dodged to the right and so did

Harper. She moved to the left and Harper followed.

Cora stood with her hands on her hips. "You can't stop me. You also can't stop me from getting Jackson back so you might as well get out of my way now."

"That's never going to happen, Cora," Harper said and then looked to her aunt. "Call Det. Granger."

"No!" Cora yelled so loudly the whole neighborhood could have heard her.

"Scream all you want." Harper stood, blocking the door. "You are not going to show up here and implicate us all in a murder. Over my dead body will Jackson or any one of us be charged with accessory to a crime."

"All Jackson has to do is come with me and it will all get sorted."

"I'm not going with you," Jackson said, walking over to Harper and standing next to her. "Harper's right, you're not leaving until Det. Granger gets here."

Hattie pulled her phone from the pocket on her skirt and found Det. Granger's number. It was late and she hoped she wasn't disturbing his sleep. He answered on the second ring.

"Hattie, are you okay?" he asked.

"Det. Granger, we got back from New Orleans and found Jackson's ex-wife sitting on his stoop. She is covered in blood and admitted she might have killed a man after he attacked her in her hotel room."

Det. Granger groaned loudly. "You two can't stay out of trouble. I'll be right there."

Hattie hung up and turned to Jackson and Harper. "He will be here soon."

Cora stamped her feet and threw herself on the floor in a heap. Hattie had never seen a grown woman throw a tantrum like a toddler but that's exactly what Cora was doing. Hattie couldn't even picture how Jackson had ever been married to the woman.

Chapter Two

Harper refused to leave Jackson's side even after Det. Granger arrived. Hattie had gone home after she made the call and was assured that she and Jackson would be fine remaining with Cora. It was clear by the look her aunt had given her that Hattie didn't trust Cora any more than Harper did – which was not at all.

Harper's only focus was to make sure Jackson was okay. He had paced around the living room and muttered to himself what a catastrophe this was. No matter what Harper said, she couldn't calm him down. Harper wasn't buying Cora's story. There was something that wasn't adding up. The blood on Cora's pants and shirt had already dried. That meant some significant time had passed since the incident.

When Det. Granger finally arrived, he asked to speak to Cora alone. Jackson walked them to his downstairs home office and shut the door so they could speak privately. They remained in there for more than an hour.

"Do you believe her?" Jackson finally asked after a long while.

"Would I be a horrible person if I said no?" Harper offered him a sympathetic smile.

"You'd be a sane and rational person. I don't believe her either. I want Det. Granger to hear the story firsthand and make his own determination before I tell him that Cora is a liar and manipulator. In the entire time I've known her, I've never known her to be truthful. It's like she's allergic to the truth. She'll tell whatever story puts her in the best light or say what she thinks will manipulate someone to give her what she wants."

Jackson dropped the frustrated tone and looked over at Harper. "I appreciate you being here, but this is mortifying for me."

"There's no reason to be embarrassed. You know my ex-husband, Nick, called me while we were in New Orleans and said he was out of prison and on his way to Little Rock to speak to me." Harper sat back and sighed. "Let's just admit it right here and right now. We both made bad marital choices."

Jackson laughed. "That's the understatement of the century."

The sound of Jackson's office door creaking open echoed in the living room. Det. Granger walked out with Cora, who had her head down and wouldn't make eye contact with anyone.

"Harper, I need to take Cora's clothing as evidence. We're going down to the hotel to check the scene. Do you have any clothes she can borrow?"

Harper wanted to explain that nothing she had would fit Cora who was significantly heavier, but there would be no point making the situation worse. She stood. "Let me go home and find something."

Det. Granger turned to Jackson. "Cora would like you to come down to the hotel with us. I'm not going to be able to let either of you in the room while I assess the scene, but I'll allow you there for moral support. Harper, too, if she'd like to go."

"I don't want her there," Cora said.

"If you want me there, you're getting Harper, too." Jackson's tone didn't leave any room to negotiate.

Harper left quickly and ran over to the house. She called out for Hattie as she walked in the door. Hattie called back that she was upstairs in her bedroom unpacking. Harper raced up the steps and down the hall toward the back of the house to Hattie's bedroom.

7

Harper explained the situation and the plan with Det. Granger. "I need some clothes for Cora. Det. Granger has to take hers into evidence."

Hattie pointed to the closet. "Your clothes will be too small, Harper, but I have some shirts and pants that might work."

Harper rushed to the closet and began pulling out items. Hattie chuckled behind her. "Remember the witches code. Do no harm. That means do not pick something hideous as much as you'd like to."

Harper turned back to her aunt. "You know me too well. I wish I had your talents. I'd have already turned her into a toad."

Hattie smiled and shook her head. "That's not a thing."

"I wish it was." Harper found an old pair of jeans Hattie probably hadn't worn in twenty years and a green pullover shirt. "Will this work?"

"I think that's perfect." Hattie went over to her niece and hugged her. "Don't stress yourself over this. It isn't your responsibility or Jackson's. Be there as support for Jackson, but don't take this on as your own."

Harper would try to heed her aunt's advice and raced back to Jackson's. She walked in and found them all in the same place she left them. Harper handed the clothes to Cora who didn't say thank you or even acknowledge Harper. Jackson told her the bathroom was down the hall and across from the office.

When Cora was gone, Jackson asked, "Did she really kill a guy?"

Det. Granger rubbed a hand over his head. "I don't know. Her story doesn't make a lot of sense, and she's been driving your sister crazy over the last week. Sarah has been too busy running Hattie's shop to deal with her."

"Who attacked her?" Harper asked.

"I can't make heads or tails of it. Cora said she heard a knock on her door and there was a man. He rushed into the room and attacked her. She said she didn't know him. She said they struggled, she stabbed him and left him dead on the hotel room floor."

Jackson turned his head in the direction of the hall to make sure Cora wasn't out of the bathroom yet. "She told us she stabbed him with a letter opener, but there's too much blood for that."

"I agree. We aren't going to know anything until we are at the scene. I have a team on stand-by. I already checked her pants pocket and searched her but found nothing. I told her to leave the clothing in the bathroom and I'd get an evidence bag." With that, Det. Granger headed out to his car.

Jackson turned to Harper. "You don't have to go with us to the hotel. I know you're probably exhausted."

"I'm going. Her story doesn't add up. I don't want you to go on your own. Hattie reminded me that this isn't our issue and not to take it on."

"You think it's going to be as simple as that?" Jackson looked at her skeptically.

She shrugged. "No, but it's a good reminder."

Det. Granger returned and went to the bathroom door and knocked. He collected Cora's clothing and returned to the living room. "Cora can drive down with me and Jackson and Harper will follow in their own car."

Cora started to protest but one look from Det. Granger and she closed her mouth. Harper assumed he had that effect on most people. He was the biggest detective she'd ever seen. His arm muscles strained nearly every shirt he had. Harper was fairly certain he could bench press a bus. He was a softie though, once you got to know him. Sarah, who had been dating him for several months, said he was a closet romantic, which made Harper giggle at the time. She couldn't picture it.

The four of them left Jackson's house and headed for the Marriott in downtown Little Rock. The hotel sat along the Arkansas River and was just a few steps down from the Old State House Museum.

Once there, Det. Granger escorted Cora through the lobby with

Jackson and Harper following. They didn't alert anyone at the desk yet because Det. Granger wanted to assess the scene and figure out next steps. They took the elevator to the fifth floor and went down the hall to the room where Cora indicated the incident happened.

Harper couldn't help but notice that Cora had remained calm and didn't seem afraid. She talked amicably with Det. Granger and, some might think, even flirted with him. He remained immune to the charm she thought she had.

Det. Granger motioned for them to stay in the hall. He pulled gloves from his back pocket and snapped them on. He took the keycard from Cora and, unlocking the door, stepped inside.

Harper, Jackson, and Cora stood in the hall in silence as they waited. Cora leaned against the wall with her arms folded over her chest. A few minutes later, Det. Granger stepped out of the room.

"Are you sure he was dead when you left him?" Det. Granger asked.

Cora blinked rapidly. "I don't know. I ran out as soon as I could."

Det. Granger shifted his eyes to Jackson and Harper and opened the door behind him so they could all see. "There's no body and no blood anywhere. It doesn't even look like a struggle happened here."

Jackson cursed under his breath and turned to Cora with anger in his eyes. "What kind of game are you playing now?"

Chapter Three

The next morning Hattie woke to the smell of fresh coffee brewing and the sounds of conversation from downstairs. Harper and Jackson were discussing something Hattie couldn't quite understand only hearing a word here and there. She had gone to bed well before Harper had arrived home, so she was eager to get downstairs and find out what had happened with Cora.

Hattie made herself presentable and went down to join them. She found Harper and Jackson at the kitchen table eating bacon, eggs, and toast.

"I want to hear all about what happened last night," she said as she entered the kitchen, which was situated in the back of the house. She helped herself to the leftover bacon and eggs in the pan and poured some coffee. She carried her breakfast to the table and sat down with them. Both Harper and Jackson looked like they hadn't had much sleep. "Don't keep me in suspense. Where is Cora?"

Finishing a bit of egg, Harper explained, "She is in another hotel right now."

"Det. Granger didn't arrest her?" Hattie asked, surprised.

"No body," Jackson said. "We got to her hotel room and there was no body in her room. There was no blood. Det. Granger said it didn't even look like a struggle had occurred. He went down and watched the surveillance video and saw Cora walking out of her room with the clothes she had on last night, minus the blood."

Hattie scrunched up her face and shook her head. "That makes absolutely no sense. Was it a ploy for attention?"

"Probably." Jackson rested his head in his hands. "Cora has always done this so I shouldn't be surprised."

Harper took a sip of her coffee. "That doesn't explain where the blood came from. I know Cora has done things for attention, but she had blood all over her. That came from someplace."

"You said last night Det. Granger took her clothes. Will they test it to see if the blood is human?"

"Yes," Harper said. "Det. Granger told her not to leave town, but he couldn't make an arrest or anything until he knew a crime had been committed. We all knew she was lying, but what we don't know is if there's any truth to what she said. Maybe she was attacked someplace else."

Jackson shook his head. "It's all dramatics. I'd bet you money right now that nothing happened to her. She has always done this to play on my sympathies and manipulate me into helping her. Not this time. Cora can handle her mess – whatever the mess might be. I'm not interested."

Jackson got up and carried his dishes to the sink and rinsed them off. He turned back to Harper and Hattie. "I'm heading back home. I have a work call and a few things I need to get done." He walked over and kissed Harper before he left.

After the back porch door closed, Hattie focused on Harper. "How is he doing?"

"About as well as can be expected." Harper locked eyes with her aunt. "Jackson is angry, probably angrier than I've ever seen him. I didn't know he could get that angry. He is always so mellow and low-key with us."

"I noticed that last night. He's been through a lot with Cora and that anger and resentment builds up over time." Hattie took a bite of her eggs and popped a piece of well-done bacon in her mouth. "When I get to the shop today, I'll pull some cards on the situation and see what I can figure out."

Relief washed over Harper's face. "There was a time when I didn't think your gifts were valuable. Now, I don't know what I'd do without them." Harper got up and wrapped her arms around Hattie's shoulders and kissed her on the cheek.

Hattie patted her arm. "Don't forget you have gifts of your own. If you can get ahold of Cora's clothes from last night you might be able to touch them and use your psychometry gift to see if you can pick up an imprint. A vision of what Cora was doing when she wore them might give you more insight than my cards."

"I can try but I'm not sure Det. Granger will allow it." Harper carried her dishes over to the sink.

"Is there a reason you didn't try that last night?"

Harper turned back and looked at Hattie. "It didn't even occur to me. I'm not used to having this gift and sometimes I forget."

"Is there a chance you didn't want to do it in front of Cora?" Hattie assumed that's why Harper didn't tap into a vision last night. When Harper didn't respond, Hattie said, "You know, even for as many years as I've done this, when I'm outside of the shop, sometimes I still get nervous about letting people know about my gift. You open yourself up to judgment, and that's not always easy."

Harper walked back over to the table and sat down. "That might have been part of it. It wasn't so much about Cora, but I didn't want to embarrass Jackson. It's obvious Cora and I will never get along and I didn't want to give her any ammunition to use against him."

Hattie smiled. "I think you need to talk to Jackson about that. I'm sure he will understand and reassure you." Hattie paused not sure she should ask the next question given how stressed and tired Harper appeared. "I don't want to add more stress to your plate, but have you heard from Nick?"

"I can't deal with him right now. He's called and left me messages and then texted me. He is in Little Rock someplace and has asked a few times to come over and speak to me. I have no desire to see him."

Harper took Hattie's plate from the table and the pans from the stove and put them in the sink. She stood there washing the dishes and left them in the drainboard to dry. Hattie wasn't sure what to say to her, but it was obvious from Harper's pained expression that she was struggling with Cora and Nick.

When she was done, Harper grabbed her bag and headed out the door for work at *Rock City Life Magazine*, where she had been helping run the local lifestyle magazine for more than a year now. She had been the editor-in-chief of Ryan family magazine *Charlotte*, which had gained international fame in its more than one-hundred-year history. That was all before Harper's life fell apart and Hattie's brother and Harper's father, Max, had fired her. It happened at the same time Harper's husband, Nick, had been implicated in financial crimes tied to the mob and had cheated on her, getting his mistress pregnant.

Hattie sipped her coffee thinking about all that had transpired over Harper's life in the last couple of years. She had no idea how Harper had made it through. The best thing Harper did was move to live with Hattie, but even she couldn't help her niece as events of the past reared their ugly head. Hattie needed insight and there was no better place to get it than at her shop.

Hattie finished getting ready for the day and walked the few blocks to Hattie's Cauldron: Potions & Pastries, which sat on Kavanaugh Boulevard in the Heights neighborhood of Little Rock. Hattie had run the shop on her own for many years. About two years ago, when business boomed, she had hired a college-aged assistant, Beatrix, who reminded Hattie of herself at that age.

Last year, Jackson's sister, Sarah, had come to work for her, too. Sarah had even better mediumship skills than Hattie but remained hesitant to read for paying customers. Hattie hoped that would change, but she wasn't going to push.

Hattie crossed the road and entered her shop. The smell of freshly brewed coffee and chocolate croissants hit her nose. "It's so good to be back!" Hattie yelled from the door with her arms open wide as if hugging the whole room.

"We've missed you!" Sarah called from behind the counter as she poured tea into cups on a tray. She arranged several pastries next to the cups and carried the tray over to a group of older women who were regulars at the shop.

Hattie put her things behind the counter and glanced at the appointment calendar of readings that had been scheduled. She scanned down the list. Five one-hour readings today. "That will take up nearly my whole day."

Sarah came back around the corner and looped her arm around Hattie's shoulders. "I'm sorry. People are clamoring to get here to speak with you. You have a few full weeks in front of you, but the rest of the week it's four readings a day and not all are an hour. Some are thirty minutes."

Hattie tapped at the book and smiled. "Can you believe there was a time not too long ago I wondered if the shop would survive?"

"That's hard to believe. While you were gone, both Beatrix and I have been working together because it's been too busy for just one of us. I reordered supplies, too. All the crystals and gemstones need to be replenished and the Reiki candles sold out the day after the last shipment came in. The baker has been working overtime to keep up with the demand."

Hattie turned to the back counter and made herself some lavender tea. "Have there been any issues with the shop or the dogs while I was gone?"

Sarah had been watching Hattie's two Golden Retrievers, Sparkle and Shine, while she was away, which thrilled Sarah's daughter.

"The dogs were perfect. I don't think Anabella is going to want to give them back. The shop has been busy but all running smoothly." Sarah sighed.

"You sound like something didn't go well."

Sarah leaned on the counter and looked up at Hattie. "Cora has been a nightmare to deal with. She came into the shop each day asking why Jackson hadn't called her back and trying to pry information from me about his life. She wants him back and will do anything to make that happen." Sarah told Hattie that she had heard about the events of last night from Det. Granger. "I'm worried for Jackson and Harper."

Hattie finished making her tea and took a sip. She looked over the rim of the cup. "I'm worried about them, too."

A look of surprise came over Sarah's face. "You never get worried."

"I know." Hattie took her tea and headed for her reading room.

Chapter Four

Harper stopped at the deli below her office in downtown Little Rock and grabbed a sandwich and coffees for herself and Dan Barnes, her business partner. As she climbed the stairs to the office, her mind filled with work needed for the next edition of the magazine. She hoped Dan had made some progress while she was away.

He had texted Harper and told her that the article she had written on the best places to see the real New Orleans had garnered serious attention on the website and social media. Dan had encouraged her to write more articles like it.

Harper hit the landing of the loft space and almost ran right into Dan. She handed a coffee and sandwich to him. "Thanks for giving me the break last week."

Dan laughed. "Break? You wrote us one of the best articles we've ever had. I think we should stop paying freelancers and let you write the magazine for us."

Harper stepped around him and headed for her office. "I have no desire to be the primary writer. I thought you brought me on for strategic direction."

Dan followed behind her. "I wouldn't go in your office if I were you."

Harper turned on her heels and faced him, fearing the worst. Dan had no design taste whatsoever. "What did you do to my office while I was away?"

Dan spoke quietly. "It's not what I did. A man claiming to be your ex-husband showed up about fifteen minutes ago. I was just on my way out of the office to call you from my cell so he couldn't hear me when you showed up."

Harper let out a string of soft curses and debated leaving the office altogether. She couldn't deal with Nick Warren right now.

Dan laughed at her. "I take it this isn't a social call?"

Harper shook his head. "He is out of prison, got a mob boss's daughter pregnant while we were still married, and tried to have me killed. It's not a social call."

"I never tried to have you killed," Nick said, standing in the doorway to Harper's office.

Harper closed her eyes and took a few deep breaths before turning to face him. "You and I have always had different perspectives, Nick. Why are you here?"

He had lost weight in prison and his dark hair had grayed in spots. His face, though, had remained as handsome as the day they married. Harper felt nothing for him – no disgust or hatred and certainly no traces of regret or love. She had achieved total indifference to him.

"We need to talk. Alone." Nick motioned for Harper to step into her office.

Harper laughed. "No, Nick. You no longer have the right to demand anything from me."

"Harper, please don't test me. I've had a trying few weeks."

"I don't care. You shouldn't even be here." Harper's voice remained calm and steady. Dan walked toward his office but turned back to make sure Harper was going to be okay.

Harper nodded once and then walked toward Nick. "You need to go." Harper entered her office, put her bag on the floor, and set the coffee cup on top of the desk. She slid into her chair. "I'm just getting back from New Orleans and have a lot to do. I'm going to ask one more time before I kick you out. Why are you here?"

Nick remained standing and looked down at Harper. "You have something I need."

"What would that be?"

"If you sold it, you need to give me the money."

Harper sat back in her chair and raised her eyes to him. "Sold it? What are you talking about? What money?" She had no idea what he was going on about.

Nick slammed the door shut and turned to her. "I know you found it, Harper. After I was arrested, you were the only one in our penthouse. The necklace was in the safe under the floorboards in my office."

Harper had no idea what Nick was talking about. She had never found any safe in his home office nor did she take any necklace. Had she found the safe, she would have turned over the contents to the FBI who had been investigating Nick at the time.

She narrowed her eyes at him. "The FBI and New York State Police did a thorough search of the place when you were arrested. I never heard mention of a safe in your office. I sold the penthouse shortly after you were sentenced. I left for Little Rock as soon as I cleared out. It sold within days. Have you checked with the new owners?"

Nick smirked at her. "Yes. I checked with the new owners. I explained there was a safe in the floorboards and I left some important documents there. They knew nothing about the safe, but when I pulled up the floorboards and put in the security code, imagine my surprise when the safe was empty. Where is it, Harper?"

"Nick, I have no idea what you're talking about. I never knew there was a safe in your office, and I certainly didn't steal any necklace."

Nick ran a hand through his hair. "I need it back now. Stop playing games."

"Who did the necklace belong to, Nick?"

19

Nick sat down in the chair across from Harper. "I just need to know what you did with the contents of the safe."

"Nick, I'm telling you for the last time, I never knew the safe was there. I don't think I stepped foot in your office after you were arrested. I hated everything you did to me and couldn't wait to get rid of every reminder of you."

Nick sat back and crossed his arms over his chest. "I know you're angry. That's why you're trying to get back at me now."

Harper blew out a breath. "Don't flatter yourself. I was angry at you for months after the divorce and had every right to be. Right now, I don't care about you at all. I don't even care enough to make you angry or to upset you."

"This is serious, Harper. More than you know."

"It's not my problem."

Nick stood and shoved his chair back as he did. "This is going to be your problem. I'll make it your problem."

Harper leaned forward. "Don't threaten me. We both know I didn't take anything. I'm not the thief, you are." Harper stood and walked around her desk toward him. "You need to get out of my office right now or I'll call the police. I don't want you anywhere near me again."

Nick shook his head and raged. He glared down at her. "I'm not leaving town until I get what I came for. Harper, I want those diamonds back now!"

Harper looked at him like he'd lost his mind. "A minute ago, you said a necklace. Now it's diamonds. Did you have loose diamonds in that safe or a necklace made of diamonds?"

"Both," he said in a frustrated breath. "It's an emerald necklace that originally belonged to some princess in Russia and is worth more than four million. The diamonds are worth ten million. None of it belongs to me."

Harper took a step toward him and looked Nick dead in the eyes. "I don't have any of it. Who does it belong to?"

"Carmine De Luca."

"Where did he get it from?"

Nick glared at Harper not saying a word.

Harper sighed, knowing she would only get half the truth. "Carmine is in prison, Nick. With his conviction, he'll die in prison. You have nothing to worry about."

"You know nothing, Harper. Just because the boss is behind bars doesn't mean the family isn't still active. His son, Marco, has taken over. I have a week to bring the jewels back to him." Nick closed his eyes. "You know what's going to happen to me if I don't."

Harper wasn't sure if he was being dramatic or serious. "Aren't you married to Lola? How's your baby? Would Marco kill his brother-in-law?"

"Marco is more ruthless than Carmine ever was. Lola and I got married the week I got out of prison and my daughter is fine. Marco is still going to kill me."

Harper hadn't known until that moment that Nick and Lola had a girl. "I'm glad your daughter is doing well. I still don't know what to tell you. I didn't take those jewels."

"I don't believe you, Harper. You're the only one that had access."

"It's been close to two years since I lived in that penthouse. There have been many people that had access." Harper looked at Nick. "Even if I knew the safe was there, which I didn't, I wouldn't have known the combination to open it."

"It was our anniversary date." Nick ran his hand through his hair. "Harper, you have to agree to help me. If you don't, I'm going to force you and you're not going to like that one bit."

They stood locked in a standoff. The only thing that broke it was a knock on the door. Harper glared at Nick as she opened it. Det. Granger stood there, his massive width taking up the doorway. Harper had never been so happy to see him.

"I didn't mean to interrupt," Det. Granger said. He stepped into the office and saw Nick. "I can come back."

"Good. We are in the middle of something," Nick said.

Harper smiled at Det. Granger. "Please come in, Det. Granger. Nick was just leaving."

Nick's eyes shifted over the detective, who wore his badge around his neck and gun at his hip. Harper raised her eyebrows. "I'm sure Det. Granger might be interested in our conversation."

"I'm going," Nick said stiffly. "I'll be back, Harper. This conversation isn't over. I meant what I said." With that, he stormed out of her office and through the loft space to the stairs.

After Nick was gone, Harper went to her desk and Det. Granger sat down across from her. "You want to tell me what that was about?" he asked, his voice tense and serious.

Chapter Five

Harper took a deep breath and let it out slowly. She repeated the slow breathing three more times to calm down. She may not care about him anymore but he certainly changed the energy of a room.

"Det. Granger, you just had the displeasure of meeting my ex-husband."

"That was your ex-husband?" he asked, surprised. "He seemed shady and slick. I can't believe you were married to him. You must not have had good taste back then."

Harper tipped her head back and laughed. Det. Granger knew her well enough to tease her like that. "You're right, but we all make bad choices at some point or another. He's the one I turned over to the FBI and sent to prison. The sentence was supposed to be longer, but somehow, he got out on good behavior."

"If I'm not being too nosey, why is he here? He seemed angry when he left."

"Wait for me," Dan yelled from the other room. He hurried into Harper's office at a slow jog, slapped Det. Granger on the arm as he passed, and then took a seat next to him. "If you're going to tell the story, you might as well only have to tell it once." He noticed the look on Harper's face. "Don't give me that look. You know you would have told me anyway. The walls are thin. I heard bits and pieces but not enough to make sense of it."

"As you might remember, I came to Little Rock to escape from all the scandal—"

"It seems to follow you though," Det. Granger interrupted. "I've never met someone who gets involved in so many murders."

"Don't interrupt," she admonished, trying to hold back laughter because Det. Granger was right. "As I was saying, Nick got himself involved with the mob – Carmine De Luca, the head of one of the New York City crime families. Nick was money laundering and a whole host of other things that I probably don't even know about. It all came to light when one of Nick's friends was murdered. The FBI came to me and demanded my help. During this same time, I also found out that Nick was having an affair with Lola De Luca, Carmine's daughter. Nick got her pregnant. All my father, Max, could focus on was the scandal so he fired me."

Det. Granger grimaced. "That's cold. Firing your own daughter like that when her life is falling apart."

"You'd think so, but it was what brought me here. It was the best decision for me." Harper leaned onto her desk. "Nick has shown up here, newly out of prison, to tell me that in a floor safe in his home office he had loose diamonds worth ten million and a necklace that belonged to a Russian princess worth four. He believes I stole them and he wants them back."

Dan interrupted and spoke with excitement in his voice. He practically bounced up and down in his chair. "Is the necklace made of emeralds and diamonds?"

"Possibly," Harper said. "Why?"

"There is a cursed necklace made of emeralds and diamonds that once belonged to Grand Duchess Olga Nikolaevna of Russia. She was the eldest child of Emperor Nicholas II, the last Tsar of Russia, and Empress Alexandra of Russia. She was also the great-granddaughter of Queen Victoria."

"I'm sure there is a story that goes with this," Harper said dryly.

"Is there ever!" Dan smiled, happy to share. "Duchess Olga had many suitors, but she never got a chance to marry. She died when she was twenty-two along with her sisters and parents. They were arrested after the Russian Revolution in 1917 and later assassinated. Olga was known to be compassionate and had a desire to help others, which she did by helping soldiers in a hospital during World War I. But she was also known for her temper, blunt honesty, and moodiness."

Dan waited to see if they had questions. Harper motioned for him to continue. "It was rumored that Olga had received a beautiful necklace from one of her suitors, a prince from someplace or another. I'm not sure where, but he gave her the necklace and promised he'd marry her. After the family was arrested, Olga and her sisters were sent on a ship that took them from Tobolsk to Yekaterinburg. As the rumor goes, Olga sewed the necklace into the hem of her dress to hide it from the Bolshevik soldiers, but they were searched and the necklace found. A soldier took it from her and it was right then and there she cursed it. Later, as you know, the family was assassinated."

"What happened to the necklace?" Det. Granger asked, looking at Dan wide-eyed.

"It was lost to history for some time but resurfaced in London where it was authenticated and then sold at auction for millions. The buyer died a tragic death and it changed hands several times – each owner suffering their own catastrophe. Last I heard, it was swiped from the penthouse of some wealthy New Yorker. That had to be about two years ago."

Harper was fascinated by the story. "That's probably when it ended up in the hands of Carmine De Luca."

"You never heard about this before?" Det. Granger asked.

"You'd think I would have, but my family's magazine didn't cover jewelry specifically. We wrote about the social scene in New York and real estate with a smattering of articles on the who's who of prominent and up and comers in New York."

Det. Granger zeroed in on Harper. "You have no idea where this necklace went?"

Harper laughed, knowing he was suspicious of her. "You sound like Nick. I had no idea he had a safe built into the floor. I wasn't allowed in his office and rarely went in there. When I did at the end, I found evidence of his crimes but never knew about a floor safe. So no, Det. Granger, I did not steal a necklace from my ex-husband."

"What are you going to do about it?" Dan asked, leaning back in his chair. He turned his head to Det. Granger, who nodded along. They both wanted an answer from her.

"What is there to do?" Harper asked. "I don't have the jewelry and I have no idea where it is. It's not like I can turn over a necklace I don't have. Besides, it's not Nick's. If it's the necklace you told us about, Dan, then it's stolen property and doesn't belong to my ex-husband so I'd turn it over to the police."

"Finally!" Det. Granger said with a big ear-to-ear grin. "You're finally learning not to get involved in criminal matters."

Harper had purposefully said what she had to throw off Det. Granger. She had no idea where the necklace was, but if Nick kept insisting Harper had it, she was going to have to do a little digging of her own. She'd have to protect herself from Nick and the only way to do that was to find the necklace before him.

"What did you find out about Cora?" Harper asked, hoping to change the subject. When Dan's face fell in confusion, she explained the events of last night.

"Both of your exes are in town at the same time?" Dan whistled. "That sounds like more than a little bit of trouble."

Det. Granger agreed. "What's with you and Jackson? You're perfectly reasonable people. You both married criminals."

That got Harper's attention. "So, the blood on Cora's pants was human?"

"Yes," Det. Granger confirmed. "We have a blood type but are still waiting for further DNA analysis to see if we can match it to anyone in the system."

"You said there wasn't a struggle at the hotel. What do you think happened?" This didn't make much sense to Harper and she fought the desire that bubbled up inside her. She hated to admit it, but she wanted Cora to be a criminal and locked away – far away from Jackson.

Det. Granger clasped his hands in front of him. "I think there was an incident someplace else and she stabbed a man. I think she told us the truth about that but not much else. Nothing happened in that hotel room. I'd stake my career on it. That leaves the possibility Cora was randomly attacked, which I also tend to doubt. I'm leaning toward an altercation with someone. I can't say whether she knew them or not."

"No body found or bloody crime scenes discovered?" Dan asked.

"Nothing like that. We are going on close to twenty-four hours now since Cora claimed this happened. She said she left the hotel after the incident and went right to Jackson's house, which is where she was found last night." Det. Granger stood and brushed down the front of his pants. "I stopped in because I wanted you and Jackson to be aware this was human blood. I don't know what his ex is up to, but I wouldn't trust her if I were you. While she claims she was the victim, we have no way of knowing that for sure. I'd watch your back."

Harper had the sinking feeling she'd have to watch her back on more than a few things. After Det. Granger left, Dan headed back to his office. He turned around and smirked at Harper. "You can find most of the research on the necklace under Princess Olga's cursed emerald."

Harper smiled as she raised her eyes to his and winked. Dan knew her far too well.

Chapter Six

That afternoon, Hattie finished with her last reading of the day and slumped down in her reading chair. She wiped her hand across her brow and yawned. She was getting far too old to keep this kind of schedule. Hattie needed some coffee and a snack. As she planted her hands on the arms of the chair to push herself up, Jackson appeared in the doorway.

"Hattie, do you have a minute?"

"For you, always. I have as much time as you need." Hattie lowered herself back down on the chair. "Are Sarah and Beatrix doing okay out there? They have been swamped all day."

"It's quiet now," Jackson said, sitting down on the couch across from Hattie's chair.

"How are you doing?"

Jackson offered a shy smile. "Not too well. Last night, I handled everything that happened with Cora okay, but Harper called me earlier and told me that Det. Granger stopped by her office. It was human blood on Cora's clothing. There's no confirmation yet whose blood it is."

Hattie reached for the bottle of smokeless sage she kept on a small table near her chair. She spritzed a few shots in the air. "I had a few readings in here today and it's better to clear the energy. I assume you want me to use my cards."

"I hoped you would, but if you want to just give me advice, I'll take whatever I can get. I need to figure out why she's here and if she killed a man."

"Let's look at the cards first." Hattie reached for her Celtic Tarot cards and shuffled, focusing her energy on Cora. She placed the cards down on the table one by one. They didn't look good. She glanced up at Jackson as he stared down at the cards. She knew that Jackson had no idea what they meant, which was just as well. Hattie took in the entire spread at once. Individual cards told her one thing. Seeing them in the spread told the whole story.

Hattie raised her eyes to Jackson. "Do you want me to sugarcoat it or tell you what I see?"

"You know me well enough by now. Give it to me straight. Don't hold anything back."

Hattie pointed to each card as she spoke and explained the situation. "What it comes down to is Cora is here to win you back and she will do anything to make that happen, even if it means lying, manipulating, and seeking out someone to cast a spell on you."

"I don't think I'm susceptible to spells. I don't believe in them."

Hattie motioned with her hand. "Your belief in them has no bearing. Depending on the spell, at a minimum, it can cause you confusion. I can counterbalance that for you. What concerns me the most is the lengths she will go to get you back. That aside, Cora is involved in things she doesn't understand and she is in over her head without even realizing it."

Jackson focused on the cards. "That doesn't surprise me. She was never the smartest woman I knew. What specifically has Cora gotten herself into?"

Hattie read the cards again to make sure she understood. "It seems she came here to Little Rock to get you back. In the meantime, she met someone here in the city. I think at first, she assumed she'd use this man to make you jealous, but he had other plans in mind. He is after something. I'm not sure what – money or property maybe. There was a theft and he is after what was stolen. I don't know if it's his or not, but he is after it. He promised Cora great wealth if she helps him find it. They are working together."

Jackson furrowed his brow. "Did Cora kill a man?"

"She believes she did, but he wasn't dead. She injured him, and when she ran, so did he."

"There was no blood at the hotel. It didn't even look to Det. Granger that there had been a struggle."

Hattie picked up the cards and shuffled them again. She focused on Cora and the incident and then put the cards down one by one. The message became clearer and Hattie explained, "This man who Cora was helping was being followed by someone else. This second man thought Cora had information he needed and he went after her when she was alone. He had a knife with him when he approached her. In the struggle, Cora got the knife and stabbed him and ran."

"Are you able to see where it happened?"

Hattie shook her head. "Not specifically, but it was outdoors. That much I can see." She studied her cards more carefully and closed her eyes to see if she could pick up anything else. Hattie asked for help from her guides and waited for a response. She opened her eyes. "All I'm seeing is a wooded area, but I can't make out much more."

"There's a lot of wooded area in Little Rock. It could be anywhere."

Hattie sighed. "Unfortunately, that's all I can see." She didn't explain to Jackson what she did next, but Hattie shuffled the cards one more time and placed them down in a different style spread. She shook her head and cursed under her breath. This didn't look any better.

"What's the matter now?" Jackson asked with hesitation in his voice.

Hattie wasn't sure she should tell him, but raising her eyes to his, she knew she'd have to. "I pulled some cards on your relationship with

Harper and how all of this will impact you both. It doesn't look good, Jackson. I see fighting and discord coming from all sides. Another man is influencing Harper and I think that's Nick. Cora will do everything in her power to break you up. In fact, I think that's the spell she had cast." Hattie tapped at two of the cards. "I know this won't make a lot of sense, but there are cards here indicating that, whatever criminal trouble Cora has found herself in, it's connected to Nick."

"Is that who attacked her?" Jackson asked.

"No," Hattie said. "I don't see a direct tie but indirect. I don't have any idea what this means. The cards aren't revealing everything to me right now." She tapped another card. "This one here shows there are more secrets to be revealed."

Frustrated, Jackson shifted in his seat. "Is there anything I can do to make sure Harper and I don't have disagreements or is it set in stone?"

"The future is never written in stone," Hattie explained, leaning back in her chair. "What I'm seeing right now is the current path based on circumstances as they are today. You have free will to change your future."

"I don't care about anything else, but I need Harper and I'm sure she needs me."

Hattie smiled and shuffled the cards again. She placed them down one by one and finally smiled. These cards told a much better story. "The good news is you and Harper will ultimately be fine. Your connection is strong, but the cards tell me to avoid fighting and arguing, you must communicate. If you think you shouldn't tell Harper something, you should. Don't hold anything back from each other. Even if you think you're protecting her, it will all come out and you both should hear the information from each other rather than an outside disruptive force."

Hattie knew that was fairly commonsense advice but even spirit guidance was logical and straight-forward at times. She also knew that what she said wasn't in Jackson's nature. He'd hide things to protect Harper and she'd do the same.

"I'm serious, Jackson. It's the only way you two will come out on the other side together and stronger than before. Please heed this warning."

Jackson assured Hattie he would and took out money to pay her for the reading. Hattie waved it away like she always did. As Jackson left the reading room, Hattie said, "Come by the house tonight so we can all talk. I'll do a spell to counterbalance what Cora did and a protection spell on the two of you."

Hattie put away her cards and fixed the couch cushions, leaving the room as neat as when she had entered that morning. She went out into the shop for some afternoon tea and a treat. As she crossed the threshold from the backroom area to the shop, Hattie stopped short. The place, thankfully, was empty, but Sarah stood at the counter flirting with a familiar ghostly face. It seemed Charlie Baker had returned.

Charlie had first appeared to Sarah a few months back. He was attached to a local mystery writer and acted as her muse for her mystery series about a 1940s private investigator in Chicago. It turned out, Charlie fed her stories about his own life, which was cut short on a case that went bad. Now, it appeared he was back again.

"Charlie, what are you doing here?" Hattie asked as she approached. "I thought you had reconnected with your writer friend and were back feeding her stories."

Charlie turned to Hattie and tipped his fedora. "I'm here this time for you, doll."

"For me?" Hattie asked pointing a finger at her chest. "Why ever for?"

"You called for help and there's no better help than a private investigator."

Hattie laughed. "I called for help in my mind. I didn't say the words aloud. Please tell me spirits can't hear my thoughts? If so, we are in trouble."

Charlie moved to a table and took a seat, dropping his fedora on the tabletop. "Nothing like that. You asked for help from your spirit guide who heard you and called me for help. It's how it works on the other side. Besides, what's a bored private eye to do on the other side? I have all the time in the world."

Chapter Seven

Hattie had been too tired to stay at the shop even after Charlie's grand announcement that he was there to help her. She had no idea what he could do at the moment. Nothing in the reading she did for Jackson made any sense, especially that Cora and Nick were somehow connected.

Hattie had the feeling that once she saw Harper, she might know more. That wouldn't be until later this evening and Hattie had dinner to cook and a nap to take. Sarah promised to bring Sparkle and Shine back to Hattie as soon as she closed the shop.

Her assistant, Beatrix, had left to go to a late afternoon class after gathering all the supplies Hattie would need to reverse the breakup spell done on Harper and Jackson. She carried home the small bag of magical supplies, unlocked the back door, and dropped the bag in a heap as she entered the kitchen.

Hattie exhaled, pleased with how the energy of her house always made her feel. A calm peaceful vibe wrapped her in a hug as soon as she entered the space. Hattie made her way through the kitchen into the living room and then climbed the stairs to the second floor. She took off her sweater and dropped it on a chair in her bedroom. She unfastened her skirt, let it drop to the floor, and stepped out of it by the side of her bed. Hattie leaned over and pulled the covers back and climbed in. She was asleep before her head even hit the pillow.

Hours later, when Hattie opened her eyes, the room had grown dark. She raised her head, but all she could see were shadows cast in the corners of the room. She felt his presence before he came into view. "Beau," she called to her deceased husband. "Are you there?"

"I'm here, my dear," Beau said, his spirit coming to sit on the side of her bed. "I didn't mean to wake you."

Hattie inched herself up in the bed until her back rested on the pillows against the headboard. "I need to get up anyway. Harper will be home soon and then Sarah and Jackson will be over." Hattie reached for his hand even though she couldn't feel anything more than their energies merging. She could tell by the concerned look on his face that everything wasn't okay. "You look worried. What's going on?"

"You know me too well." Beau sat back and crossed his legs then crossed his arms over his chest. Hattie likened the look to a grandpa about to ask his grandchildren exactly what they had been getting into. "I'm concerned about Nick being here. I've been tracking him and he is up to no good. Do you know he showed up at Harper's office this morning?"

"I haven't spoken to her all day. I'm sure Harper will tell me tonight."

"I don't like it, Hattie. He has been out of prison less than a few weeks, and here he is bothering Harper."

The news didn't come as a surprise to Hattie. Nick had texted Harper that he was coming to Little Rock to speak with her. Hattie had never liked him. She had kept her mouth shut when he and Harper first met, hoping that her niece wouldn't get serious with him. She had seen in her cards Harper would. Hattie had never been more pleased than when Harper had decided to split from him. She hated that Harper had gotten hurt in the process, but she had hoped they were done with Nick forever.

Hattie sighed, which turned into a loud yawn. "Excuse me," she giggled, "I could have slept through till morning. What did Nick want?"

"He is searching for some jewelry and he is not the only one. I saw him meeting with another man in the park and they were talking about how others are here searching for the same."

"What jewelry?" Hattie asked, thinking back to her reading with Jackson where she saw the theft. "Why would the jewelry be here?"

"He thinks Harper stole it from him!" Beau said, his voice filled with disgust. "Can you imagine that? Harper stealing from him? The nerve of that man. If I had a body, I would have kicked his behind right then and there."

"Please tell me you haven't done anything to him?"

Beau pursed his lips together. "I've tried to haunt his hotel room, but he hasn't paid any attention. He is focused on one thing and one thing only – finding the jewelry." Beau explained about the loose diamonds and the emerald necklace he had been holding for Carmine De Luca. "It is that necklace, Hattie. Duchess Olga's emerald necklace. I remember reading articles about it when I was alive. Nick has a picture of it on his phone. I'm concerned he is going to hurt you or Harper if he doesn't get his hands on it. Nick is a desperate man right now and desperation leads to foolhardy decisions."

"Okay, okay, Beau. Calm down." Hattie threw the covers off her legs and planted her feet on the floor. If what Beau said was true that's exactly what she couldn't make sense of in the cards. She had to let Harper and Jackson know immediately. Hattie went into her bathroom and splashed some water on her face. She ran her fingers through her short gray locks and mussed them about until she had them perfect. She pinched her cheeks for color so she didn't have that hallow paleness that reminded her of someone waking from their crypt.

Beau still sat on the bed watching her. "I'm serious, Hattie. I'm worried."

"You're always worried, my love. Let me go down and make dinner. I'll talk to Harper and Jackson and address it. You can come down and hover over me if you'd like."

Hattie got dressed and headed for the stairs and realized that she wasn't alone in the house. Harper's, Jackson's, and Sarah's voices carried from downstairs and it made Hattie smile. The old house, which had been in Beau's family for generations and was one of the oldest in the Heights neighborhood, was too big for Hattie alone. She and Beau never had children, and Hattie enjoyed the laughter and chatter. A house was meant to be lived in not as quiet as a museum.

As she hit the downstairs landing, Sparkle and Shine rushed from the kitchen almost knocking her back to the steps. She bent down and scratched them behind the ears as they wiggled and danced around her. "Did you miss me? I figured you wouldn't want to come home with all the love and treats you probably got at Sarah's house." Hattie pulled back and looked at them as they sat obediently at her feet. "You both look a little fatter." She laughed and then patted her belly. "I guess I can't blame you. More cushion for our old age. If I fall, I'll probably just bounce back up."

Hattie entered her kitchen pleasantly surprised to find Harper standing at the stove stirring a big pot. Sarah was putting together a salad and Jackson, as usual, sat at the table overseeing the whole operation. "Business as usual," she joked, looking at Jackson.

"They banished me to the table. I tried to help. I cut all the sweet potatoes for the chili, but Harper said I cut them wrong. I'm useless," he joked.

Hattie went back to the stove. "Sweet potatoes in a chili?"

Harper nodded. "New recipe – turkey sweet potato chili. You'll love it."

Hattie had no idea if she'd love it or not, but it didn't matter. She went over to Sarah and squeezed her. "My dogs look fat. How much did Anabella feed them?"

Sarah smiled. "Every scrap she could find. She didn't want to let them go. I think we are going to have to get a dog."

"You should get my niece anything she wants," Jackson teased.

Sarah angled her head to glance over her shoulder at him. "Then Anabella can come live with you."

Hattie raised her hand. "I'll take her! It's been a while since I had a child in the house. I'd love the noise..." Hattie didn't get a chance to finish her sentence because a knock at the back door quieted them all. She went through the back porch and looked out the window to see Det. Granger standing there.

Hattie opened the door. "Have you come for dinner?" she asked but then saw the look on his face and realized whatever he was there to tell them wasn't good news. Hattie stepped out of the way so he could enter and then followed him into the kitchen.

Det. Granger came up behind Sarah and kissed her on the cheek. He leaned back on the counter facing all of them and cleared his throat. "I don't mean to disturb you all at dinner, but I figured you'd want to know before it hits the news. There's been a body found in Allsopp Park just off one of the hiking trails. Preliminary evidence at the scene indicates it might be the man that Cora stabbed."

Chapter Eight

"Why do you say that, Det. Granger?" Hattie asked, sitting down next to Jackson at the table. She waved Det. Granger to sit down with them.

As he took a seat, he explained, "We found Cora's name and cellphone number in his pocket. The victim, Vinnie Ruggiero, is from West Palm Beach, Florida. He has connections to a crime family that operates down there. I have no idea why he was in Little Rock."

"Tyson, do you think Cora killed him?" Sarah asked, bringing the salad to the table.

"Ruggiero had multiple injuries, more than I think Cora could have inflicted. It looks like he had been roughed up pretty good. He does have a stab wound to his abdomen though so that part of her story checks out, but the medical examiner didn't think that's what killed him."

"What killed him?" Jackson asked, his lips drawn in a firm line.

"Bullet to the head."

"That would do it. Have you brought Cora in?"

Det. Granger shook his head. "We can't find her. She's not at the other hotel in the room she checked into last night."

Wide-eyed, Sarah asked, "Do you think she's in danger?"

"I have no idea. I need more information to figure this out. I've got a dead mobster connected to Jackson's ex-wife, a story that doesn't make any sense, and no other suspects. It's going to take some time."

Harper carried over the large pot of chili and put it on a warming plate in the middle of the table. She set it down and then stood back with her hands on her hips. "Is there any chance this mobster has anything to do with mine?"

"Nick?" Hattie asked her voice raised.

Jackson groaned. "Let's hope she only knows one."

"Yes, of course, Nick," Harper said, rolling her eyes at Jackson. "He had mob connections in New York. He said his boss is after that jewelry. It sounds like Carmine De Luca stole that necklace. Maybe word got out that it's been stolen and others are searching for it, too."

"How would Cora get tied up in that?" Jackson asked, turning his head to look up at Harper, but his attention quickly turned to his sister when she laughed out loud.

"Jackson, I love you, dear brother, but for a military man, you can be naive at times. How does Cora get involved with anything?" Sarah waited for a response and when she didn't get any, she slapped her hands down on the table for emphasis. "Money! She's not working. She's living off your alimony and on your health insurance and has all the time in the world. Cora sniffs out drama like Hattie's pups sniff out treats."

Hattie, who had been sitting quietly listening to the exchange, tapped her spoon against the bowl. All eyes turned to her. "I did a reading earlier on the situation," Hattie started, leaving out the reading was for Jackson. "At the time, nothing made sense to me. I saw Cora connected to Nick and to a man she was helping. Then I saw another man trying to get information from her. I believe Vinnie was this third man. He followed Cora or she met with him under some pretense and when he didn't get what he wanted, I think he might have gotten rough with her. That's when she stabbed him."

"You know I can't investigate based on psychic readings," Det.

Granger said, leveling a look at Hattie.

She held her hands up. "I'm just telling you what I saw. Is there a way to find out if others are here searching for those jewels?" As Hattie said the words, her spine tingled and her hair stood on end. She felt the presence before she saw him, and the energy didn't feel positive. The energy snapped and sizzled like a hot burning flame.

"I don't like people talking about me," a man said from behind Hattie.

Sarah saw him first and moved back in her seat. Hattie could see the fear in her eyes and swallowed hard. She had fought demons; she could certainly handle an angry dead mobster.

Mustering all her might, Hattie rose from her seat and turned in the direction where Sarah had her eyes fixed. Pointing her finger, she barked, "I don't appreciate grown men sneaking up on me and you're not welcome in my home." The only problem was that Hattie was yelling at dead air.

While all eyes were on Hattie, from the other end of the table Sarah coughed and cleared her throat. Her voice came out raspy and tinged with fear. "He was just there, Hattie. His energy was vile, that's the only word I have for it. It put off a horrible red glow around him."

Det. Granger reached for Sarah to comfort her and Hattie shook with adrenaline and fear. "I'll handle it, Sarah. Don't worry," Hattie reassured. "He is not welcome here or anywhere else."

Harper and Jackson shared a look, neither of them quite comfortable with ghosts. Harper had never developed the gift to see or hear them and Jackson wanted no part of it at all. Harper asked, "Who was it?"

Hattie sat back down but couldn't shake the feeling that someone was watching them closely. "I assume it was Vinnie. He said he didn't like people talking about him. He must have heard mention of his name and our conversation drew him to us. That can happen, especially with the recently departed." Hattie reached for the spoon in the pot. "Let's eat before it gets cold."

When Det. Granger got up to leave, Hattie wouldn't let him. "You're eating before you leave. You might have a long night in front of you." Det. Granger sat back down and did as Hattie said.

They ate without talking about Cora or Nick or the spirit that had shaken Hattie to the point of distraction. She ate and chatted and pretended like everything was fine, but the last thing she needed was an angry ghost in her home.

Later, when the dishes were cleared and Sarah and Det. Granger had left, Hattie asked Jackson and Harper to follow her into the living room. They sat together on the couch while she took her favorite chair. The dogs sat at her feet. Hattie kept her tone serious. "Listen, as I told Jackson earlier, you're about to face some rough road ahead. If you want to make it together to the other side, you're going to have to be a team. You're going to have to communicate with each other and not hide information or how you're feeling."

Their faces fell knowing that they were both guilty of doing exactly what Hattie said, which is why she had corralled them into the living room to give this little talk. "Harper, I did a reading for Jackson earlier. Cora wants him back and will do anything, including putting spells on you both, to break up your relationship."

"Can someone do that?" Harper asked.

"There's some debate about that," Hattie said. "Real witches have a code so whatever spell caster she is using is not someone ethical. What the spell will do is bring discord into your lives, sow confusion, arguments, and so forth. Ultimately, it can't take away the love you have for each other, but it can make circumstances difficult. It's up to the both of you how you handle it."

Jackson reached for Harper's hand. "I'm confident we will get through it together, and we will heed your advice."

Harper scrunched up her face. "Can't you hit Cora back with a spell? Make it so awful for her here that she goes away?"

"The code, Harper," Hattie said frustrated. "Didn't you hear what I just said? We have a code that we live by. We don't cast bad spells like that. Isn't Cora having a hard enough time right now? She is wanted for questioning by the police, not to mention tied up with mobsters."

Harper shrugged. "That's of her own doing."

"A little compassion, Harper, please." Hattie stood and went to gather her supplies to do the protection spell around them. She hoped Harper wasn't falling into the trap of many new witches. They go overboard, using witchcraft to solve every little problem and abuse the power they have.

Hattie had already instilled in Harper that what she sends out into the world, good or bad, will come back to her threefold, but that was only part of the witches code. Harper needed to know her craft inside and out and know her power. She needed to keep her thoughts and intentions focused on good and keep the balance at all times. There were so many things Harper needed to learn. It might be time for Hattie to start instructing her on the family grimoire.

Hattie gathered her supplies from the kitchen and carried everything back into the living room. Seeing Hattie's hands full, Harper and Jackson jumped up to help. They pulled candles, stones, red string, a container of salt, and glasses of herbs from her hands and set the items down on the coffee table.

Jackson looked at the items with a mix of wonder and skepticism. Hattie figured she'd have to turn herself into a cat in front of his eyes before he fully believed, but that was okay. She liked that he was skeptical. It kept the rest of them grounded.

Hattie had them stand side by side in the middle of the living room and drew a circle of salt around them for protection. She tied the red string around them and made a knot. She handed each of them a piece of rose quartz and an emerald. Then Hattie lit a black candle and said a few words. When she felt the energy was right, she snuffed out the black candle and then lit four red candles and one white one. She mixed herbs into a glass mason jar and added a few drops of rose and lavender oil.

Hattie had grabbed a photo of the two of them earlier that day and folded it so they were facing each other and dropped that into the jar as well. She held the jar in her hands and said more words to the spell. Before she closed the lid, she walked to both Jackson and Harper and had them breathe into the jar, each of them giggling as they did.

Hattie would have scolded them but pouring happiness into this kind of spell would only serve to make it stronger. She said more words and poured her energy into the jar and then sealed it shut. She'd put the jar on a love altar she had brought home from the shop.

"Are we done?" Jackson asked, still smiling.

"I'm done with you if that's what you're asking. But now it's time for the hard part – what I talked about earlier. You both have work to do to keep your relationship strong."

"You broke Cora's spell?" Harper asked, starting to untie the string.

"It wasn't a strong one, but yes, I did. I also did a relationship protection and reinforcement spell. The rest is up to the two of you. Hold onto the stones I gave you and if you encounter trouble, meditate with them," she said eyeing them and hoping they would at least take that seriously.

Chapter Nine

Harper stumbled into work the next morning like she had been drinking heavily the night before and couldn't shake the hangover. In reality, she had only stayed up late talking to Jackson about everything that had transpired. After Hattie's spell, they went to Harper's bedroom and sat in bed discussing everything so they could clear the air and get everything out into the open.

Hattie had been right to warn them. They each tended to keep secrets from the other. Nothing terrible just embarrassing incidents from past relationships, their failings in their previous marriages, and insecurities that often caused them to hold back on expressing how much they loved each other. Battle wounds of a life lived as Jackson called it. No one who had loved and lost and took risks in their lives made it to their forties without them.

Harper couldn't bounce back from an all-nighter the way she could in her twenties or even thirties. She was barely over the threshold into her forties and in great shape and already her eyesight failed her from time to time. Although, she was sure they were making labels smaller and it wasn't her eyes at all. Her joints ached in ways they hadn't before, and now, she couldn't even stay up late without feeling like she'd been run over by a train. She wouldn't have it. She simply refused to get old as she had told Jackson that morning. He laughed at her and told her to embrace it because it was either aging or death and he much preferred her alive.

Harper stopped at the deli and grabbed coffee and breakfast sandwiches for her and Dan. The egg and ham sandwich on the buttery croissant smelled so good she barely made it up to the office without taking a bite. She found the office empty of freelancers who sometimes used the open loft space to work on their assignments.

"Dan!" Harper called out as she walked toward his office. "I have coffee and breakfast for you." She nudged open his office door, which had been shut halfway, and found him hunched over his laptop, his head stooped and eyes glued to the screen. She cleared her throat, announcing herself again. "What has captured your attention so much that you're not racing over here for your favorite breakfast?"

Dan slowly raised his head but kept his eyes focused on the screen "Huh?" he murmured and then lowered his head back to the laptop.

Harper went to her office and dropped her bag and the rest of her items on her desk and carried the coffee and breakfast back to Dan. She scurried behind his desk and looked over his shoulder. On his computer screen, there was a photo of Princess Olga's necklace and a recent newspaper article about the theft. Harper should have known. Dan couldn't let it go any more than she could.

Harper patted him on the shoulder. "I figured you'd find me some good information." She sat down across from his desk and sipped her coffee and unwrapped her sandwich. "Don't keep me in suspense, what did you find?"

Dan raised his head and let his eyes meet hers. He smiled impishly. "It's a good story," he started. "That necklace could be anywhere, but imagine if it's right here in Little Rock. That would be amazing!"

"I think it is," Harper said regretfully. Dan's eyes lit up in excitement. "Slow down, think about it," she cautioned. "If that necklace is here and it was stolen from someone who stole it, then it's going to bring all sorts of criminals here looking for it. Not to mention putting me and those around me, including you, in danger."

"Yes, I understand that," Dan said, still excited. "Think about the stories we could write though! Don't you think if we put it out there that we know the necklace is here and they are searching for it, it will keep you safe? Who is going to come after you if you're public about it? Wouldn't that protect you?"

Harper belly laughed. "Dan, you're crazy! Tell me what the article said about the latest theft."

Dan flipped the plastic lid on the coffee cup and took a sip, thanking Harper. "First off, this isn't a news article in mainstream media. I had to search around until I found a website that traces historical artifacts like the necklace. It seems they did their own digging so I can't verify facts for you. I'm only telling you what they have dug up."

"Understood, go on."

"A few years ago, George Lennox, a New York City finance mogul who lives on the upper east side, bought the necklace at an auction at Christie's New York for close to three million. Here's the catch, almost as soon as he buys it, two of his business ventures fail and his wife becomes sick with some obscure neurological condition. George tried to sell the necklace but couldn't get any takers. At first, he didn't put any stock into the curse, but then all this happened and suddenly he didn't want any part of it. He was trying to unload it even at a loss. What do you think happened next?" Dan asked, leaning forward on the desk grinning.

"I have no idea," Harper said, but she had some ideas mulling around in her head.

Dan slapped his hand down on the desk hard. "Bam! The necklace is stolen and Georgie-boy is collecting the insurance money. As soon as it's out of his hands, his wife's condition improves within a few months and he goes on to make other investment deals recouping his losses and then some."

"You think this was a setup all along? Not really stolen but fake theft for insurance money?"

"Sounds like it to me," Dan said, taking another sip of coffee. He was so excited over this revelation he couldn't sit still. He jumped up out of his chair and came around to the front of the desk, standing in front of Harper. "This could be a huge story!"

Harper raised her eyes to him. "A huge story for us? We are a society magazine. We don't break crime stories and this was all found on websites that are not reputable news sources. You don't know that's how the story went. We've been through this before, Dan. Our readers like what we write. They can get hard-hitting crime stories from the nightly news."

Harper was trying to hold back her smile because she didn't want to encourage him. Dan had been doing this for a while now. He had been editor-in-chief of the largest newspaper in Little Rock several years ago and then took over *Rock City Life*, which he thought at the time was a step up in his career. It turned out he was relegated to going to social events and talking to socialites, something he soured on rather quickly.

Everything changed when Harper came along and agreed to work with him as a full partner. She brought new readership and advertisers in and the magazine took on a new life, but Dan still tried to pull them in a more hard-hitting news direction. Where once, Harper had been a forward thinker pushing the envelope at her family's magazine *Charlotte*, now she had taken on the role of holding the reins and slowing down Dan's wild ideas.

Dan sighed and pouted but he wouldn't quit. "Remember how we took on the author Lanie Dunham's story and that murder investigation? We wrote about it from an arts and literary perspective, but we still covered it. That's the kind of thing I'm talking about. Readers loved that. We never had better hits online and magazine sales other than your New Orleans story."

Harper felt her resolve start to crumble because Dan was right. They had taken a crime story and put their spin on it. "What's your angle on the necklace?"

Dan planted himself on the edge of the desk. He had a twinkle in his eyes knowing that, without much of a fight, he had won her over. "I want to cover the history of the necklace first along with the curse, obviously, and then we can talk about the theft. Once we know more, we can talk about how it might be in Little Rock. We can do this online and then maybe do a big splash in the print edition if it's found." Dan winked at her. "That's code for go out and find the necklace. You're going to have to do something. Your ex-husband has already called here three times this morning looking for you."

Harper sighed. "You could have led with that."

"Then you would have been distracted." Dan hopped off his desk and went around to his laptop. "I'm going to print you off a photo of the necklace so when you get the time you can do that thing where you touch an item and get a vision."

Harper was still iffy how well her gift worked with photos rather than the item itself, but she had developed her psychometry gift more than she had ever thought possible. "If you insist we cover this story, I'm going to call George Lennox and see if I can get any information directly from him. We need to confirm the facts."

Dan narrowed his eyes at her. "You think he'll take your call?"

Harper held back her grin. "I don't see why not. He lives in the same building as my father. He was one penthouse below ours." Harper watched as Dan's face shifted from shock to excitement. His eyes lit up like a little child on Christmas morning.

"You sat there that whole time not saying a word as I rambled on about George Lennox." He laughed. "You enjoy shocking me like that, don't you?"

Harper stood and grinned at him. "You're so easily shocked, it amuses me. Now let me go and call George."

Chapter Ten

Harper shut the office door behind her and sat down at her desk. She couldn't remember the last time she had spoken to George Lennox. She thought back and it seemed to be right around the time she had left for Little Rock. They passed each other in the lobby of her father's building where they both lived. He had a look on his face that told Harper he knew about the scandal unfolding in her life. It had been a look of pity and concern. Of course he knew. Practically all of Manhattan knew, but now after what Dan told her, she wondered if George and the necklace had been among the first dominos to fall in her life.

As Dan had told her about George Lennox, what Harper didn't disclose was that she remembered her father telling her about the theft. Maxwell had told her that George's penthouse had been robbed. At the time, Harper hadn't asked any questions because she hadn't been interested. She didn't know what had been taken, and she was sure she didn't care other than slight pity for the man. Harper had worried about her father's safety for a short period after the theft, but the crime quickly faded from her memory. If she recalled correctly, it was about six months before her own life fell apart.

A sinking feeling spread in her stomach as Harper thought back to the connection George had with her family, including Nick. Harper recalled her father telling her that George had made a police report about the robbery but had shunned media attention. Harper hadn't given it a second thought then. Who wanted the media hounding after a theft? She certainly wouldn't, but now, a more sinister reason came to mind for George dodging the media. Harper had no facts in front of her, but the nagging in her gut told her all she needed to know.

Harper scrolled through her cellphone looking for George Lennox's phone number and was pleased when she found it. She couldn't remember why she had it in her contacts, but she was glad it was there. She placed the call, and after a few rings, a woman answered. Harper identified herself, asked for George, and was put on hold.

After a few moments of silence, George picked up the call. "Harper, so lovely to hear from you. I hope all is well." He was met with silence. "Harper, are you there?"

Harper took a deep breath and used the angriest most indignant tone she could muster. "I'd like to know, George, why you staged the jewelry robbery at your penthouse and involved my family?"

"Harper, I don't...I don't know what you're talking about." His stammering said otherwise.

"You know exactly what I'm talking about. You can either discuss this with me or I'd be happy to send my father to speak to you." Harper's father was old money in New York City and among the rich and powerful. Few dared to go up against him, and once you got on his bad side, you were as good as ruined.

"Please, that's not necessary," George said, his voice dropping. "You don't understand."

"Yes, I do." Harper tapped her pen on the table as she spoke. "You bought Duchess Olga's necklace for your wife and then things started to go wrong in your lives. When you saw an opportunity to unload it, you took it and claimed the insurance money, offloading the problem to someone else. Did I say anything incorrect?" The question was more rhetorical than anything.

Harper pressed on. "The only thing I don't know is how you came to give Duchess Olga's necklace and the diamonds to my ex-husband. That's what you're going to tell me now. Did Nick come to you or did you go to him?"

"Hold on, Harper," George said with a hint of confusion. "I don't know what you're talking about. Yes, Duchess Olga's necklace was stolen from my penthouse, but I swear to you I don't know anything about diamonds."

"That still doesn't answer my question. I know the robbery was fake. Did Nick come to you or did you go to him?"

George hesitated. "He came to me," he said slowly as if waiting for Harper to explode.

"Why would he come to you? You're leaving something out." That didn't make any sense to Harper at all. Until the final days of their marriage, most people knew Nick as a respectable guy.

George didn't respond at first and Harper threatened her father's wrath again. "Fine, fine, I went to Carmine De Luca with a proposal. He arranged to keep the necklace, and you can't imagine my surprise when your husband showed up to collect it from me. I swear to you, Harper, I didn't know early on that Nick was involved."

Harper believed that. "What was the plan?"

"Do you need to know all that?"

"The plan, George. Tell me the plan."

George whined, which was quite unbecoming for a man of his stature. "I called Carmine and we worked out a deal where he could keep the necklace and I'd claim the insurance money. I told him how much he could get for it and we agreed. Of course, he'd have to keep it hidden away for a few years before he could do anything with it, until people forgot about the robbery."

"Why not sell it?"

"No one wanted it, Harper. The rumor of the curse had been long-standing. I can't tell you the number of people who told me not to buy it, but I didn't believe in such things." George exhaled loudly. "I was wrong. By the time I admitted it, the damage had been done. No one wanted to go anywhere near it, except for Carmine who didn't believe in the curse either. All he saw was the millions he could make for doing nothing but holding onto it for a few years."

Before Harper could respond, George let out an ironic laugh. "You see where that got him now, don't you? It didn't matter if he believed in the curse or not. It got him. What's he doing, ten to twenty years in state prison?"

Harper didn't think that had anything to do with a curse. "George, the man runs a criminal empire. He was bound to get caught."

"He'd never been caught before, Harper. For years and years, this man committed more crimes than anyone in the city, and no one, not even the FBI could touch him. Mark my words. That necklace is a hazard to anyone who comes in contact with it."

"What was the plan, George? Nick came over to get the necklace. Did he help you stage the robbery? What was he going to do with the necklace after he took it?"

"Harper, I'm pleading with you. You shouldn't be involving yourself in this. Nothing good will come of it."

The man tested her last nerve. "George, if you don't spill what you know right now, not only will my father be at your door, but you can count on the police and an insurance fraud investigator. Now, tell me and stop dragging this out!" If Harper had been in front of the man, she might have grabbed ahold of him and shaken him by now.

"All right, calm down. Nick planned the whole thing. Carmine sent him over and he planned the robbery and took the necklace. He told me what to say and how to act. I had no idea what he was going to do with the necklace after it was stolen. I still don't know. I didn't ask and he didn't tell me."

"Is there a reason you didn't bother to tell me or my father that you knew Nick was involved with a known mob boss?"

"That should be fairly obvious. If I had told you, you would have asked how I knew. Getting rid of that necklace was more important than anything." George got quiet for a moment and the implications of involving Nick sunk in. "Oh no, Harper. Do you think Nick kept that necklace at your residence? Is that why your life fell apart?"

Harper hadn't thought of that until the words were out of George's mouth. No, she didn't think that. If anything, the curse was a blessing in her life, exposing a husband who was both a criminal and a cheat. If all that hadn't happened, she wouldn't be with Hattie, would never have met Dan, and certainly would never have the loving happy relationship she had with Jackson. It wasn't a curse to her.

"That isn't my concern." Harper wasn't sure if she should tell George about the current state of affairs, but the need to know what he knew overrode her hesitation. "Duchess Olga's necklace is missing. It seems that Nick did keep it in a safe in our residence. I had no idea until Nick showed up here a couple of days ago accusing me of taking it. Since then, there have been other nefarious happenings."

"I know the necklace is beautiful, but if you have it, you must get rid of it immediately before it's too late."

"George, I assure you, I do not have that necklace. I didn't even know anything about it until Nick showed up here. Do you have any idea where it could have gone?"

"No idea. When I handed the necklace over to Nick, a weight lifted off me. I never saw it or even heard about it again." George paused and exhaled. "The value of Duchess Olga's necklace has only increased over time. If the word is out that it's missing and there is some hint at where it could be, it will bring out every black-market dealer and criminal. It's a rare find and the curse only makes it more alluring."

That's exactly what Harper had been afraid of. The call with George ended with her more worried for her safety than she had been only an hour earlier. If Nick thought she had the necklace, there was a chance others did as well. They'd all be coming for her.

Chapter Eleven

As the clock struck ten in the morning, Hattie pulled open the door to her shop and was met with a flurry of activity. Her eyes darted back and forth not sure where to land. Sarah had a line of customers at the counter. Beatrix pulled cups and dirty dishes off a table and swept them into a bin as a customer waited for the clean table. Hattie waved to her regulars as she made her way back behind the counter.

"Has it been this busy all morning?" Hattie asked, as she checked the pastry display case and saw that it was nearly empty. A lone chocolate chip muffin sat on the top shelf and a cheese Danish sat on the second. The third shelf was barren of the usual sweet treats.

Sarah turned her head to Hattie only briefly. "You have no idea. It's like everyone in Little Rock decided to wake up and come to your shop. I opened at eight for the regulars who stop in at that time but I've been barely able to keep up. Thankfully, Beatrix made it in by nine and has been able to clear some tables. I called the baker back to make more treats and called the dishwasher in early. It's been a madhouse."

Hattie jumped right in and made tea and a fresh pot of coffee before checking on the progress of the baker in the back. She never micromanaged her employees because it wasn't her style and she didn't need to. They cared about her shop almost as much as she did.

Hattie opened the door to the kitchen and watched as the baker pulled trays of fresh sweets from the oven. Other trays ready to be delivered to the front of the shop sat on the counter. Hattie rolled up her sleeves and grabbed two trays, offering her thanks as she left. She carried them down the hall and nearly collided with Beatrix. Hattie pulled up short and wobbled a bit trying to keep the trays steady.

"I'm sorry, Hattie," Beatrix said embarrassed. "I was on my way to grab some treats for customers who have already paid." She took one of the trays from Hattie and they both turned and walked to the counter. Beatrix set the tray down and moved over to allow Hattie room to walk to the display case. "I don't have a class until four this afternoon so I can stay most of the day if needed."

"I don't know what I'd do without you." Hattie refilled the first shelf of the display case and set the metal tray back on the counter behind her as a man cleared his throat. She spun around, smiled over the glass case, and introduced herself as she did to all her customers. "Can I get you something?"

The man had small round glasses that sat on the edge of his nose. He peered over the rims of them to look at Hattie. "While those look wonderful," he said, pointing at the treats, "that's not why I'm here."

"Tea maybe or coffee?" Hattie asked, wiping her hands on a dishtowel.

The man, who looked to Hattie to be in his late fifties or early sixties with a tuft of graying hair on his head and wrinkles around his brown eyes, smiled at her. "I'm a collector of sorts and I heard there is a precious gem that needs finding. I'm here on a hunt for it."

"Here in Little Rock?" Hattie asked, not sure she had heard him correctly. The man had an accent from the south she couldn't quite discern. He was southern for sure but not local.

"Indeed." He unfolded a piece of paper that he held in his hands and passed it to Hattie across the top of the display case. "Duchess Olga's treasured necklace. There is a finder's fee of $500,000 and it's believed to be here in Little Rock. It mentions checking with Harper & Hattie Ryan. That's why I'm here. Do you have the next clue or maybe the necklace?"

Hattie stared down at a picture of the necklace and the call for interested parties to help locate it. There was an email address at the top – a generic one that didn't tell Hattie much about who had put out this call to find the necklace.

"Can I make a copy of this?" she asked and navigated her way past Sarah and Beatrix to come around the counter. The man didn't object so Hattie carried it to the backroom of her shop to her small office and made a photocopy of it. Hattie didn't have Harper's skill of being able to touch an item and get a vision, but she hoped her niece could hold this call to action to find the necklace and make sense of it all.

She made a few copies while she stood there and tucked them away in the top drawer of her desk. Hattie made her way back to the man and handed the paper back to him, thanking him. "I'm not sure how I can help you. If you'd like to sit down, we can discuss."

Hattie had to wait for Beatrix to clean off a table for them. "The shop is busier than it usually is," she said sitting down. "Tell me about yourself."

The man introduced himself as James Wiggins from Atlanta, Georgia. "I'm an antique and vintage jewelry collector and have been following Duchess Olga's necklace for years. I'm interested in both its history and the curse. When it was stolen a couple of years back, we were all flabbergasted that such a piece could go missing. Now, there is a chance for it to be found again and reward money for it, too."

"Do you have any idea who set up this search for the necklace?" Hattie asked, knowing now this was exactly what she had seen in her cards.

James smirked. "I know it must seem silly to you, but no, ma'am, I have no idea who set this up. If I find the necklace, I should send a message to the email mentioned and arrange to meet them. At that point, I give them the necklace and receive payment."

"How can you be sure you'll be paid if you find the necklace?"

"Well, I'll have the necklace, and if they want it back, they will have to pay me for it."

"I see," Hattie said but she didn't see at all. What she saw was a man in over his head. "Do you have any idea who stole the necklace?"

James shook his head. "No one knows."

"So, you have no idea what kind of people you're dealing with. Risky for a legitimate businessman." Hattie tapped her finger on the table. "Let's think this through together. If someone stole the necklace that makes them a criminal and criminals don't take too kindly to being blackmailed. Now, where do you think the necklace went after it was stolen and before it was lost?"

"I don't think anyone knows, which is why it's lost." James smirked at Hattie.

He probably assumed she was a daft old woman who didn't under-stand. Hattie didn't care. She had a point and she was going to make it. "I would imagine the people who stole it either sold it to someone willing to buy stolen jewelry or it was stolen from them. Either way, you're trying to hunt down a necklace for someone without any morals and I assume a criminal record. Do you want to deal with those kinds of people?"

James sat back and appraised Hattie, his eyes roaming over her face. "What do you do for work besides run this quaint little shop?"

Now Hattie looked at him like he was daft. She turned and pointed to the sign over the counter. "Hattie's Cauldron: Potions & Pastries. I'm a psychic, witch, spiritualist – whatever word suits your fancy. Spells, tarot, and the best sweet treats and tea you'll find in town."

"Perfect!" James said and leaned in on the table. "I'd like a spell then. You can help me find the necklace."

"That's not how it works."

"You're selling spells and I want one. They sent me here for a reason. If you don't have the necklace or a clue, maybe that's why." He leaned back and looked down his nose at her. "The customer is always right."

Hattie laughed and stood. "Not in my shop they aren't."

James persisted. "I don't think a bad review will help you much. You're a small business and just one review could ruin you."

Hattie let out a sound that was half a laugh and half a grunt. Leaning over him like a parent scolding a child, she said, "You old fool. Look around this shop. You can't change that. My customers are like my family and no one messes with that." She pinned her eyes on him. "I don't know anything about the necklace and I have no spell to help you. Now, you can order some tea or coffee and a treat and sit here and enjoy the ambiance or you can be on your way. Those are your only options."

With that Hattie turned and walked to the counter without looking back. As she approached, Sarah looked at her astounded at the exchange. "Nearly everyone in the shop is staring at you, Hattie."

"Let them stare," she said with a swish of her hip. "No one bullies me or demands service in my shop and walks away unscathed."

"Feisty." Sarah laughed. "What did he want?"

Hattie poured herself some coffee because she needed it after dealing with James. She explained to Sarah what he was doing and what he wanted. "He isn't the first looking for that necklace and won't be the last. We need to call Charlie. He offered the other day and we should take him up on it."

Chapter Twelve

The day dragged for Harper even though she kept herself busy checking off items on her to-do list. By five, she scrambled to get out the door. She waved to Dan who was still at his desk. She sprinted down the stairs and pulled open the front door and bumped into Nick. Her head hit his chest.

Harper shoved herself from him and raised her head. "You are the last person I want to see right now," she barked as she sidestepped around him.

Nick tried to grab her arm but she shook free of him. He walked fast to keep up with her. "I need to talk to you, Harper. I'm not the only one here searching for the necklace."

Harper stopped and turned on him. "The necklace that you took from George Lennox and then helped him stage a robbery." She watched as red crept up his neck and cheeks and his face fell. "You think I'm still the same woman you were married to, Nick. I'm paying attention now, and trust me, you aren't getting away with anything."

Harper started walking but stopped in her tracks. "What do you mean you're not the only one looking for the necklace? I assumed there'd be others, but what do you know about it?"

"Marco De Luca called me and said someone put word out that the necklace is here in Little Rock and that I better find it before anyone else does." Nick kept the same intense eye contact with Harper as he did in their marriage when he tried to control her.

Harper broke the eye contact and looked away not because she didn't want to look into his eyes, but she had learned long ago she couldn't give Nick any control because he'd take it all. She watched as a car drove down the block and turned at the cross-street. "Who else knew the necklace might be here?"

Nick reached his hand out and gripped Harper's jaw and turned her face to look at him. She smacked his hand away and stepped out of his reach. "I hate when you won't look at me," he said, frustration evident in his voice.

"Never touch me again."

He held his hands up in surrender.

Harper glanced up at him. "What do you want, Nick? Why have you brought all this trouble to my door?"

"I didn't do anything, Harper. The last place I saw the necklace was in our safe at home in New York. I got out of prison and it's gone. You tell me what happened."

Harper turned and started walking toward her car with Nick following. "As I've said several times now, someone else took it. What I don't understand is who would tell people the necklace is here? Who did you tell you thought it was here?"

"No one, I swear." Nick pulled out his phone and tried to show Harper the screen. She pushed his hand away. "Look at this, Harper. It's the email message that went out. Whoever sent it is offering people a reward if they find the necklace."

"It was probably Carmine or Marco," Harper said although she had no proof. "I'll ask again. Who else thinks it's here? Who did you tell?"

"I didn't tell anyone. Marco told me that I better find it and that was the end of the discussion. I need to find it, Harper. He'll kill me otherwise."

Harper turned on him so quickly he bumped into her. "I have no desire to help you. You've left me with no choice though. Who knew where you hid the necklace?"

Nick stared off into space. "There were a few people. Carmine and Marco knew. Of course, I told Lola and a few of the guys working with me. I'm sure Carmine might have told some of the other guys."

"Then any one of those people could have stolen it."

"Carmine was in jail. He couldn't have."

Harper tossed her head back and rolled her eyes. "He could have sent someone. Our place was empty for at least a month in between me moving out and the new couple moving in. There was plenty of time for that safe to be robbed." Harper locked eyes with him. "I'm going to ask one more time. Who knows you're down here searching for the necklace? Who did you tell you thought I stole it?"

Nick ran a hand through his hair and avoided Harper's gaze. She knew immediately that he hadn't been truthful before. He had told someone. She pressed harder. "Nick, I've had enough with the lies. I need to know or I'm calling Det. Granger and telling him you're harassing me. You saw him yesterday. Do you think he's going to stand by and do nothing?"

Nick didn't answer her. He changed the subject. "Where's your boyfriend? I thought you were involved with someone. How come I haven't seen him yet?"

Harper shook her head. "Trust me. Jackson is the last person you want to meet."

"Are you going to help me or not, Harper?"

"I can't help you if you won't tell me the truth." Harper turned and walked away from Nick. This time he didn't follow. Harper made it to her car, and once inside, locked the door. Nick had invaded her city and an overwhelming feeling that she wasn't safe came over her. It wasn't just Nick. There were others out there watching her. She knew it.

Harper turned on the ignition and backed out of the space. She drove through downtown Little Rock and up Cantrell to the Heights neighborhood where Hattie's shop was located. Once she got close, Harper could see that Hattie's lights were still on. Instead of making the right to the house, Harper drove straight and found a spot to park at the curb.

She grabbed her bag from the passenger seat and got out of the car. Through the window of the shop, she saw Hattie sitting at a table talking to someone. From Harper's angle though she couldn't see who. As Harper got closer, she realized that Hattie was alone.

Harper pulled on the door, but it didn't budge. She rapped once on the glass, which startled Hattie who turned quickly to see who was there. Hattie got up and walked to open the door, all the while talking. Hattie unlocked the door and pulled it open for Harper.

"I'm glad you're here," she said. "I was about to call you. We have a problem."

Harper stepped inside and scanned her eyes around the shop. Just as she suspected. Hattie was alone. "Who are you talking to?"

"Charlie," Hattie said, pointing to the table where she had been sitting. "He appeared to me earlier and offered his help. From what I heard, we are going to need it."

Harper narrowed her eyes. "What did you hear?"

"Take a seat and I'll get us some snacks and tea. You look hungry." Hattie hurried over behind the counter.

Harper's stomach growled as if agreeing with her. "I didn't have any lunch. It's been a long day." While Hattie was behind the counter making them tea and putting chocolate chip cookies on a plate, Harper filled Hattie in on her day, including the call with George Lennox and interaction with Nick as she left her office.

"I've known that man since my twenties," Hattie said as she set down the tray of teas and treats in front of Harper. She took a seat across from her niece. "I can't believe that he would do that. I've never known him to be unscrupulous in any way."

Harper took a generous bite of cookie. "George was freaked out about the curse, came to believe it was true, and wanted to get rid of the necklace as quickly as he could. Given his run of bad luck, he couldn't find anyone to buy the necklace. I guess he felt like he didn't have another choice. At least we know now how it ended up in Nick's possession."

"We need to figure out who stole it from your penthouse and who put out a call for people to find it." Hattie sipped her tea and explained her visitor earlier today. "While I didn't get a criminal vibe from James Wiggins, I believe that man would do just about anything to get his hands on that necklace. He seemed obsessed."

"What did James Wiggins want from you?"

Hattie toyed with the cup. "The call to find it mentioned us. He wanted another clue like it was a treasure hunt."

Hattie got up and went behind the counter again. She came back to Harper and handed her the page she had copied from what James had shown her. Hattie pointed down at the page. "Whoever sent this out believes the necklace is here in Little Rock and connected to us. James never mentioned where he thought it might be."

Harper read the page line by line and then once more. She raised her eyes to Hattie. "I think it's time I used my gift to see if I can tap into who is causing all this trouble."

Chapter Thirteen

Harper pulled a photo of the necklace from her bag and laid it flat on the table. She stared down at it, trying to connect to its energy. Hattie had closed the front blinds of the shop and turned the lights down in the hopes people would realize the shop was closed and wouldn't disturb them. She also let Harper know that Charlie was still there with them.

"You have to shake me out of the vision if it gets too intense," Harper told her aunt. That was the one thing Harper hated about her gift. She had no idea when she touched an object and zeroed in on a vision how intense it would be. Most propelled her through time and space and she ended up feeling like she was a part of the vision.

Harper placed her hand over the necklace and focused her attention on Nick's home office in New York City. That was the other trick Harper had learned over time. If when she touched the object, she had a time and place in mind, she could direct the vision to show her that. Without that vision, Harper would be taken to whatever energy was most prominent from the object she touched. It may be significant or not.

She slowed her breathing and focused her intent. A moment later, Harper stood in her old residence in Manhattan. It had the same smell, look, and ambiance as when she had lived there.

Harper took a step toward Nick's office, which was the first door on the right off the hallway. The door was open and Nick was on his hands and knees hunched over a spot on the floor. Harper walked into the room to see what he was doing. The floorboards had been removed and the safe door opened. He had a small black bag in one hand and loose diamonds in the other. He slipped the diamonds into the bag and tucked them into the safe. From a large black bag, Nick pulled out the necklace. The beauty of it made Harper suck in a breath. She had never seen anything quite like it in person. When Nick had secured both items in the safe, he closed the metal door, clicked it in place, and tried to open it. With it secure, he replaced the floorboards and then walked out of the room.

Harper refocused her attention, and the vision changed rapidly, almost like watching a movie in fast forward. She watched herself packing and preparing items for her move. Her real estate agent brought several people through to look at the penthouse. Movers came and removed furniture and boxes. No one touched the safe during that time.

Harper stood alone in the empty penthouse and let time continue to slip by. As the afternoon sun beat through the windows, a time-of-day Harper loved on the weekends when she was home to experience it, someone stood on the outside of the door turning the handle back and forth. The lock clicked and the door pushed open.

Harper turned to the door as a man entered. It wasn't one of Nick's friends that she knew. She didn't believe it was anyone the real estate agent had brought through. Harper was sure she had never seen him before.

He was dressed in crisp khaki pants, a pressed blue shirt that was tucked in, and a brown pair of shoes. The man had short dark hair and stood a little taller than Harper. There wasn't much distinguishing about his face. He had dark eyes and thin lips and a straight pointy nose. He knew exactly where he was going because he didn't waste any time. The man walked from the front door directly to Nick's office. He counted floorboards and then dropped to his knees and used his hands to pry up two boards where the safe was hidden.

With the safe exposed, the man pulled a slip of paper from his pocket and turned the combination dial on the safe until it unlocked. He made quick work of grabbing the two bags with the diamonds and the necklace. He put one in each pants pocket and closed the safe. He dropped the boards back in place and left as if he had never been there at all. In total, he was in Harper's home less than ten minutes. It was clear he knew what he was after and where to find it.

Harper took a deep breath and headed for the doorway, but she couldn't get past it in her vision to follow the man. She was blocked for some reason. She mentally propelled forward to try to see where the necklace went next, but the vision brought her outside of Hattie's house.

Harper stood on the sidewalk and looked all around, trying to figure out why her vision had brought her there. The house was dark and quiet. Harper's SUV sat midway up the driveway.

Suddenly, the vision moved her forward again. Harper stood still as the world moved around her. People she knew came and went from Hattie's house. She watched herself go back and forth across the street to Jackson's house. Then the vision stopped advancing and all stood still. It was late afternoon with the sun almost setting. Harper's SUV was gone and Jackson wasn't home either.

A moment later, a four-door gray sedan pulled alongside the curb in front of Hattie's house. The same man she had seen taking the jewelry from Nick's safe climbed out of the car, looked up at Hattie's house, and went to the front door. He tried the door but it was locked. Hattie rarely used the front entrance. It was the side entrance off the driveway that took visitors into the enclosed back porch. The man tried that door next, and when the door wouldn't unlock, he gave it a hard shove with his shoulder. The door popped open. Harper had been telling Hattie for a while that the door wasn't safe or secure. This only proved her right.

Harper tried to approach the house in her vision, but she was only able to walk as far as the driveway, and again she was blocked. It frustrated her and she tried again, nearly bouncing back as if she had hit an invisible wall. She couldn't see what the man was doing in Hattie's house, but she had an idea. Harper wasn't sure how long she stood there, but there wasn't another soul in sight. Even Sparkle and Shine didn't seem to care that a man had broken into the house. Nearly fifteen minutes later, the man returned, closing the door behind him. He walked down the driveway passing right by Harper and got into his car. He started the car, adjusted his mirror, and drove away without looking back.

Harper jolted back to the present. Her eyes flicked open and she struggled to catch her breath from nervous excitement. She took a sip of tea. It had grown cold, but it didn't matter, her throat was dry.

Harper set the cup on the table and looked at her aunt. "I think the necklace is in your house." Harper explained the series of visions from start to finish. "That man stole the necklace and then planted it in your house. I'm sure of it."

Hattie didn't seem to understand. "What do you mean it's in my house? Where?"

"I don't know. My vision would only allow me certain access. This happens sometimes and it always seems like it does at the most critical moments."

Hattie reached her hand out to Harper's. "That's the way it goes sometimes. I can't read cards for myself. We have these gifts for others. The more we want to know something, it seems the more we are prevented from knowing."

Hattie turned her head to look to her right. "Charlie wants to know if you saw the man bring the necklace into the house?"

"No. When he stole it, he put the necklace in his pocket. He didn't have anything in his hands when he went into the house, but he'd have no other reason to be there."

"That makes sense," Hattie said. She listened to something else Charlie said. "We are going to need to search the house."

"Before we get to that, we are calling someone to put in a new side door and lock."

Chapter Fourteen

The next morning after she finished breakfast, Hattie sat at the kitchen table and pored over her grimoire for a spell she had remembered late last night before she fell asleep. The spell was designed to have an object reveal itself and bring it close. She never had use for such a spell before.

Once when her friend Lottie had lost her wedding band, Hattie thought she might need the spell, but she had looked in her cards and saw that the ring was in a coat pocket. Sure enough, when Lottie checked, it was there.

With the necklace potentially in the house, Hattie wanted to find it. She had barely slept the night before knowing that someone had been in her house roaming around and hiding stolen property. She had asked Charlie to ask around on the other side to try to find out how many people were in Little Rock looking for the necklace. Both Hattie and Harper wanted to know just how many people they were up against.

Hattie carefully turned page after page until she found the spell. She read the instructions and while it seemed easy enough, she didn't have many of the ingredients the spell called for at home. She'd have to go into the shop and make the mixture and perform the spell later that day. As Hattie closed the grimoire, the feeling that she was being watched overcame her.

Hattie scanned the room, but no one was there. She shrugged it off and stood. As she planted her feet under her, a wave of dizziness took hold and she reached back for the chair and lowered herself into it. Hattie took a few deep breaths and shook the feeling. Again, she tried to stand and couldn't. It was almost like an invisible force held her in place.

"I know you're here. Show yourself," Hattie demanded, her eyes scanning over her kitchen again. "I won't help you if you don't show yourself to me." Hattie assumed the spirit of the dead mobster that had come to her house before was there again.

Hattie summoned all her energy, envisioned a white bubble of light protecting her, and then she planted her hands on the table and forced herself upright. Hattie fought the dizziness that tried to take hold again and she put one foot in front of the other. It was a bit like walking through quicksand. Hattie knew the more she fought the energy the stronger she'd become. The first time against a negative spirit was always the hardest. If she allowed herself to have fear, it would only feed off that energy and grow stronger.

"Vinnie, I know that you're here. You have no power over me." Hattie stepped into the middle of the room and spun around checking every direction. She didn't see him, but she knew by the hair that stood on the back of her neck and the chill that ran down her spine that his energy was present. It wasn't like when Beau or Charlie appeared to her. Their energy was soft and pleasant almost like stepping out into the sunlight after being stuck inside for a few days.

This was something different – cold, draining, and heavy.

"I know the necklace is here, Vinnie. Is that why you're here?" Fingers poked into Hattie's back and she spun around to face him.

"You took it, didn't you?" he asked, his face contorting in rage.

"I didn't take anything. I didn't even know until last night that it was here." Hattie planted her hands on her hips. "You're dead, Vinnie. Even if we find it, you can't have it."

"I can take it if I want to."

"How?" Hattie asked with a laugh. She turned around and pulled open her silverware drawer and grabbed a spoon. She turned back to Vinnie and held it out to him. "Take this."

Vinnie tried but his hand swiped through it unable to grasp the object. He tried over and over again, growing more frustrated and angrier by the second. His anger made Hattie's dishes rattle and cabinet doors fly open.

"That's enough," she said, pulling the spoon back and tossing it on the counter. "Do you see now that you're dead and dead men can't steal necklaces? There are no pawn shops and black-market dealers on the other side. Who sent you here?"

"I don't know." Vinnie stepped back, a look of confusion replacing his anger now. "Did you say I'm dead?"

"Yes, you're dead." Hattie wasn't going to pull any punches with him. The times when Hattie would have to inform a spirit that they were dead, she normally tried to do it gently. It could be quite jarring for some who didn't understand what had happened to them. This guy hadn't garnered any of Hattie's pleasantness. He had been a mobster in life – stealing and taking what wasn't his by force if necessary. He wasn't going to do the same thing in death and certainly not in Hattie's home.

"Did you kill me?" Vinnie asked.

"No. I don't know who did."

"Why am I here?" Vinnie said, finally opening his eyes wide and looking around her kitchen. "I don't even know where I am."

"My kitchen in Little Rock, Arkansas. Where are you from?" Hattie asked even though she already knew.

"Chicago originally, but I was living in Florida. All I remember is that I came here to find a missing necklace. I wanted the money."

"You were murdered in the process."

Vinnie held his hands out in front of him and turned them over inspecting them. They had been covered in dirt and blood when he first showed himself to her. He had a bullet wound in the middle of his forehead and other bruising around his face. Now that he was acknowledging his death, the wounds and dirt disappeared. It was often one of the first steps spirits took after death. They were able to stop appearing as they had when they died. They could choose how they showed themselves to people. As the transformation took hold, Vinnie's energy changed as well.

It still pulsed hot but had tempered some. "What can I help you with?" Hattie asked now that he was calmer.

"I don't know. Why can you see me?"

"I can see spirits. I can help them, too." Hattie went to her table and sat back down. "You can't come in here like you were though. You're not allowed to use your energy to try to hurt me."

Vinnie rubbed a hand over his dark slicked-back hair. "I didn't mean to do that. Someone told me you stole the necklace and that I had to get it from you."

"Do you remember who told you that?"

Vinnie stood there for several moments thinking it over, but it never came to him. "I don't know why I can't remember."

"It happens sometimes when you die. It takes a while for you to adjust and start remembering things about your life. Some things you'll remember more quickly than others."

Vinnie slumped down in the chair across from Hattie. "I never even got to get married or have kids."

Hattie had to hold back a laugh because she had thought Vinnie was well into his fifties. "How old are you, Vinnie?"

He sighed. "I turned fifty a few months ago."

"When exactly did you think you were going to get married and have kids? Most people have done that by now."

"I know," he said regretfully. "I was focused on my career."

A laugh escaped Hattie and she covered her mouth, pretending to cough. "Well, maybe next life you can focus on a family."

"Next life?" Vinnie asked, his confusion evident. "I don't believe in all that reincarnation crap."

"Okay," Hattie said. "Why are you here?"

Vinnie pointed down and made a jabbing motion with his finger. "You think I'm going to end up down there?"

Before their recent trip to New Orleans, Hattie hadn't believed in the underworld. She had thought there was a version of heaven that was more like a waiting room where you hung out and reviewed your life, saw how well your karma had balanced before you were sent into a new life. She had met demons face to face and they had to hang out someplace.

Hattie shrugged. "I don't know, Vinnie, but that's something you're probably going to have to figure out on your own. I can't help you with that."

Vinnie raised his head and took one last look around the kitchen. Before he disappeared, he said, "I'm not going anywhere until I figure out who killed me, and you're going to help me with that."

Hattie sighed so loudly her dogs came into the kitchen to see what was going on. Hattie smirked at them. "You come out now that the bad guy is gone?"

Chapter Fifteen

T he last thing Harper wanted was to be at work. What she wanted to do more than anything was dig out the email that had directed people to search for the necklace in Little Rock and see what kind of vision she'd tap into. She had been too tired to try the night before and Harper hadn't had a moment all morning to focus on anything other than *Rock City Life* business. Two freelancers had missed deadlines for their articles and that sent Dan and Harper scrambling for content. By the time they each had written an article, it was time for lunch.

Dan popped his head into Harper's office. "Can I get you something from the deli?"

Harper asked for her usual turkey wrap and kettle chips and then put her head back down to tackle another item on her to-do list. She wanted to wait for Dan to get back before she tapped into a vision, but Harper couldn't hold out anymore. She pulled the photocopy of the email from her bag and scooted her chair back from her desk to give herself room.

Harper closed her eyes and placed a hand over the top of the email. Her vision took her to an unfamiliar office. Harper stood alone for several minutes glancing around to see if anything looked familiar. She moved behind the desk and scanned the documents on top. Marco De Luca's name sat atop one of the invoices. Harper wasn't surprised that it was Marco. If she were in Marco's shoes, she wouldn't trust Nick to get the job done either.

As Harper stood behind the desk, Marco pushed open his office door and entered. Lola, his sister and Nick's wife, strode in behind him. She hadn't lost any of the baby weight and looked like a disheveled mess. There was a part of Harper that was pleased with that. She wouldn't admit it to anyone, but if she was going to be cheated on at least she could be far more attractive than the other woman. Harper hated that petty side to herself.

Lola followed Marco into the office and continued to argue with him. She put her hands on Marco's back and shoved him as she berated him. "You can't go after Nick like that, Marco. Dad wouldn't be happy with that. He accepted Nick into the family and you should, too. He's the father of my daughter. You have to accept him."

Marco fell forward and turned on his sister, his face registering anger that worried Harper, but thankfully, he didn't lay his hands on her. "Don't touch me again. Nick is a lying cheating thief. He'll find what was stolen or he'll end up at the bottom of the river."

"He didn't steal it," she pleaded. "It was probably Harper. You know how she sent Dad and Nick to prison. She probably took it to mess with us some more."

"Nick said he didn't think Harper would do that."

Lola stood defiantly with her hands on her ample hips. "Let's be honest. Nick isn't the sharpest tool in the shed. He didn't think Harper would ever find out about me or that he was working with Daddy."

Marco laughed and shook his head like his sister was an idiot. "Lola, the only reason Harper found out was because you went to her office and told her. That set off a chain reaction. If anything, you're the reason Dad and Nick went to prison."

Lola picked up a stapler from his desk and threw it at his head. He ducked in enough time that it didn't hit him. "Go home, Lola, and take care of your daughter. Leave the business to me. I have a plan."

"What's the plan?" Lola demanded.

"I'm not telling you. You'll tell Nick." Marco turned his back on her and went to sit down at his desk.

"Tell me, Marco, or I'm going to the prison and telling Dad how you're destroying the family."

Marco cursed. "You're a grown woman. Are you ever going to stop running to Daddy?" he mocked.

"Tell me now!"

"I've sent someone down there to help Nick find it. Only he doesn't know."

"Who did you send?"

Marco shook his head. "I'm not telling you that, but he'll get to the bottom of it with Harper."

"What if someone gets hurt?"

Marco shrugged. "That's not my problem."

"What about Nick?"

"What about him?"

"What if he can't find it?" Lola asked cautiously.

"He should have thought about that before he let it get stolen. If Nick had been more careful, I wouldn't have to be going through this right now. He's costing me time and money, Lola." He locked eyes with her. "Be grateful I've already let him live this long."

The vision ended when someone touched Harper's arm. Her eyes flew open and she jumped in her seat at the same time she let out a scream. She turned her head and came face to face with Cora who was bent down staring into Harper's face.

"What are you doing here?" Harper asked, catching her breath.

"I could ask you the same question." Cora pointed to the paper in Harper's hands. "What were you doing?"

Harper didn't dignify her with a response. She set the paper down on her desk. "What are you doing in my office? How do you even know where I work?"

Cora strutted to the other side of Harper's desk and sat down in a chair. She crossed her legs and laughed. "I know more than you think I do. I've been checking you out. I bet there are things you wouldn't want Jackson to know."

"Jackson knows everything about me," Harper said, realizing quickly what Cora was doing there. "What do you want?"

"I want Jackson back and you're going to get out of my way so that can happen."

Harper leaned back in her chair. She was a forty-one-year-old woman. She wasn't about to have a cat fight over a man even if it was Jackson. "Cora, let's be real. Your relationship with Jackson was over long before he met me. Even if he and I weren't together, he wouldn't be with you."

Cora clicked her tongue and shot Harper a dirty look. "You think you're so much better than me with your fancy education and big job. Jackson needs to feel needed and you won't do that for him. You're too independent You don't need anybody."

Harper didn't show it on her face or body language, but Cora's comment hit right to the center of an insecurity. Harper had always been too independent for some men. She wasn't good at showing anyone they were needed. Her father had said the same thing to her when Nick cheated on her and her marriage imploded. If only Harper had been more of a submissive wife and not so focused on her career, she might have noticed her husband's dissatisfaction with their marriage sooner.

Cora smirked at Harper's silence. "You know I'm right. Jackson told me as much. He said you were smart and independent. He may complain about having me around, but he likes that I need his help. It makes him feel useful. Like he's a hero again."

Harper shook off the insecure feeling growing in her gut. "Jackson and I are happy together, Cora. I'm sorry that you're still chasing after a man and a marriage that ended a long time ago. There's nothing I can do to help you. You should leave."

Cora didn't budge. She crossed her arms. "Jackson and I slept together recently while you two were together. He told me not to tell you. You aren't enough for him, Harper. Just like you weren't enough for your ex."

It took Harper longer than she'd like to admit that Cora's comment stung. It was like a punch to the gut she hadn't seen coming. Even though Harper knew exactly what Cora was doing and didn't believe her for a second, there was still doubt and fear that crept up her spine.

"I don't believe you."

Cora smirked. "It happened whether you believe me or not."

Harper picked up her cellphone from the desk and sent off a quick text.

Cora smiled. "See, you're checking with Jackson right now. You know how much he cares about me. You're going to get hurt when he leaves you for me. I'm trying to save you from the pain."

Harper ignored Cora as her cellphone pinged, alerting that a text came through. She picked up her phone and read it. When she was done, Harper sent off another text and then refocused her attention on Cora. "You said when you sat down that there were things about me that I didn't want Jackson to know. What are the things you think you know?"

"I'm not telling you that."

"Then I can assume you don't know anything."

"I do, too," Cora said like a petulant child who wasn't getting their way.

Harper shrugged like she didn't care and pulled her laptop closer so she could get back to work. Cora sat watching her. Harper wasn't sure what the woman was going to do, but she wasn't going to feed into the drama. She focused all her attention on editing an article for the magazine while Cora sat there fidgeting and huffing and puffing trying to get Harper's attention, which she wouldn't give.

Finally, Cora blurted, "I bet he doesn't know you're a witch and that your aunt does spells and you have visions. Trust me, if he knew that, he'd leave you."

Harper held back a laugh. "Why do you think Jackson would be bothered by that?"

"He doesn't like that sort of thing."

"Sarah is a medium," Harper said and watched as Cora's face registered surprise. She had been married to Jackson for years and he had never told her. Harper leaned forward on her desk. "I guess if Jackson doesn't like that sort of thing, he wouldn't be too happy that you used a spell to try to break us up."

Cora's eyes got wide and she fumbled for a response. "I did no such thing!"

"I'm a witch who has visions, remember?" Harper wiggled her fingers at her and made a woo sound. "I see all, Cora. Everything," she said, laughing. When Cora didn't say anything, Harper admitted. "Jackson knows all about my aunt and my visions. He also knows you tried to break us up. As I said, Jackson knows everything. We don't keep secrets from each other."

Cora stood. "Does he know you stole a necklace belonging to the mob?"

Chapter Sixteen

"Harper didn't steal that necklace," Det. Granger said, standing in the doorway. "You seem to know all about it though. We found the guy you stabbed. He's dead and we need to talk. You're coming down to the station with me." He motioned for her to follow him.

Cora collapsed back down in her chair and turned on the waterworks. She fake sobbed, but no tears fell from her eyes.

"This isn't going to work with me," Det. Granger said with an exasperated tone. "You told me the other night you killed a man. I don't think you did, but you know more than you told us. I want to take you into the station of your own will. Don't make me do it by force."

Cora stopped fake crying long enough to shift her eyes up toward him.

"He's not kidding," Harper said, leaning back in her chair.

Det. Granger winked at Harper. "Thanks for the tip and for keeping her here."

"You did this?" Cora asked, standing. "You told him I was here."

"Yes." Harper had a smug smile across her face.

Cora launched herself across Harper's desk and swung her arms, missing Harper's face by inches. "I'm going to kill you!" she shouted.

Harper shoved her chair back and stood out of Cora's reach. She wasn't sure how to respond, but she had never thought this would be

Cora's reaction. Det. Granger pulled Cora off the desk and held her in place until she stopped cursing and screaming. Det. Granger shoved her toward the doorway.

Before they left, Cora turned and hissed at Harper. "I'll get you for this."

Harper believed her. She witnessed first-hand what it must have been like for Jackson to be married to this woman.

"What was all that about?" Dan asked walking into Harper's office.

"That was Jackson's ex-wife. You didn't hear her come in?"

"I was on a call with my door closed." Dan stepped closer. "Are you okay? You seem a bit shaken."

"I'm fine." Harper gathered her things to go, shoving her laptop in her bag and picking up her keys and wallet from her desk. "Everything is all set for the next edition. I'm also halfway through editing an article to go online tomorrow. I'll finish it up tonight."

"I can take care of it, Harper. You're upset. Take some time and go do what you have to do."

Harper expelled a breath and looked to Dan with gratitude. "It's that obvious?"

Dan smiled at her. "Your face is flushed and your hair is all messy. Plus, I heard all the yelling. You're bound to be shaken up. Jackson's ex sounds like more than a handful."

Harper set her laptop bag on the desk. "She sounded completely awful, right? I feel so bad for Jackson having been married to her, but then I keep wondering why on Earth he'd marry someone like that to begin with."

"People make all sorts of crazy relationship decisions." Dan blushed and ruffled his hair. "I had the same question about you. How could you have married someone like your ex? I assume you were in a different mindset when you made that decision."

"Fair enough," Harper said. She picked her bag back up off the desk.

"Where are you running off to?"

"I need to speak to Jackson and then I want to look up a spell to banish Cora."

"Is that all?" Dan laughed. "I'd be careful with that. You should probably ask Hattie to help you."

Harper agreed except she wasn't sure if she was planning to tell Hattie anything. She had already warned Harper that she shouldn't try any spells to negatively influence anything. Harper didn't think getting rid of Cora by spiritual force if necessary was a bad thing for anyone though.

Harper left the office and got to her car without incident. She tried to call Jackson on her way to his house, but his cellphone went to voicemail. She turned up the radio and tried her best to belt out a few lyrics as a distraction for the anger and insecurity that rose in her gut.

She knew Jackson hadn't said any of those things to Cora, but she couldn't get a handle on the fact that the woman knew exactly how to pinpoint Harper's weakness. Jackson had to have told her something. The fact that he had spoken about her at all to Cora angered her beyond all measure.

Harper drove to her neighborhood trying to temper her anger. It wasn't working and she knew she should go into Hattie's house, calm down, and talk to Jackson later. The growing fire in her belly was in control of her decision-making now.

As Harper pulled to a stop, she noted Jackson's truck parked in the driveway. She left her bag in the car and got out, slamming the door behind her. She marched over to his house, crossed the lawn, and pounded her fist on his door. The fact that it took him more than two seconds to answer galled her that much more.

By the time he pulled the door open, wiping the sleep from his eyes, Harper fumed. He smiled, clearly happy to see her, and reached his arms out to wrap her in a hug. Harper shoved past him into the house and then turned on him, getting right up in his face pointing her finger.

"How dare you tell that woman anything about my life! How dare you tell her that my ex-husband cheated on me! Do you have any idea how embarrassing that is?" Harper felt the hot tears spill down her face and she turned away from Jackson, not wanting him to see that she was crying. She slapped at her face until they were gone and wouldn't turn back around. As angry as Harper was when she arrived, once the words left her mouth, she instantly felt foolish for accusing him of anything. Cora had gotten the better of her.

Jackson reached his hand out and gently touched Harper's shoulder. He tried to pull her back into him. She remained rigid in place so he moved to her and leaned against her back while he wrapped his arms around her. He brushed her hair out of the way and brushed the side of her neck with his lips.

"I don't know what happened to you today. I assume it was pretty awful to get you as angry as you are. I've never seen you like this, but I never told Cora anything about you. I'd never betray you, Harper."

She wiped the tears away. Foolishness and shame replaced the anger. Harper turned around and raised her eyes to his. "I'm sorry," she said softly, barely above a whisper.

Jackson wrapped her in a hug and kissed her forehead. "Tell me what happened today."

Harper stepped out of his embrace and sat down on the couch. Jackson sat next to her, tracing his fingers along her palm. She told Jackson all about Cora coming to her office and the things she said, including indicating Jackson and Cora had slept together recently.

Jackson looked at Harper with concern. "I hope you know that's not true."

"I believe you. I didn't think that part was true anyway."

"Did you have any doubt?" Jackson didn't let her answer because he said, "Trust me, Harper, that kind of physical intimacy was barely a part of my marriage."

The mixed emotion of what Jackson said hit her at once. She felt bad for him and at the same time was glad. Harper wanted to ask why he had married her and stayed married for so long, but Dan's words about her marriage echoed in her head. "I appreciate you telling me that. I trust you. Cora just got in my head."

He reached for her and wrapped her in a hug and kissed the top of her head. "That's what Cora does. She did it to me for years in our marriage. It was always mind games. She sent me a letter when I was at war to tell me she'd had an affair. Please, never take anything that woman says with any level of credibility."

Harper pulled back from his embrace to look Jackson in the eyes. "I think it's time I made up for all the good loving you missed out on for all those years without me." She leaned in and kissed him passionately on the lips.

When they broke apart, Jackson grinned. "There's so much to make up for."

Chapter Seventeen

Hattie never got the chance to do the spell to find the necklace because the shop was full of people all morning. Sarah couldn't handle the crowd on her own. Hattie helped with the morning rush and then attended to her scheduled readings for the majority of the day.

Even in her downtime, Hattie had to make three money spell kits and one for love. She had assembled all the items and worked with each of her clients. Hattie had to explain more than once to a client who wanted a love spell that she couldn't make someone fall in love. She could, however, work her magic to clear any blockages standing in the way, boost the energy to make love more favorable, improve communication, and give a confidence boost.

Love though, or any emotion, wasn't to be manipulated and it wasn't what Hattie did. Her clients said they understood. One young woman though had a look of hope in her eyes that Hattie knew meant she had only heard what she wanted. In this case, Hattie wasn't too worried.

Before any spell work, she did a reading to see if the outcome was in the cards and what blockages might be in the way. It's how Hattie had such a success rate with her spells. She was able to hone in on what was preventing something from happening. As Hattie told more than one client, you can't debate fate. If something wasn't fated to be, no begging, pleading or spell work was going to change that.

The most challenging part of her day, other than again running out of treats and calling her baker to come back to the shop, was Vinnie, who stuck by her side for most of the day. Even Charlie had tried to stop Vinnie from being so persistent. It hadn't worked. They got into such a heated debate the energy swirled around the shop like a mini-indoor tornado, knocking newspapers off tables and causing such a ruckus that a few customers gathered up their things and left the shop.

Hattie had scolded Charlie and Vinnie in her back office and then tried to convince customers that these things sometimes happened when dealing with spirits on the other side. Hearing about it was one thing – witnessing it first-hand was something else entirely.

At the end of the day, Hattie walked home, wanting a long hot shower and a bowl of the chicken and dumplings she had made the night before. Hattie had told Vinnie that he wasn't allowed inside her home. She also told him that there was no way she would help him if he continued to make such a nuisance of himself. He had disappeared after that, but Hattie knew she wasn't off the hook quite yet.

As Hattie unlocked the back porch door, the dogs ran up to her, wiggling their tails and dancing with excitement in front of her. Hattie didn't bend to pet them just yet. "Come on, come on," she said, "let's go see what Harper is up to."

"How do you know I'm up to anything?" Harper called from inside the kitchen.

Hattie came through the kitchen door and set her bag on the counter. She found Harper sitting at the kitchen table with Hattie's grimoire opened in front of her. "What are you doing with that?" she asked.

Hattie had no problem with Harper reading it. She had practically begged Harper to start learning some basic spells, but to date, her niece had never taken an interest.

"I'm looking for a spell to get rid of Cora," Harper said, not even looking up at her aunt. She flipped a page and kept her eyes focused on the grimoire.

"We discussed this. You cannot use a spell to make her go away." Hattie pulled a cup from the cabinet and opened the fridge, pouring herself cold sweet tea. She bumped the fridge door closed with her hip and joined Harper at the table. "Why do you want to banish Cora?"

Harper finally looked up from the book and explained to Hattie what had happened earlier in the day when Cora showed up at her office and began trying to bait her with information about Jackson. "I knew she wasn't telling the truth, but she still got to me. She's toxic and I need her far from me and Jackson."

Hattie didn't disagree, but spell work wasn't the way to go. It would have repercussions. Banishing spells, which is what Harper needed, always did. "The question you should be asking yourself is where did Cora get the information from?"

"I don't know. Do you think Jackson was lying to me?"

Hattie laughed. "No. You're being insecure. Think this through for me, please."

"I don't understand—" Harper started to say.

Hattie interrupted her. "Think, Harper. Stop being so dense."

Harper sat there for a few moments, a frustrated look on her face. Then suddenly all at once, it was like someone flipped on a light switch in a darkened room. "You think Nick told her, don't you?"

"That would be my guess. Now where Cora and Nick met up or how the information was exchanged, I have no idea. There are very few people who know your past, Harper." Hattie leveled a look at her. "I think it's a safe assumption to think Nick might have given Cora the ammunition. Why is anyone's guess."

Harper said back but didn't close the grimoire. "I don't understand where they could have even met up. I don't think it's a coincidence that they are here in Little Rock at the same time though. I've been thinking that's odd."

"Has Nick said anything about wanting to get back together?"

Harper nodded. "He has said things, but I don't think he's serious. His main focus seems to be on finding the necklace, which is a good thing because Marco wants to kill him."

"Marco?" Hattie asked with raised eyebrows.

"Before Cora interrupted me, I tapped into a vision. I didn't confirm it was Marco who sent the email, but I think it was him. He said he was sending someone down here to help Nick." Harper motioned with her hand. "You know they are all still angry that I'm the one that got Carmine arrested. He missed the birth of his first grandchild. I'm lucky they haven't come after me. It's one of the reasons I moved down here. I figured they wouldn't find me, but Nick figured out where I was and told them."

"How dangerous do you think they are?" Hattie grew up in New York City and was there in the seventies at the height of the Italian mafia hold over the city. She knew FBI operations had busted up the stronghold, but they still retained some power.

"Carmine was willing to kill me that night. It was only you helping me tap into my intuition that got me out of the situation. I figured Nick would be in prison longer and then consumed with Lola and the baby. I didn't give much thought to them coming after me here."

"What happens if we find the necklace?" Hattie asked.

"We turn it over to the police."

"Won't that make Marco angrier?"

"Of course, but it's the right thing to do."

Hattie knew it was, but she couldn't shake the feeling that they'd need to do more to squash the threat from the De Lucas. "I was going to do a finding spell this morning and never got to it because Vinnie interrupted me. He also spent the day trailing around after me at the shop." Hattie told Harper about the interaction between Charlie and Vinnie earlier in the day. "We are going to have to keep them apart."

Harper smiled for the first time. "I know nothing about keeping spirits away from each other. That's on you. Maybe I can help you with the finding spell."

"You want to learn spell work?" Hattie asked surprised. She had been wanting to teach Harper since she moved to Little Rock, but she had never shown any interest before.

Harper shrugged. "Don't you think I should?"

"I've been wanting to teach you for a long time, Harper. It comes with responsibility though. I told you there is a witches code and once you go down this path, you have to understand there are consequences to your work. With spells, you're putting energy out into the world. There is a balance that must be maintained. Negative spells can come back on you quite easily. Even a love spell is dangerous if you're using it to attempt to force the will of another person. It can come back to bite you."

Hattie reached for the grimoire. "I'll teach you, but I'm also going to instill responsibility in you for the spells that you do. I need you to promise me you're not going to try to banish Cora - or Nick for that matter."

Harper contorted her face. "With all this power we have, I'm supposed to sit here and let Cora mess with my relationship with Jackson? That doesn't seem productive to me."

"That's exactly what I'm talking about, Harper." Hattie sat back and sighed. "You can't control Cora. The only thing you can control is your reaction to her. There are many tools in our arsenal for that. You can do spells to help how you feel when dealing with her. There are spells to shore up your relationship with Jackson if you feel the need. Protection spells. Calming spells. Love and communication spells. You have to fight the negative with positive."

Harper was starting to look like she understood. Hattie knew she'd have questions and that was fine by her. "I know what you're thinking,"

Hattie added. "You want to know why doing a binding and banishing spell in New Orleans was okay but not now."

Harper smiled. "The thought crossed my mind."

"I was binding and banishing truly bad people who had corrupted their souls. They made themselves immortal through terrible deeds. I restored the balance. I meditated long and hard to make the decision I made. The spell I did was for the good of all, not only to benefit me. Do you see the difference?"

"Don't be a selfish cow." Harper laughed. "Got it."

Hattie playfully swatted at her. "Help me with this finding spell. Consider it your first lesson."

Chapter Eighteen

Harper hadn't slept well the night before. She had tossed and turned thinking about the necklace in Hattie's house. She didn't want to tell Hattie but she had been fascinated by the spell they had done. A little candle magic, a special jar with some herbs and oils enchanted by Hattie's words from the grimoire, and then a strong meditation imagining the necklace being found. When Hattie finished, she snuffed out the candle and left the jar on a special altar she had in the library off the living room. It wasn't a space anyone went into often.

When they finished the spell, Hattie thanked her spirit guides and the universe for finding the necklace. She said it as if it had already happened. For good measure, she said the prayer to St. Anthony to find lost objects. When Harper asked her about closing with a prayer, Hattie had smiled and said that St. Anthony had never failed her yet.

They had done a cursory search of the house but found nothing. This morning on the way to work, Harper had asked when the spell would work. Hattie said to have patience and that it wasn't like magic on television. The energy needed time to percolate.

Harper trudged off to work and was now sitting at her desk finishing the article she had promised Dan she'd edit the night before. He didn't need it right away so she had time before he came into the office. She finished the last line and attached it in an email to Dan. As Harper leaned back and rested her eyes, an overwhelming sense of dread came over her. She couldn't quite pinpoint where it came from but it rose in her gut until her throat constricted.

Harper sat forward in her chair and opened her eyes. There was no one there that she could see. What she sensed was something different. Harper got up from her desk and walked to the edge of her office and looked out to wide-open loft space.

"Hello!" she called out but was only met with silence.

As Harper sat back down at her desk, the stairs that led to their office space creaked once and then twice. Someone was coming up the stairs. Their loft space was old, but the stairs didn't creak on their own. As soon as anyone put their weight on the fifth step from the top, it creaked and popped. Harper grabbed her cellphone and then rushed toward the stairs.

"I know someone is there," she said with anger in her voice. "Identify yourself now or I'm calling the police."

The dark-haired top of a man's head appeared just over the wall as he ascended the rest of the stairs. "Hold your horses, lady. No need to get yourself all worked up," the man said as he reached the landing and took a few steps into the loft space.

"Most people don't linger on the stairs. They come up to the office like normal people." Harper still felt on edge and didn't make a move toward him. He stood about six-foot, had an athletic build, and nearly black hair that was slicked back with too much gel. He was dressed in pants and long sleeve shirt. As soon as he got a good look at her, he turned on his charm.

"You must be Harper," he said smiling and extending his hand. "I heard you were beautiful. That was an understatement. You're an absolute knockout."

Harper didn't take his hand and he dropped it after a moment. "Can I help you with something? Advertising in the magazine, maybe?"

"Nothing like that. But you can help me." He stepped closer to her and Harper stepped back. He narrowed his eyes. "You seem afraid of me. There's no need for that."

"You still haven't told me your name."

He relaxed his body posture and extended a hand to her again. "My apologies. I didn't even realize. I'm Sam Franza."

It was just as Harper had expected. "What crime family are you with?"

He rolled his eyes to the ceiling. "You think everyone with an Italian name is connected to the mafia?"

"Not at all, but you are." Harper held her ground.

Sam shrugged and a little laugh escaped. "It is what it is. I assume you know why I'm here then."

"The necklace, right?" Harper said, wanting to call someone but she wasn't sure who could get there in enough time. Dan was never late for work so she hoped that he'd be bounding up the steps at any time. "I don't have it. I know Marco is looking for it and thinks it's here, but it's not."

Sam narrowed his eyes. "Marco De Luca?"

Harper nodded. "I assume you either know Marco or got that ridiculous email."

"The email didn't say anything about Marco De Luca. It was sent by an anonymous person with a call to find the necklace. If we find it, then we meet up and exchange the jewels for the money."

Harper moved over to the high table that was positioned in the middle of the loft space that some of the freelancers used from time to time. She rested her phone on the table because she wanted better access to it. "Several people are looking for it. As I said, Marco thinks it's here but he's mistaken. Sorry, you wasted your time."

Sam glanced around the office space. "Are you alone?"

"No. Dan Barnes, the editor-in-chief of the magazine, is downstairs at the deli. He'll be right up," Harper lied hoping that Dan would be there at any moment.

"I'm going to have a look around." Sam walked away from Harper, not in the direction of their offices but across the loft space. There was a library room and another office space that was rarely used. Both doors were closed.

"You can search all you want. You're not going to find anything." Harper took that opportunity to send Det. Granger a text, telling him that he was needed at her office as soon as he could get there. He responded almost immediately that he was tied up on a case but he'd send a uniformed officer over right away. She also texted Dan.

Harper wasn't sure if she should let Sam continue his search or stop him. Letting him do what he pleased seemed the smarter idea since she was alone. She could at least take the opportunity to question him.

"Sam," she called, walking toward him. He had entered the library room but had yet to reemerge. "Sam," Harper called again, standing at the edge of the doorway.

"What?" He stood bent over a box of books that sat on the floor near a bookshelf.

"Do you know Nick Warren?"

Sam dropped the book in his hand and turned to face her. "I've heard the name. Why?"

"He's my ex-husband and is trying to find the necklace, too. He's in trouble with Marco De Luca. Don't you think if I had the necklace that I'd just turn it over to him?"

Sam shrugged. "You're his ex. Maybe it's easier for you with him out of the way."

He had a point, but that's not how Harper went about things. "Do you know Cora Morris?" She thought that was her last name anyway. It occurred to Harper after she asked the question that she had no idea if Cora had taken Jackson's last name.

Sam smirked. "I've come across her recently. Is she dating your ex?"

Harper shook her head. "My ex is married to Lola De Luca. Cora is someone else. How did the two of you meet?"

Sam folded his arms over his chest. "Why should I tell you?"

"Why wouldn't you tell me? It's a simple enough question." Harper was doing exactly as she had planned – buying time before Dan and the cops arrived.

"I don't have to tell you anything," he said defiantly.

"Sure, you don't. I'm curious though because Vinnie Ruggiero was murdered. I think Cora might have had something to do with that."

"I don't know anyone named Vinnie, and what Cora may or may not have done has nothing to do with me."

Harper stepped toward him. "Did Cora tell you that she killed him?"

He ran a hand down his face. "Cora told me that she got mixed up with some real bad guy and that someone is dead as a result." Sam looked back at the bookshelf that he still hadn't searched.

Harper gestured with her hand. "Keep searching if you want, but I need to know everything you know about Cora."

As she stood there and watched Sam turn to the bookshelf and begin his search, Harper reached into her pocket and gripped the arfvedsonite stone and whispered the incantation to a spell she had read in Hattie's grimoire the night before. Harper had read the spell and memorized it before Hattie had arrived home and caught her with the book. It was a truth spell – causing the target of the spell to be overcome with the need to tell the truth. It would make them unable to speak if they were to lie.

Harper finished the incantation. "Sam, I'll ask you again. How do you know Cora?"

With his back still turned, he said, "I met her in the hotel bar. She told me she was from Virginia but had been contacted by Nick Warren to come to Little Rock. They had a plan to break up their exes. He told her that there would be money in it for her if she succeeded."

"Did Cora kill Vinnie?" Harper asked, reciting the incantation quickly again to give it more power.

Sam turned to her. "What are you whispering?"

Harper ignored the question. "Tell me what you were going to say about Cora and Vinnie."

"I wasn't going to say anything." Sam's hand rubbed his forehead. "What are you doing to me? You're making me feel strange." He stepped toward her. "What's in your pocket?"

Harper let go of the gemstone and pulled her hand out of her pocket and showed him. "Nothing. Nothing is going on. I asked you a question you still haven't answered."

Sam stood there and tried to speak but no words came out. He reached for his throat as he tried to speak and couldn't. Sam's eyes grew wide and he groaned loudly.

"What's going on?" Dan asked from behind Harper.

She turned sharply, startled and unnerved by his presence. "Nothing," she said too quickly.

"Harper, what's wrong with him?" Dan asked, shoving past her and going to Sam who looked like he was choking on something. Dan didn't seem to know what to do so he stood there and watched the man.

Harper trembled as Sam's face contorted and his eyes started to bulge. She had no idea what to do. She didn't think this would be the effect of the spell. She only had one idea on how to break the spell. "What are you looking for, Sam?"

Just as quickly as the man tensed up, he relaxed. "The necklace," he said and his eyes darted between Dan and Harper. He didn't say another word though. He moved quickly out of the library room and ran down the stairs.

"Explain," Dan demanded. When she didn't say anything, he stepped closer. "Now, Harper."

Chapter Nineteen

"Calm down, Dan." Harper walked away from him, moving swiftly back to her office as he followed. She wasn't going to turn around and see the frightened look on his face again. The first time was too much to take. The guilt of what she had done pitted in her stomach.

"Who was that guy?" Dan walked into Harper's office right behind her and took a seat. He didn't get to sit for more than a second when a cop yelled for Harper from outside of her office door.

Harper walked back out and greeted the young, uniformed officer. "I'm so sorry to have wasted your time. I had called Det. Granger because there was someone here who I thought meant me harm. He's gone now."

"Are you sure you're okay, ma'am?" the cop asked.

Dan poked his head out of Harper's office. "I'm here now, officer. The guy is gone. I don't think he'll be returning." He shot Harper a look of annoyance.

The cop turned his attention back to Harper. "If you're sure you're okay, I'll go. Det. Granger said he'd call you when he's done in the field."

"Thanks so much for checking on me. I appreciate it." Harper walked with the cop to the top of the stairs and watched him descend. He turned once and waved to her before walking out of the building.

Harper knew she had to go back and face Dan. She still wasn't sure what she was going to say. Could she explain that she had tried a spell that nearly choked a man to death? The way his eyes bulged and he gripped his throat – that image would haunt her forever.

Harper found Dan still waiting. "That man was Sam Franza. He's searching for the necklace and thought it might be here. He insisted on searching the library and I was alone so I let him."

"What happened to him when I came in? He looked like he was choking on something."

Harper didn't mean to but she shifted her eyes to the side and tried to think of a reasonable explanation. Dan caught the look.

"Level with me, Harper."

She leaned her arms on her desk. "I tried a truth spell I learned from Hattie's grimoire. I hadn't intended on using it. I was going to use it on Nick the next time I saw him. But then Sam showed up here and I figured why not try it."

Dan's eyes grew wide. "What did it involve? It looked like you were killing him."

"That was his own fault." Harper leaned back and bit her lip. "He told me the truth on the first question I asked and he was fine. The second question he started to lie and that's what happened. He was choking on his lie. That's why I asked him the question I did because I figured he'd answer it truthfully since I already knew the answer. It seemed to break the spell."

"What are you doing learning spells, Harper? I didn't think you were interested in that."

Harper wasn't sure how to explain to Dan. She held back tears and fought the urge to spill her guts. She wanted to tell him she was afraid of Nick and that she might lose her relationship with Jackson. She wanted to say she was angry with Cora and wanted revenge and wasn't thinking straight. Harper couldn't vomit her emotions onto Dan like that.

She went with the simplest answer she had. "Hattie has been wanting to teach me and we started last night with a spell to find a lost item. The necklace hasn't shown up yet. I had looked through the grimoire and figured the truth spell was easy enough."

Harper reached into her pocket and pulled out the gemstone, explaining to Dan what it was. "All I had to do was hold onto this and chant an incantation while directing it to Sam. I had no idea he'd have that kind of reaction."

Dan rolled his eyes. "Did you at least get something from that insane experiment?"

Harper set the gemstone on her desk. "I found out Nick was in contact with Cora and he asked her to come down here to try to break up Jackson and me. He told her about the necklace as a way to get her to come. She met Sam at the hotel bar and was chatty with him. It sounds like she'd trust anyone."

Dan cursed under his breath. "I'm not sure if your ex is worse or if it's Jackson's. Two peas in one messed up pod." He laughed. "What about the murder? Did Sam tell you anything?"

"That's what I had asked before you came in. I asked him directly if Cora killed Vinnie. He never answered, but he knew something because his first instinct was to lie. I'm going to need to speak to him again."

"He's not going to get within five feet of you, Harper. Did you see the way he took off out of here?" Dan shook his head. "I'm sure he's afraid of you now. You might have blown your only shot."

Harper slumped down in her seat. "I know. I thought he might know something and would be willing to tell me. I guess my intuition was a little off on that one."

"You were afraid. Sorry I was late. I had an early meeting across town with a potential advertiser. I should have let you know." Dan's face registered a regret Harper didn't want him to feel.

"It's not your job to look after me." Harper rubbed her temples, the stress of the day setting in. "I think we might want to consider locking the downstairs door for a while at least until this is all sorted out."

"Good idea. I'll let the freelancers know and make some copies of the keys for them." Dan stood and walked out into the loft space. Harper couldn't see what he was doing, but he came back into her office a moment later. "I think I'll call the alarm company, too. The landlord never gave me the correct code and I kept setting it off. Eventually, I stopped using it. I'll call them this afternoon. Maybe they can reset the code for us."

"I think that's a good plan. Hattie and I need to find that necklace and figure out who killed Vinnie."

"You need help with that?" Dan asked, leaning against the doorjamb.

"I think Jackson is coming over to the house tonight to help us search. Hattie said something about the spell showing us when the necklace will be ready to be found." Harper realized now how silly that sounded and she laughed. "I know nothing about spells so I think I'm going to leave that to Hattie."

Dan smiled. "I didn't want to say that, but it's a good idea. I don't want to have to post signs about no witchcraft in the office."

"Right. I can't even imagine what I was trying to do. Hattie told me not to do any spells until she taught me." Harper fiddled with a pen on her desk. She had so much to do before she could go home for the day.

Before Dan left her office, he asked, "Do you have any suspects yet?"

Harper considered for a moment because that hadn't even been a question that she had asked herself yet. "I'm not sure. Nick and Cora are definitely on the list. I think Sam is now, too. Hattie said something about a guy coming to her shop. I don't remember his name though. I'll have to ask her. I think anyone trying to find the necklace has to be considered. Who else would kill him? Vinnie was from Florida. I can't see someone tracking him to Little Rock just to bump him off."

"That makes sense. What was Det. Granger up to when you called him?"

"He didn't say. Do you need him for something?"

Dan shook his head. "I was just surprised he didn't come to your rescue."

Harper scanned over her desk and then double-checked her to-do list for the day. The tasks had been piling up. She loved her job and never minded the work. Today, though, she wanted to be at Hattie's figuring out where the necklace was and who killed Vinnie. Her mind wasn't anywhere on the tasks at hand. Dan was right. She needed to step back and assess who might have killed Vinnie.

She reached for her phone and texted Jackson asking if he wanted to meet after work for a good strategy session about who the killer might be. Harper was about to set the phone back down on the desk when he texted her back. It was a simple sweet text:

Anything you want. I'll pick up dinner.

Jackson was a foodie, but the man never cooked. He was great at ordering dinner though so Harper readily agreed. She could do with a good night in with him.

Chapter Twenty

Hattie finished the last reading of the day and slumped down in the chair in her reading room. She and Sarah had sat down that morning and ironed out a new schedule for the baker and for Beatrix, who helped behind the register and handled the ordering of magical supplies for the shop. Hattie decided they'd need to hire some extra help behind the counter for orders of tea and coffee and to give customers their sweets.

This would allow Sarah to focus on more of the magical offerings the shop had available. Sarah had let Hattie know there was no way she could run the register and address the needs of the customers who wanted gemstones, candles, spells, and readings. Although it was Hattie who made the spell bags and did the readings, there was still a good deal of work to gather all the information, which had been left to Sarah when Hattie was busy.

Hattie had used the opportunity to ask Sarah if she'd like to offer some mediumship readings. Sarah had hesitated at first but then admitted she was excited by the idea. She wanted to pick and choose the readings she gave until she warmed up and became more comfortable with it. What scared her the most was giving readings to someone who recently had a loved one pass. Sarah wasn't ready to handle the emotion of that and Hattie understood. For now, it was decided, Sarah would give a handful of readings a week.

Hattie started to drift off into an afternoon nap when a familiar voice brought her back to the present.

"I didn't mean to wake you," Charlie said from the doorway.

Hattie angled her head to look at him. "Come on in. I wondered where you'd gone off to."

Charlie stood near the end of the coffee table. "I was trying to get some information for you about the necklace. No one over here seems to know where it is in your house. I even took a peek and can't find it."

"I did a spell so I'm hoping it will show itself to me soon." Hattie sat up in the chair. "Any idea how many people are here in Little Rock looking for it?"

Charlie frowned and nodded. "I counted upwards of ten – all mobster-type figures from around the United States. That guy you had in here, James Wiggins the jewelry collector, is an odd duck. He's not mob-related, but I can't quite figure him out either."

Ten was too many for Hattie to keep track of. It was too much for her to even wrap her head around. They had to find that necklace fast and turn it over to Det. Granger. "What about who killed Vinnie? Did you find out anything about that?"

"Nothing," Charlie said defeated. "I don't think that's the only murder though."

Hattie snapped to attention. "What do you mean?"

"That's why I'm here. I was hoping to ease you into this slowly." Charlie shrugged. "The dead guy isn't getting any deader, you know what I mean."

Hattie rubbed at her forehead. "Please, tell me what you're talking about."

Charlie sat down on the couch across from Hattie. "I went to Allsopp Park, back to where Vinnie's body was found. I looked for evidence the cops missed. I always did that when I was working as a private investigator. I started looking around the area and that's when I saw him – another dead guy."

Hattie sucked in a breath. "Oh my, another one? That's terrible." She caught the look on Charlie's face and realized why he was telling her. "You were there right before you came here?"

Charlie nodded. "I think we are the only ones who know."

Hattie raised her eyes toward the heavens. This meant she'd have to make a call to Det. Granger and explain once again she knew something that no one else knew and hadn't come by the information from normal means. After dating Sarah for several months, she had hoped he'd be used to their craziness by now. Det. Granger was so hardheaded though. It was all facts and reports and such. No room for magic.

She glanced back at Charlie. "Is there anything you can tell me about where you found him or the state of the body that I can tell Det. Granger so he can find him more easily?"

"He's right off the main path. They found Vinnie to the right of the path. Tell him to look left in the same area. Guy had on a tan jacket and jeans. His boots are black and thick-soled."

Hattie thanked him for the information and Charlie disappeared. She pushed herself up off the chair and sighed because her bones felt heavy today. Hattie laughed at herself for thinking that. It wasn't her bones. It was the extra thirty pounds she carried about with her. Hattie would have to find a spell to turn her off sweets or zip her mouth closed. Maybe, she'd just join senior water aerobics.

As Hattie moved aside the curtain that separated the back work area, she caught sight of Sarah chatting with Charlie. "I thought you were leaving," she said to him as she approached. The two had been flirting with each other since the first time he had made an appearance. Charlie was downright smitten with Sarah.

Hattie understood it. Sarah was one of the few people who could see him. She had a lovely dark complexion and gorgeous deep brown eyes. Today, she had her hair braided and wrapped up in a knot at the top of her head. Red earrings, the same color as her lipstick, dangled from her ears. Sarah was, as men sometimes said, curvy in the right places. She was dating Det. Granger and attachments of any kind in the spirit world led nowhere.

Charlie turned to Hattie. "I couldn't leave without saying hello to my favorite girl."

Sarah batted her long eyelashes and giggled. "I should get back to work," she said, catching Hattie's eye.

Charlie winked and smiled before vanishing. Sarah apologized to Hattie for talking instead of working. Hattie waved her off and told her there was no need to apologize. She went behind the counter, grabbed a clean cup from the shelf and poured herself some coffee. Hattie leaned back against the counter and took a sip, savoring the taste. Hattie loved her tea, but there was nothing like an afternoon cup of coffee after a long day. It was the jolt she needed.

"Don't worry. The place is empty and thank goodness for that. It gives us a chance to regroup before we close for the day." Hattie checked her watch. It was nearing three and she knew there were afternoon customers who came in later in the day for some tea and cakes. "At least, the place is cleaned up."

"Beatrix cleared the tables and wiped them down before leaving for her afternoon class. I don't know what I'd do without her." Sarah dried the last few teacups that sat in a drying rack the dishwasher had left for her. As she toweled the inside of a cup, she looked over at Hattie. "I know what you said about flirting with Charlie. It's harmless. He makes me feel fabulous though like I'm the prettiest woman in here."

Hattie laughed. It had been a long time since a man had made her feel like that. "You are the prettiest woman in here."

"Don't be silly," Sarah said, offering a broad smile. "Anyway, he's a ghost. In the real world, he and I would have never worked out."

"Why because you're a medium?" Hattie asked. When Sarah nodded, she said, "Enjoy the attention – even if it's from a ghost."

Sarah smiled. "I'm still going to flirt with him when he's around. Let's just not tell Tyson."

"Speaking of Det. Granger. Do you know if he's around today? Charlie has been a big help and there's information I have to pass on. Det. Granger isn't going to like my call." Hattie explained to Sarah what Charlie had found.

She groaned. "Tyson has had a rough day. He was at a crime scene earlier today, but I'm not sure where he is now."

"I might as well get the call over with." Hattie pulled her cellphone from the pocket of her skirt. Det. Granger's phone rang and rang. When he didn't answer, she hung up and sent him a quick text that he needed to call her as soon as possible, that she had information about another possible murder. She considered calling 911 but how would she ever explain how she knew the body was in the park. No, Hattie wouldn't risk it. As Charlie said, it's not like the dead guy could get any deader. She'd feel horrible though if a jogger or family walking along the trail found him.

Hattie held the phone in her hand and debated what she should do. She never got the chance to make a decision though because the front door of the shop opened and Nick sauntered in. His slicked-back black hair appeared stiffer than usual and she wanted to smack the smug grin off his face. It surprised Hattie he'd dare show his face in her shop.

Chapter Twenty-One

"What do you want, Nick?" Hattie said, drawing Sarah's attention with the edge in her voice.

He walked over to the counter, flashed the smug grin again, and held his arms open wide. "Come over here and hug me. It's been too long."

"It hasn't been long enough," Hattie grumbled and Sarah choked on the coffee she had just sipped. "What are you doing here?"

"I want you to talk some sense into Harper. She doesn't want to talk to me. I'm sure you know she took a necklace when she left our home in Manhattan and I need it back."

Hattie wasn't in the mood to pull any punches so Sarah was in for a show. She pushed herself off the counter and walked around to where Nick stood. She raised her head and looked at him. "I couldn't talk any sense into Harper to prevent her from marrying you. What makes you think I can talk any sense into her now?"

Nick frowned and clutched at his heart. "You wound me, Aunt Hattie. I know you don't hate me that much. I admit I wasn't the best husband... " Nick didn't get out the rest because Hattie cackled at him.

"Not the best husband? You were downright terrible!" Hattie sat down at a table, hoping to show disinterest in continuing the conversation. She checked her phone again to see if Det. Granger had replied, but her text to him was the only communication there.

Nick said hello to Sarah and tried to sweet-talk her, but she went back to drying dishes, ignoring his interaction. He gave up and joined Hattie at the table.

"Fine," he said sitting. "I accept that you don't like me and never will. I need your help though or some bad men are going to show up at your house. I don't want that for you or Harper."

Hattie brought the cup to her lips and took a long sip, watching him over the rim. She set the cup down on the table and assessed him. His desperation wafted off him like the smell of New York City sewer on the hottest day in August. "I don't know what to tell you, Nick. Harper doesn't have the necklace. She never brought it with her when she moved. I've never once seen it."

"I need to search your house." Nick sat back and folded his arms across his chest.

"That's not happening, Nick. I don't want you in my home and I'm sure Harper wouldn't want you there either. I think you better go back to New York. It doesn't seem like you're going to get what you came for." Hattie locked eyes with him. "You're not going to get anything you came for."

By the look on his face, he knew what Hattie meant. "I guess if I asked for your help to get back together with Harper you wouldn't be interested."

"Not for all the money in the world." Hattie toyed with the cup much in the way he was trying to toy with her. She wasn't taking the bait though. "You and Harper have been over for a long time, longer than before you went to prison."

Nick shifted his eyes to Sarah who had remained quiet doing busy-work behind the counter. Hattie knew that Sarah wasn't going to leave her alone with Nick and she appreciated it. Not because Hattie was afraid of Nick. No, she was more worried about what she'd do if left alone with him.

111

"You don't need to look at Sarah. She knows all about your past with Harper and what you did. Sarah is Jackson's sister. You know, the new man in Harper's life – the one that isn't going anywhere."

Nick sat back and gave Hattie that smirk she wanted to reach over and smack off his face. "I guess we'll see about that. Things change all the time."

It hit Hattie all at once. "You brought Cora here, didn't you?"

Sarah dropped the cup in her hands and it smashed into pieces on the countertop. Her eyes grew wide and she came around the counter. "How dare you mess around in my brother's life!"

Hattie had never seen Sarah so enraged, but she wasn't going to do anything to stop her.

Nick scooted his chair back from her, a tinge of fear in his eyes. "She wants Jackson back and has every right to try."

Sarah got right in his face with her finger. "I don't know who you think you are, but no one messes with my family and gets away with it. Jackson and Harper are happy together. I've never seen my brother happier or more content in life. Cora has no chance with him and you had no right to contact her or get her involved in this."

All at once, Charlie appeared next to Sarah. He placed a hand on her shoulder. "You okay, doll? What's the commotion here?"

Sarah fumed. She sucked in deep breaths and Hattie could tell she was trying to calm herself. "I'm fine," she said, turning her head to Charlie. "I think it's time the trash is taken out."

With that, she turned on her heels and walked back to finish drying the dishes. She glared over at Nick as she picked up the towel and cup.

Hattie wasn't sure what to say because Sarah had said everything. "I think you should leave, Nick. I'm not going to help you with anything."

Nick refused to move. "Don't make me do this the hard way. You will allow me to search your home or I'll do it without your permission. I'm getting in there one way or the other."

Hattie raised her eyes to Charlie who stood over Nick with his arms crossed. Nick hadn't reacted when Sarah had told him she was fine. Hattie suspected that Nick thought Sarah was talking to her. Now, Charlie's face registered the anger that Sarah had only moments before.

"Who is the blowhard?" Charlie asked.

"It's Harper's ex-husband. He's a wannabe mobster who just got out of prison."

Nick turned his head to see who Hattie was talking to but no one was there. He looked back to Hattie and snapped his fingers toward her face. "Have you lost it already, old lady? You see things that aren't there?"

Sarah was about to throw down the dishtowel again and come back around the counter, but Hattie held her hand up to stop her. This insignificant man was a Ryan family problem. "You've known about my abilities. Harper told me how afraid you were of me. I have additional skills now including speaking to the dead. While I may be an old woman, I'm highly skilled. You're lucky I just gave Harper a lecture about using our powers for good. Otherwise, I might not be so patient and accommodating with you. I've asked you once, and now I'm telling you – get out of my shop."

Hattie stood even though she wasn't sure what she was going to do. She didn't have the strength to shove him out of her shop.

She didn't have to worry about it. Charlie gave Nick a hard shove and knocked him out of the chair, sending him sliding across the hardwood floor. He scrambled to his feet and turned around in every direction.

"What..." he started to say but couldn't get out the words.

Charlie walked over and shoved him again, this time toward the door. Nick tripped over his feet as he tried to keep his balance. Normally, Hattie wouldn't allow a spirit to interact with the human world this way, but she was quite enjoying it.

"Give him one more shove right out the door!" Sarah shouted smiling from ear to ear.

Charlie winked. As Nick reached for the door and pushed it open, Charlie gave him one more hard shove sending him crashing to the ground on the sidewalk. Sarah hooted and then clammed up fast as Det. Granger appeared standing over Nick.

He looked into the shop. Hattie was laughing so hard that she couldn't stop. Det. Granger shook his head at Nick but didn't help the man to his feet. He simply stepped around him and walked through the open door.

"What was all that about?" he asked, looking at Sarah and then at Hattie.

She wiped her face and caught her breath from laughing so hard. "It was a ghost friend taking out the trash for us."

Det. Granger smiled. "I don't think I want to know."

"You're better off not knowing," Sarah said. "You look exhausted. I'll get you some coffee."

As Sarah went about fixing his coffee and selecting a sweet treat for him, Hattie motioned for him to sit at the table where she and Nick had just been. "I'm glad you stopped by, Det. Granger. Face to face is easier than trying to explain over the phone."

"I figured as much. What's going on?"

There wasn't any point sugarcoating it. "Our ghost friend, Charlie Baker, the private investigator from Chicago, has been looking into the necklace disappearance and Vinnie's murder. While he was doing that, he stumbled over another body."

Det. Granger nodded. "We know about the guy down on the river trail. A jogger called that in earlier today and I've been out there all afternoon."

Hattie hated breaking the news to him. "I wish I could tell you it was him, but this is another dead guy in Allsopp Park."

Det. Granger rubbed his forehead. "Are you kidding me with this? He saw a dead body today?"

Hattie was glad that he had stopped questioning the validity of the information she gathered even if it was by sources he didn't understand. "It was about an hour ago." Hattie watched his face fall. "I didn't want to call 911 because it's difficult to explain how I know."

"I get it. I'm glad you called me. I'll head out there now." He turned to Sarah. "I'm sorry. I'm not going to be at dinner tonight."

Sarah came around the counter and leaned down to kiss him. "I understand. Work comes first, but if you want to stop by when you're done, I'll save some for you."

"Thank you. I'm missing Anabella, too. I promised I'd take a look at a science project she's been working on."

Anabella was Sarah's daughter. "There's plenty of time for that."

Hattie knew when Sarah had made the decision a year ago to move to Little Rock after her divorce that she'd have success in all areas of her life. With Det. Granger, she had found a wonderful boyfriend who adored her daughter. Jackson had been the main role model in his niece's life so far and it was nice to see that Anabella had another one.

"Det. Granger, is the dead man you found by the river connected to Vinnie's death?" Hattie asked.

He turned his attention back to her. "I'm not sure yet, but the guy is from Philadelphia and he was shot so it could be. I won't know more until tomorrow."

Hattie had the sneaking suspicion that one of the people searching for the jewelry was bumping off his competition. She kept that to herself for now. Det. Granger had enough on his plate, for tonight anyway.

Chapter Twenty-Two

Harper sat snug on Jackson's couch waiting for him to return from picking up dinner. They had decided to order from Heights Taco & Tamale, one of their favorites. After work, she had gone home and changed her clothes, seeing Hattie only briefly. Her aunt had told her about Nick's visit to the shop and the bodies that Det. Granger had found. Hattie also told her about Sarah's reaction to Nick admitting his involvement with Cora.

Harper smiled thinking about it now. There was a time she worried about her reputation outing Nick for the liar and cheater he was, but people here saw Nick for who he was. She was glad that Sarah liked her so much.

Jackson's SUV pulled up in the driveway and Harper got up from the couch to open the door for him. She had on her favorite cardigan and leggings and her hair had been twisted on the top of her head. Jackson wasn't the kind of man who cared if she dressed down for an evening. He didn't much care what she wore. Earlier in the relationship, Harper had bought nice lingerie for a special evening and Jackson admitted that he much preferred it on the floor. Harper had giggled at the time, but she liked the comfort she felt with him.

Harper held the door as he walked through with dinner in his hands. He kissed her quickly on the cheek. "I'm starving. We need to eat before we get down to work," he said and went directly to the kitchen.

Harper followed and told him about Det. Granger finding two other bodies. "He wouldn't tell Hattie that he thought they were connected to Vinnie's murder, but she was sure they were. That makes three."

Jackson stood at the counter and pulled the containers from the bag and opened them. He transferred the food to plates. "I don't think my ex-wife is a serial killer," he said with a smirk.

Harper had her doubts. Cora seemed far more diabolical than Jackson believed. "Maybe not a serial killer because she doesn't seem like she could physically pull it off, but that doesn't mean she wasn't involved."

Jackson tried to hold back a smile. "What about Nick? He could be a serial killer."

"He's not smart enough." Harper grabbed a chip and dipped it in hot cheese and popped it in her mouth. Her nutrition had gone to the wayside living in the south. "Being a serial killer takes planning. You and I could be serial killers if we were into that sort of thing. Nick doesn't have the brains or patience or planning ability to pull that off."

Jackson raised his eyes to her as he spooned some black beans onto his plate. "And you think Cora does?"

"No. I don't like her so it's easy to see her as evil."

"I'm not saying she's not evil, but she's not serial killer evil." Jackson finished arranging their plates and slid Harper's toward her. "Besides, who said anything about a serial killer. This is probably a mob guy taking the hunt too far."

"That's true," Harper said and carried her plate over to the coffee table. She set it down and sat on the floor cross-legged while Jackson sat on the couch. "Is that what you think then – that it's a mob guy knocking off his competition?"

"They are after a good deal of money. That's always a motive for murder." Jackson dug into his dinner and moaned at the first bite. "I can't believe how good this tastes."

Harper smiled up at him but her thoughts were still on the killer. "Do you think it's one person or do you think it might be more than one?"

"What do you mean?"

"Do you think the same person who killed Vinnie killed the others?" Harper scooped a spoonful of black beans into her mouth.

Jackson squinted. "What are you thinking, that it's an all-out mob war in Little Rock over the necklace?"

"Stranger things have happened." Harper continued eating without saying anything more. She allowed Jackson to finish his dinner without bothering him about it further. She had no good suspect list anyway.

When they were done eating, Jackson picked up his plate and Harper's and carried them to the sink. He rinsed them off and dropped them in the dishwasher. As he closed the dishwasher door and raised his head, Harper stood there smiling at him.

"What?" he asked.

"I appreciate how you take care of things." Harper wrapped her arms around Jackson's neck and gave him a tender kiss on the lips. Harper hadn't intended for it to be quite so passionate a moment but it quickly turned to that.

Jackson kissed her more passionately and trailed his hands down her sides resting them on her hips. When he pulled back from the kiss, his eyes said it all. Harper reached for his hand and led him out of the kitchen and through the living room. She turned again at the bottom of the stairs and kissed him again. Jackson leaned into her and nearly toppled them over.

He laughed as her lips were against his. "You're teasing me."

Harper grinned and pulled the rubber band from her hair and let her tresses fall over her shoulders. "I don't tease...for long anyway."

Jackson groaned and turned her around playfully and patted her bottom in a gesture to move her up the stairs. They made it about halfway, giggling and laughing when there was a knock on the front door. Jackson cussed like a man interrupted.

"I think we should ignore it," he said, glancing down at himself. "I'm in no condition to answer the door."

Harper would have agreed but the knocking became louder. She smoothed down her hair. "I'll go get it." She leaned into Jackson and gave him a peck on the lips before she went to the door.

Harper looked out the living room window and spotted Det. Granger. "I'm coming," she called to him through the window. She pulled open the door. "Is everything okay?"

"I need to speak with you, Harper. Hattie said that you were over here."

Harper stepped out of the way and let him enter. "What's going on?"

"Does the name Brendan Miller mean anything to you?" Det. Granger asked as Harper led them into the living room so they could speak.

Harper thought for a moment, but she was sure it wasn't a name she had ever heard. It seemed like a common enough name, but still, she couldn't place it. As she sat down on the couch, she said, "I don't believe so. Why?"

Det. Granger sat on the other end of the couch and turned his body to face her. "His body was found in Allsopp Park. There were photos of you on his phone and we had someone come forward accusing you of being involved with him."

"Involved?" Harper asked, her voice rising an octave higher. "What does that mean?"

Jackson walked into the living room and looked at Harper with his eyebrows raised. Both he and Det. Granger stared at her, and she stammered for a response because she had no idea what was happening.

"I don't care who told you I was involved with this man. I've never even heard of him." Harper raised her head to Jackson. "You're the only person I've been involved with since I moved to Little Rock. Before that, I was married and faithful. It's been more than ten years since I've even had a date otherwise."

Harper worried that Jackson might not believe her since Cora had cheated on him and his mistrust still reared its head sometimes. Jackson surprised her this time.

"If Harper says she wasn't involved with this person, she wasn't involved," Jackson said with conviction. "Can I see the photos he has of her?"

Det. Granger pulled out his phone and swiped across the screen until he pulled up an image. He turned the phone around so Jackson and Harper could see it. The photo was of Harper sitting in a restaurant smiling. It appeared the person sitting directly across from her had taken the photo. She couldn't quite remember when the photo had been taken but it wasn't recent.

Harper pointed. "Look at the highlights in my hair and how much makeup I'm wearing. I don't even own that dress anymore. This photo is from years ago when I lived in Manhattan."

"These too?" Det. Granger asked, swiping through four more photos from different settings and times.

Harper looked at each photo. "All of them are from Manhattan."

"Do you know who you were with when these were taken?"

Harper expelled a breath. "I don't remember. I went out to lunch nearly every day for the magazine. I had business meetings and lunches with freelancers and photographers. Nick and I rarely ate at home. We always went out to eat either with his work colleagues or our friends. There were some nights we were alone, but more often than not, it was work related."

Det. Granger glanced down at the photos. "You have no idea who took these?"

"No," Harper said, shaking her head to emphasize the point. "I'm not even looking directly at the camera. I have no memory of this at all. I can't see enough of the background to figure out what restaurants these were taken in. If I could, it might jog my memory."

"I don't understand," Jackson said, sitting down in the chair across from them. "Even if Harper knew this guy in New York, it doesn't mean she killed him here. Not to mention, if he was someone searching for the necklace, they were all told to connect with Harper. I'm sure someone gave them photos. How else would they recognize her?"

Det. Granger nodded conceding the point. He scrolled through his phone until he reached another photo. This one wasn't of Harper. It was a man with blond hair and a round pleasant face. He turned the phone to Harper. "Do you know him?"

Harper assumed it was the victim. She looked closely at the photo, but he didn't look familiar at all. That isn't to say she had never met him through work or even Nick. That might have happened. Harper couldn't be sure. Brendan wasn't someone she had spent much time with though. She knew that to be true. She didn't even remember meeting him. She told that to Det. Granger.

"What else connects us besides the photos he had of me?" Harper asked.

"We have a witness who says you were recently seen with Brendan. The witness said he met with you and you tried to kill him."

Harper's stomach dropped because she knew the answer to the question before she asked it. "Who is the witness?"

"Sam Franza. He said he visited you at your office today and you admitted that you have the necklace. He said then you used some sort of voodoo to try to kill him."

Harper stood. "That most certainly did not happen!"

His voice calm and steady, Det. Granger raised his eyes to hers. "Then tell me what did happen."

Chapter Twenty-Three

Harper tossed and turned in her bed later that night. After being forced to admit what she had done to Sam in her office, both Jackson and Det. Granger had been left speechless. Det. Granger thanked her for the information, said he'd be in touch, and then left the house.

Jackson had been a different story. He had looked at her with pity and a little bit of fear. Since they met and Harper learned of her gifts, Jackson had been supportive. What Harper saw in Jackson's eyes earlier reinforced what she had done was a step too far out of his comfort zone.

They talked for a while after Det. Granger left and Harper tried to explain her actions. The truth was her jealousy over Cora had gotten the better of her. Jackson said he understood, but Harper wasn't sure. This was twice now Jackson had seen her give in to her anger and jealousy.

Jackson had asked Harper to stay and they tried to recover the magic they had before the interruption, but it was clear neither of them felt the same. He kissed Harper goodbye at the door and she went home for the night.

Once in bed, Harper couldn't sleep. She tossed and turned and ran through who Brendan could be and wracked her mind trying to figure out if she had met him at some point. Sleep had been impossible. Around two-thirty, she finally slipped on her bathrobe and made her way down to the kitchen. She found Hattie sitting at the table having a glass of milk and a cookie.

"You can't sleep either," Hattie said, dunking a piece of her cookie into the glass of milk.

"It was a rough night." Harper reached into the cabinet and pulled out a cup and then grabbed the milk from the fridge. She carried both over to the table and sat down. She poured herself some milk and refilled Hattie's glass. "I want to tell you about it, but I don't want you to be angry with me, too."

"Let me guess," she said, leveling a motherly look at Harper. "You tried a spell and it backfired."

Harper looked at her aunt in surprise. "How did you know?"

Hattie patted Harper's hand. "We've all been there." She pointed to the cabinet that held the grimoire. "Don't you think I did the same thing as you?"

Harper couldn't imagine Hattie ever being irresponsible with her gift. "Not really, if I'm being honest."

"I did. When my mother showed me the book and I got my hands on all those spells, I tried some before I was ready. Every young witch does it. With that kind of power at your fingertips, it's easy to go overboard and think you're ready when you're not." Hattie dunked the last of her cookie and popped it into her mouth. "What did you try?"

Harper explained the truth spell she had used on Sam and the terrifying result. "I thought he was going to die right in front of me."

"How did you break it?"

"I asked him a question I knew he'd answer honestly. He had told me the information earlier in the conversation. Once he answered that question, the spell broke and he could breathe again."

Hattie appraised her niece and then grinned. "You're smarter and stronger than you think, Harper. I'm surprised your first spell was that powerful. Normally, a truth spell is only mildly effective. It can coax out the truth if the person has a weak will. I've never seen anyone about to lie have that kind of reaction."

"Do you think I did the spell incorrectly?" Harper asked and then detailed for her aunt everything she had done including the chant from the grimoire.

"You did it correctly," Hattie explained. "I'm not sure why it was so powerful. Maybe Sam has a guilty conscience about something and the guilt is getting to him. If you undid it, why are you so worried?"

Harper explained that Det. Granger had paid her a visit at Jackson's house earlier in the evening. "I don't know how the meeting with Sam and the cops came about, but when Det. Granger spoke to him, he said I tried to kill him."

"I'm sure it felt that way, but the spell doesn't work like that. You can't kill someone with a truth spell." She locked eyes with Harper. "At least, normal witches can't. I'm starting to think you're not a normal witch at all. You're rather something quite exceptional. You might very well be the strongest witch in the Ryan family line."

Harper couldn't believe that was true. Even if it were, it wasn't the kind of power she wanted, especially after seeing what she had been able to do. Harper explained to Hattie about Brendan Miller's murder. "Sam told Det. Granger that I was involved with Brendan and there were photos of me on his phone. They were from when I was in Manhattan. Brendan Miller isn't even a name I know. When Det. Granger showed me a photo of him, I'm sure I've never seen him before."

Hattie tsked. "It seems we need to figure out why Sam would lie. I hope Det. Granger considered that Sam connected himself to Brendan when he was lying about you. I think we need to learn a little bit more about Sam and Brendan."

Harper didn't disagree. At that moment though, worrying about Jackson and their relationship was more prominent in her mind. "I don't know that Jackson will ever forgive me. When I had to explain to him and Det. Granger what happened with Sam, they both looked at me with such disappointment."

Hattie waved her off. "You know how Det. Granger gets. He was already stressed because earlier today I had to tell him a ghost found a dead guy. He probably had his fill of magic or just the Ryan women," she laughed. "As per Jackson, you'll work it out. He was very understanding when I started to see ghosts for the first time. It's a hiccup. He's probably worried you might try the spell on him."

Harper hadn't thought of that. "I think he's second-guessing things because I've been getting so jealous over Cora."

Hattie pulled another cookie from the jar and offered it to Harper. "You have nothing to be jealous of," Hattie said, taking a sip of milk. "I know it's hard being around someone's ex and Cora doesn't make liking her easy. Nick said earlier that he's the reason Cora is even here. I think you and Jackson both need to deal with your exes. Cora wants Jackson back as much as Nick wants you."

Harper knew that's what Nick was doing. He had said as much. She had thought at first that he was saying it to manipulate her into giving him the necklace. "I'd never go back to Nick. I can't even remember why I was with him in the first place. It seems like another lifetime."

"I think I'm safe in saying that Jackson feels the same way about Cora. You have no reason to believe he'd ever go back to her." Hattie stood and walked over to the cabinet that held the grimoire and brought the book back to the table. Setting it in front of Harper, she said, "You can't banish her, but I think you can find a good spell to raise your confidence."

Harper placed her hands on the book and looked up to her aunt. "There's a spell for that?"

"Sure there is." Hattie sat back down. "It's a good spell to start with. I've done confidence spells on myself and to help others have confidence. Once," she laughed, "I did a confidence spell on a loan officer at the bank when I was getting a construction loan to build out the back of the shop. I wanted him to have confidence in me that the business was legitimate and that I was a good investment. I also needed confidence in myself to make the pitch to him."

Harper smiled. "I assume that it worked."

"He offered me more money than I had initially applied for after he came by the shop and I talked through the specs of the construction. Your Uncle Beau thought I had done some magic to get him to say yes. All I did was give us both a boost of confidence in my ability. The loan manager could have said no, but I opened his eyes a little and maybe removed some of the bias against shops like mine."

Harper thought she was beginning to understand. "Is that what you mean when you talk about the witches code? Spellcasting the loan officer and forcing his will to say yes would have been wrong, but doing a spell to boost your confidence and his so he could more clearly make a decision is okay. Is that it?"

"That's right," Hattie said with pride in her voice. "Whenever you're doing a spell that will bend the will of another or cause them harm, it's against what we do. Now, those spells are necessary for certain situations, but as a rule of thumb, never a good idea. That said, you can do spells to make conditions more favorable for you and others. That's how love spells work. I can't make two people fall in love, but I can help them get out of their own way or remove blocks from them being together so they are free and confident to act on the feelings they already have."

Harper felt like the lesson her aunt had been trying to teach her finally sunk in. "You think this confidence spell will work for me?"

Hattie nodded. "Confidence is what you're missing right now. Maybe it's because Nick is back and it's thrown you off your game or because this is the first time that you're coming face to face with Jackson's past. You have a lot going on and it's only natural to feel a little off."

Hattie got up and kissed Harper on the top of the head. "You need to remember who you are and a confidence spell will help you do that."

Harper watched her aunt walk to the stairs. "Thanks for helping me."

"Anytime, kid." Hattie took a step up and then paused. She came back down and glanced over at Harper. "The truth spell isn't a bad spell for you to be doing, Harper. Practice it on Nick. I think he knows far more than he's telling us. Maybe a lunch meeting would be good." Hattie winked at her and then went back up the stairs.

Chapter Twenty-Four

While there was a steady flow of customers for Sarah and Hattie, it was a considerably slower day than earlier in the week. For that, Hattie was thankful. After she and Harper talked the night before, Hattie had gone straight to sleep. She woke up still tired but dragged herself from her cozy bed and walked the few blocks to the shop. Once out in the fresh fall air, Hattie felt more prepared to take on the day.

After a fairly easy reading with a woman who wanted to know when she'd find love, Hattie poured herself some tea and sat at one of the tables. When Sarah finished restocking a shelf, she joined her.

"I can't believe how angry you were at Nick yesterday," Hattie said, sipping her tea.

"I know I shouldn't have been. I feel protective of Harper and Jackson. My brother has been through so much with Cora. The last thing he needs is more drama."

"I wasn't complaining. I found it amusing."

"I'm relieved. I was so embarrassed about my outburst." Sarah looked around at the few customers left in the shop and then leaned toward Hattie. "Charlie did a good job of getting rid of him though."

"I think he'd do just about anything to protect you." Hattie smiled.

"What are you ladies discussing?" Jackson said as he walked up to the table startling them both. He laughed when they both jumped in their seats. "I knew you two were up to something hunched over the table like that. What are you plotting?"

Hattie swatted at him, hitting his side. "We aren't plotting anything and you should know better than to sneak up on an old lady."

Jackson apologized. "Anyone see Harper today? I figured she'd stop by this morning before work. I tried to call her but she didn't answer."

Hattie motioned for him to bring a chair over to the table. "She thinks you're angry with her about the spell she used on Sam."

Jackson lowered his eyes to the table and Hattie could tell he felt remorse for how he had acted the night before. When he looked up after a moment, he admitted as much. "I was so stunned that Harper would try a spell on her own and that she had hurt someone in the process, I didn't know what to say. She hasn't been acting like herself lately."

"What do you expect?" Sarah asked, giving her brother a look of annoyance. "Cora is here messing with her head. Her ex is causing all sorts of issues. He's the one that brought Cora here. Did you know that?"

Jackson turned to his sister. "What are you talking about?"

"Nick admitted yesterday that the reason Cora is here is because of him. He wants to get back together with Harper and Cora wants to get back together with you. I think they made some pact to break you up."

"Is that true?" Jackson asked, looking to Hattie.

"If you had been patient with Harper last night, she might have told you that Sam met Cora and she told him as much. Nick admitted it when he was here yesterday." Hattie sipped her tea. "You're not helping your cause by coming down too hard on Harper. She's learning, Jackson. I know you probably can't understand it, but when someone first starts exploring their magical abilities, it's a bit of a toy for them. Harper doesn't know her power. She's learning and we all need to have patience with her."

Jackson reached over and squeezed Hattie's hand. "I'll make it right.

I wasn't just looking for Harper today. I came in to ask you what you think I should do about Cora."

"Have you heard from her?"

Jackson shook his head. "Not a peep. I'd like to assume that's a good thing and maybe she's gotten the hint, but—"

Sarah interrupted. "You could scream at that woman until you ran out of oxygen and she still wouldn't get the hint."

"Sarah isn't wrong. I'm taking Cora's silence as a warning that she's up to something big."

"That may be true, but your focus should be on sorting things out with Harper. That way, no matter what Cora does, you have a solid united front with Harper," Hattie countered.

She saw by his expression that it wasn't enough for Jackson. She was going to make another recommendation, but at that moment, the door to her shop flew open and a disheveled man stood in the doorway, looking lost and confused.

It took Hattie a moment to realize she knew the man. It was James Wiggins, the jewelry collector who had stopped into her shop the other day. He looked to Hattie like he'd been attacked by a bear and then ran through a muddy forest for safety. She jumped up from her seat and so did Jackson.

"What happened to you?" Jackson said, reaching the man first and helping him to a table.

James pulled off his cap and threw it down. "I was attacked by someone."

Hattie rushed over to him, but she wasn't sure where to look first. He had dirt and scratches across his face, his hands were bloodied, and his shirt had tears in it. "Where were you attacked?"

He pointed his finger and shook it in her face. "In your backyard! Why do you think I'm here?"

Hattie pulled back. "What were you doing in my backyard?"

James rolled his eyes. "I was looking for the necklace and the diamonds. What do you think I was doing?"

Hattie wanted to throttle the man herself. He had no business in her backyard and she told him as much. "I told you when you were here the other day, I don't have the necklace. I haven't seen it and neither has my niece. You had no reason to go on my property."

He held his hands out to his side. "Well, your thugs made that abundantly clear."

"Thugs?" Jackson asked, glancing down at the man and then looking to Hattie for an explanation.

She shook her head not having any idea what James was talking about unless a ghost did this to him and Hattie couldn't imagine that happening. James had been attacked by a living human, someone out to do damage.

"How did you get away?" Hattie asked before James could answer Jackson's question. Hattie changed her mind. Piecemealing this out wouldn't help anything. "Start from the beginning and tell us everything," she demanded. Hattie pulled up a chair in front of him. Jackson also took a seat while Sarah went to the counter to help other customers who had come into the shop.

James held out his muddy, bloodied hands. "How about I get cleaned up first?"

Hattie sighed annoyed at the delay. She stood and pointed to the back of the shop. "Behind that curtain is a bathroom." She waited until he was gone to speak to Jackson. "Do you think he's telling the truth that he was attacked in my yard?"

"Ghost?" Jackson asked, grimacing.

"I thought of that, but I hardly think Beau is strong enough. Of course, Vinnie has been hanging around my house and Charlie did knock Nick out of his chair. He might be strong enough to do this, but it seems all too human to me."

"Me too." Jackson watched the back of the shop as they waited for James to return. He took so long pulling himself together that Jackson nearly went to check on him. Several minutes later, James returned and made his way to the counter. He ordered coffee and then sat back down at the table.

"I'm feeling a little better." James turned to Jackson. "You asked me who the thugs were. I don't know."

"I said to start at the beginning!" Hattie yelled, not meaning to lose her temper. It was pure frustration on her part. When customers turned to look, her cheeks flushed and she waved like she was okay and for them to go back to their tea and treats. "Sorry, start at the beginning, please, so I can fully understand what happened."

"As you know, we were told that to find the necklace we had to connect with you. I figured maybe you or your niece buried them in the backyard. I had a metal detector and I was out there in your yard searching. When I hit on an area of interest, I got the shovel and started to dig. I was down on my hands and knees and that's when he attacked."

"You saw him?" Jackson asked.

"No, he was wearing a ski mask and a hat like a cat burglar. He looked ridiculous," James said, folding his arms across his chest. "Who attacks someone like that? I tried to fight him off, but it was no use. He pummeled me – punching, kicking, and scratching at me." He held up his hands. "I probably just washed away his DNA. I don't even know how I got away but I did and I ran. That's when I saw the woman sitting in the car at the curb. She laughed at me as I ran by."

"Did you run all the way here?" Hattie asked.

"Yes, I did. I figured you'd know who did this to me." He locked eyes with Hattie. "I assumed it was someone protecting your house. I should call the police."

Hattie smirked. "To tell them what? That you were trespassing and were attacked? Good luck with that."

Jackson pulled out his phone and scrolled through photos. When he found what he wanted, he slid the phone across the table to James. "Is that the woman you saw?"

James glanced down at the screen and snapped his head back up. "That's her. See, I knew you'd know her. Who is she?"

"My ex-wife," he said dryly. Jackson glanced over at Hattie. "I'll go check your house."

"Wait for me. I'll go with you." Turning back to James, she asked, "Do you want me to call the police?"

James shook his head and wouldn't meet Hattie's eyes. She had thought as much.

Chapter Twenty-Five

Harper had taken Aunt Hattie's advice to heart. She hadn't gathered everything together yet for the confidence spell, but she planned to work on that later this evening. Right now, she threw her shoulders back and walked into a restaurant in the River Market District of downtown Little Rock, steps from her office, to meet Nick.

Harper had practiced the truth spell that morning on Dan, who had agreed to be her guinea pig. He was such a good sport that he hadn't even flinched when she asked him to help her. They sat in her office and she asked him a series of questions and when they hit one where he tried to lie, he simply couldn't speak. He hadn't tried to fight it like Sam so nothing bad happened.

Eventually, Dan laughed it off and they went to another question. Harper even threw him a few curve balls about his dating life that Dan hated talking about. She didn't ask anything too embarrassing, and all in all, it had been fun.

Harper, armed and ready to take on Nick, walked up to the hostess stand and looked inside the restaurant. She didn't see Nick anywhere. The place wasn't so crowded that she would have missed him.

Harper checked her phone and was right on time. Nick was a stickler for getting to meetings on time. As a young woman approached, Harper smiled and asked for a table out of the way so they'd have a little privacy.

The young woman accommodated. Harper took off her coat and draped it on the back of the chair. She sat down and patted her pocket ensuring that the gemstone for the spell was there.

A young man approached and asked Harper if she'd like something to drink. She placed her drink order and ordered a small salad as an appetizer. Then, she waited. Harper checked her phone over the next several minutes anticipating his arrival. Nick hadn't texted or called to say he'd be late.

At twenty minutes past the hour, when her drink and salad were already in front of her, Nick rushed through the door, brushing his hair back as he searched for her. She waved to him and he made a beeline through the dining room to her table.

"I'm sorry. I'm late," he said slightly out of breath. He tucked his shirt back into his pants and patted down his hair. He pulled out the chair and sat as he caught his breath.

"You seem flustered, Nick. What kept you?" Harper asked.

"I had to meet up with someone but they were late." Nick glanced down at the menu in front of him.

Harper had forgotten the spell when she asked her first question. She reached into her pocket and gripped the stone and silently said the words she knew by heart now. "That doesn't explain why you were such a mess and out of breath. Your fingernails look like you've spent the day gardening without gloves. Why were you late, Nick?"

Nick dropped the menu back to the table and looked at his hands. He raised his head and looked right at her. He didn't say a word, and a second later, he shivered with his whole body as if a chill ran through him. He shook his head like jarring his brain lose.

"We aren't married anymore, Harper. I don't have to tell you what I've been doing."

"Fair enough," Harper said and smiled. She wasn't going to press her luck. His lateness wasn't her primary focus. It was good though to know his reaction to holding back the truth. What happened to Sam the day before still weighed heavy on her mind. "Let's order then."

As soon as the server left with their lunch order, Nick excused himself to the bathroom. Harper stood slightly to see if he had left anything behind that she could snoop through, but his chair was empty. When Nick came back, his hands had been washed and he had regained his normally tidy appearance.

As he sat down, Nick smiled at her. "Why did you want to meet, Harper? I figured you'd never want to see me again."

"I heard what happened at Hattie's shop and I want to apologize," Harper said sweetly, nearly choking on her own words. "Sometimes Hattie goes a little overboard."

"I pushed her buttons," Nick admitted. "I don't understand what happened though. She said there was a ghost. How can a ghost attack someone alive? I don't even believe in ghosts." He laughed nervously.

"I don't know much about that. I can't see them or talk to them like Hattie."

He narrowed his gaze at her. "Hattie said you had powers of your own and that you're powerful. I take it this wasn't something you were doing in Manhattan."

Harper figured admitting the truth couldn't hurt. "I didn't believe I had magical powers. It turns out I did, even in Manhattan. Sometimes when I'd hold an object, I'd get impressions. I didn't know what it was then. I didn't have a name for it."

Nick scrunched up his face. "I don't understand."

Harper held out her palm. "I can hold an object and close my fingers around it and meditate. During that meditation, images connected to the object will come to me."

Nick laughed at her. "Harper, come on. I've never known you to be that gullible. None of that is real. You used to have more sense."

She wasn't surprised by his reaction. The thing that bothered her most about her relationship with Nick, other than the cheating and criminal activity, was his disdain for Hattie. Harper had thought, at first, it was just because Hattie hadn't liked Nick. It wasn't that. A couple of months after their wedding, Nick told Harper he thought Hattie was a fraud and scamming people out of money. It had been a sticking point in the marriage and something she had never forgiven him for.

"You can believe it or not. That's your prerogative." Harper took a sip of her drink and set the cup back down. "I've solved homicides using my gift. I don't need you to believe in me for me to believe in myself." Harper meant it too. She was starting to believe what Hattie told her – that she was more powerful than she realized.

"Poor Harper. Is this what life has done to you without me? You're delusional, babe."

Harper hated that he called her an affectionate name. It created an intimacy that wasn't there and would never be there. She wasn't going to address that though.

She locked her gaze on him. "I saw who stole Princess Olga's necklace."

"You did?" he asked with a hint of doubt and skepticism in his voice. "Who was it?"

"When I touched a photo of Princess Olga's necklace, I got an impression from it." Harper leaned into the table. "I watched it being stolen from our place in Manhattan. A man entered and knew right where your safe was located. He went right for it, Nick. He knew what boards to pull up and knew the combination. He took the necklace and the diamonds and left."

"That can't be," Nick said, shaking his head.

"It happened."

"What did he look like?"

Harper described the man down to the last detail she could remember.

When she did, a look of recognition came over Nick. "You know who it is, don't you?"

Nick tried to say no, but when he opened his mouth nothing came out. Harper reached back into her pocket and gripped the gemstone and said the chant to herself, stronger this time. "Tell me, Nick. You know who took it."

Nick's eyes shifted from right to left and then he gasped as if he were trying to catch his breath. "He's Marco's right-hand man. It doesn't make any sense though, Harper. Why would Marco steal the necklace and then send me to find it?"

Harper didn't have the faintest idea why Marco would do that, but a thought occurred to her and it rumbled in her gut like she had hit on something important. She took another sip of her drink and watched him over the rim of her glass.

"Maybe Marco doesn't know he stole it. If Marco knew where to find the safe, it makes sense this guy would, too. Did Marco know the code to your safe?"

"Carmine knew so it's possible."

"That's your answer then. What's the name of the guy who stole it?"

"Richie De Luca, he's Marco's cousin and Carmine's nephew."

Harper sat back satisfied with herself. "All we need to figure out is why Richie wanted to set you up and frame me."

The server brought their food over at that moment. They both dug in quickly because Harper's stomach had not stopped growling even though she had eaten that small salad. Being a powerful witch kicked up her appetite. She'd have to look at a weight loss spell or at least go back to the gym if she was going to keep this up. She laughed at herself and popped a French fry into her mouth.

Nick looked over at her plate. "Even your diet has changed."

"I'm not so concerned with the things I was concerned with when I was in Manhattan. There's more to life than being a size six."

"I noticed your new boyfriend is a little chubby. I guess it's rubbing off on you."

Harper didn't take the bait. "Jackson may not be lean like you are, but I wouldn't cross him if I were you. He's been trained to kill a man with his bare hands. For the record, I love him exactly as he is." She watched as Nick swallowed hard and lowered his eyes to his plate. She wasn't playing this game with him.

They finished eating and Harper wiped her hands on her napkin. "You've stalled enough, Nick. Why is Richie setting us up?"

Nick pushed his plate away and leaned back. "I have no idea, and I'm not convinced that he is. I still think you stole it. You need to give it back, Harper."

She shook her head. "I can't give you what I don't have. You can keep barking up the wrong tree or you can address whether Marco and Richie or just Richie is setting you up. The sooner you face reality, the sooner you can go back home."

When Nick didn't say anything, Harper asked the question that she had been dreading the most. "Why are you here, Nick? I know you got Cora to come here, too. What's your plan?"

Without missing a beat, he said, "To break up you and Jackson." His eyes opened as big as saucers. It was obvious by his facial expression that he hadn't meant to say what he did. Nick tried to recover but it was no use.

"It's never going to happen," Harper said sternly. "Jackson and I are in love and incredibly happy. Cora wasn't right for him and I wasn't right for you. I'm a different person now. We don't fit any longer, not that we ever did."

Nick started to argue and Harper held her hand up. "There's no point arguing about this. You and I are over. I'll help you find the necklace and diamonds so you can go back to Manhattan and Marco doesn't kill you. I'm only doing that because you've put Hattie and me in the crosshairs, too. That's all that's left between us though. You need to accept it and move on."

Nick locked eyes with her. "I'll never accept losing you."

Harper frowned at him. "Then I truly feel bad for you because you're going to live a lonely life full of heartbreak. We're over and were long before we divorced. The same with Jackson and Cora."

Chapter Twenty-Six

Hattie had left the shop with Jackson even though he had begged her to let him go alone. He had tried to convince her it would be too dangerous because they might catch Cora and whoever she was with in the act of digging up her yard. Hattie didn't care. She needed to see for herself.

They rounded the corner and didn't see any unusual activity. There wasn't a car parked on the corner near Hattie's house as James had indicated. It was only once they got closer to Hattie's and stepped over the curb to the sidewalk that Hattie could see her backyard had been torn apart. As Hattie got closer, her hand flew to her mouth. Not only were there holes in the ground, but her flower beds had been overturned and soil tossed in piles on the grass.

Jackson expelled a breath. "You think James showed up at the shop as a distraction to make sure we stayed there while someone did their worst to your yard?"

Hattie hadn't been thinking that, but looking at the yard now, it occurred to her how much time this would have taken. "You think he did that? Someone beat him up pretty badly."

"Surface cuts and scrapes," Jackson said. "He could have gone to the cops or back to his hotel, but he came to you and then took his sweet time telling us the story."

Hattie placed a hand on his back. "That's a little farfetched for me to believe but anything is possible. You think he made up the story about Cora?"

"No. I think he was out here and Cora was with the other guy. I don't buy that a guy in a ski mask attacked him and he fought himself free. They could have been working together. Did you see him, Hattie? He couldn't fight off a kitten."

Hattie giggled because when Jackson said it that way she couldn't disagree. "Well, whoever it was made a mess."

Jackson pulled out his phone and snapped a few photos of the damage. "I'll help you get your yard back in shape."

She patted him on the arm. "Never you mind about that. You have to repair things with Harper. I can call my landscaper and he'll fix this up in no time."

"Are you sure?"

"Yes," Hattie insisted. "Now go see Harper at her office. The sooner you two speak the better for you both."

Jackson looked around the yard and then back at the street. "I don't want to leave you alone. What if they come back?"

Hattie spotted Beau standing at the far side of the yard. "I'm not alone. I'll be fine. Please, go see Harper. She needs you."

Jackson followed Hattie's gaze toward Beau, but of course, he wouldn't see what she was seeing. She told him again to go and this time he left. It was only then that Beau approached.

"Did you see what happened to the yard?" Hattie asked as she felt his energy merge with hers.

Beau nodded. "I caught them when they were just about done. A man and a woman. I didn't recognize either of them."

"There was a third man," Hattie said. "He showed up at the shop and said someone attacked him in the yard. Did you see that?"

"I didn't see that, but as I said, by the time I got here it was a man and a woman."

Hattie tilted her head to look up at her husband. "Was it Nick, Harper's ex-husband?"

Beau had only met the man once before his death. He hadn't liked him either. While Hattie had tried to talk Harper out of marrying him, Beau supported her and assumed she knew best. "It wasn't him, Hattie. I'd love to blame this on him, but it was a different man. The woman called him Sam."

"That was the man who showed up at Harper's office the other day. He told Det. Granger that Harper was involved with a man that was recently murdered."

"That doesn't surprise me. He looked like he was no good. I tried to scare them off, but outside like this, I don't have the same control over energy as inside the house."

"You didn't have the strength?" Hattie asked, not sure what he meant.

"There was nothing to throw at him. I tried to push him and my hands went right through him."

Hattie understood. Sometimes in more confined spaces, spirits could summon the energy and use it to their will. In a wide-open space like the yard, the energy was harder to gather. Hattie started to ask Beau another question, but she caught sight of Father Peter McNeely, the parish priest from St. Joseph's Catholic Parish, coming up the dirt path at the back of her yard.

She smiled up at Beau. "We better stop talking before he thinks I'm out here talking to myself. Come see me tonight when I'm home."

When Beau disappeared, Hattie called and waved. "Fr. McNeely." She walked over and met him on the lawn. "Can I help you with something?"

He was a young priest, only in his forties, and had been a help to Hattie on previous occasions. He knew what Hattie did at the shop and had reserved judgment. She liked having him as a neighbor.

"I've been waiting for you," he said. "I was going to walk over to the shop soon if you hadn't come home. I saw the people who did this to your yard. I figured you'd want to report them."

"You saw them?" Hattie asked, grateful he had come over.

"I stopped them. I had taken my dog for a walk and was on the way back. I came down the side street here and saw them in your yard." The side street that ran next to Hattie's house led back to St. Joseph's Church where the road dead-ended. It wasn't a well-traveled road except on weekends for church services.

"I heard it was a man and a woman who did this."

"Yes, they both had shovels and were digging around your yard. I stopped and asked what they were doing. The woman told me that you told her she could be back here, but I didn't think that was right. Why would you tell them to dig up your yard like that? It didn't make sense so I told them I was going to call you and then they took off. I haven't seen them come back."

Hattie pulled her phone out of her skirt pocket. "Would you know them if you saw them, Father?"

"Yes," he said, nodding. "I think I could identify them. That shouldn't be a problem."

Hattie scrolled in her phone until she found a photo of Nick. She didn't have any of Cora or James. She turned her phone to face Fr. McNeely. "Is this the man?"

He squinted down at it and shook his head. "No, that wasn't the man I saw. The man was taller and had more muscle. He looked like a shady sort of fellow. The woman was a little heavyset in the hips. She couldn't have been more than five-foot-two and had dark hair."

Hattie wasn't sure what Sam looked like but assumed by what Beau said, it was him. He had broken into Harper's office after all, and it was likely he'd try the house. Looking around at the mess, Hattie's breathing became uneven and she lowered her head. She brought her hand up to her chest where her heart thumped.

Fr. McNeely reached his hand out and touched her shoulder. "Are you okay, Hattie? Let me walk you into the house."

Hattie didn't like to be tended to but this time she would allow it. She took the priest's arm and he guided her around to the side door of her home and she pulled out her keys and unlocked the door. Fr. McNeely helped her up the steps and into the back porch. He closed and locked the door behind them.

Sparkle and Shine ran to her from the hallway but stopped short as if sensing it wouldn't be a good idea to jump on Hattie as they normally did. They sat down in the middle of the kitchen floor and watched as Fr. McNeely escorted Hattie inside. He walked her over to the table and then stood there looking down at her.

"How about I make you some tea?"

"Father, you don't have to go to all that trouble. I'm fine really. It's just been a stressful day and then seeing my yard and all my flowers ripped up like that, it's terrible."

He waved her off. "Please, Hattie, just call me Peter. I'd love a cup of tea and I don't have any over at the rectory so you'd be indulging me if you have a cup of tea with me."

Hattie knew he was just being kind. She pointed to a bottom cabinet near the stove. "How about some Irish coffees instead? The coffeemaker is all set up. All you need to do is turn it on and I have Bailey's under the counter there."

Fr. McNeely smiled broadly. "A woman after my own heart. That does sound a bit better than tea." He went to the cabinet and pulled out the Bailey's. He found the cups and switched on the coffeemaker. "While I'm doing this, tell me what's going on. Why were those people digging in your yard?"

Hattie normally was cautious around religious people because her own beliefs and lifestyle were frowned upon. More than that, she had been accused of all sorts of things associated with the devil himself.

Maybe it was because Hattie was comfortable with Fr. McNeely or because she was in over her head, she sniffed back tears and told him everything.

He listened intently and didn't interrupt her. After he fixed their coffees, he carried the cups over to the table and then grabbed the tin of cookies Hattie had pointed to on the counter. When he sat down and took a sip, he smiled over at her. "I'm glad you trusted me enough to tell me what was going on. Anyone would be overcome with stress."

"I don't know how to protect them all," Hattie said, taking a sip.

"Did someone tell you it was your job to protect them? I've met Harper and Jackson and they seem like incredibly capable people."

"They are," Hattie admitted slowly. "They get in their own way sometimes. I don't want them to make too many mistakes and ruin their relationship though. Both of them have their exes visiting and it's too stressful for any relationship."

Fr. McNeely reached his hand over and placed it on top of Hattie's. "It's their mistakes to make. You're trying to control things too much and not letting nature take its course. They will be fine. Let them weather the storm together. They will be better for it in the end."

She didn't disagree. It was easier said than done though. She was about to tell him that when a worried expression came over his face. "What is it?"

"Do you have a photo of the necklace you said was missing?"

Hattie didn't but she reached for her phone. It didn't even take a minute to find it on a website about Princess Olga. "Here you go," she said, handing him the phone.

Fr. McNeely stared down at the photo and his face paled. He raised his eyes to her. "Hattie, the youth group at the church has the necklace. One of the girls just wore it in a school play." He slumped back in the chair, his face paling. "I thought it was fake."

Chapter Twenty-Seven

Harper checked her watch. She didn't have much time left to sit with Nick before getting back to the office for a meeting. "Nick," she said, leaning toward him at the table. "Do you know Brendan Miller?"

Nick didn't seem fazed by the question. "He works for Marco," he said absently, looking at his phone. When Harper didn't say anything, he raised his head. "You've met him, Harper. He worked at my father's financial firm."

Harper had no memory of meeting him. "When did we meet?"

"A few times. The event we went to that last New Year's Eve we were together. Brendan sat at our table with his girlfriend. We've had dinner with him as well."

Harper remembered the New Year's Eve event. She had been tired and cranky and wanted to be at home, but instead, Nick had made her go to a high-end party at The Ritz-Carlton. Her dress had been uncomfortable and her shoes made her feet and knees ache. She had spent the night listening to Nick and his friends drone on about work and then she slipped out early and had gone home before midnight. She barely remembered who sat at their table and couldn't recall Brendan.

She gripped the stone in her pocket tighter. "Did you give him photos of me?"

Nick furrowed his brow. "That's a weird question. No, why would I do that?"

"He had photos of me on his phone."

"When?" Nick set his phone down and stared across the table at her. "What are you talking about, Harper? I haven't seen Brendan since I got out of prison."

"He's dead, Nick." Harper watched his face for a reaction.

He didn't believe her. "What do you mean dead? How do you know?"

"He was killed here in Little Rock. Det. Granger found his body in Allsopp Park, just like Vinnie Ruggiero, the other mobster that was murdered." Harper lowered her voice. "Brendan had photos of me on his phone that I don't remember. Det. Granger showed me his photo and he didn't look familiar to me."

It didn't seem to make any sense to Nick. "He could have grabbed some photos of us off my Facebook page. You only met him a handful of times. I'm not surprised you don't remember him. I need to tell Marco that he's dead." Nick picked up his phone.

Harper reached across the table to stop him. "You might want to reconsider that. I assume it was Marco who sent Brendan down here. You told me yourself that the man I saw stealing the necklace is Marco's cousin, Richie. Do you think Marco is someone you can trust right now?"

"He's my brother-in-law."

Harper shook her head in frustration. "Haven't you ever seen a mob movie? I hardly think your relation to him matters. Not to mention, you got his sister pregnant and are still trying to get back together with your ex-wife."

"He doesn't know that."

Harper couldn't believe that Nick wasn't seeing what was right in front of his eyes. "Are you kidding me?" she asked, exasperated. "Marco has the necklace stolen from your office and creates this crazy story that I must have it. Then mob guys start dropping like flies. What has Marco got us caught up into?"

Nick searched her face. "You're different down here, Harper."

"We don't have time for that. What do you think Marco is doing? Aren't you concerned for your safety at all?"

"I am," he stressed. "That's why you need to give me the necklace."

"Nick, I'm going to speak slowly so you understand me." She punctuated each word. "I do not have the necklace. I have no idea where it is. I did not take it." When Nick didn't say anything, Harper yelled at him. "You are going to have to face reality! Whether you believe in my gifts or not, that's irrelevant. I know what I saw. So, you tell me, why would Richie take the necklace? Would he rip off Marco?"

"No one in their right mind would steal from Marco. He's more ruthless than Carmine ever was."

"Then Marco told him to take the necklace thereby accusing me of stealing and setting you up. None of it makes sense. What's his endgame?"

"I don't believe this is all true," Nick said, but the look on his face indicated he was starting to believe her at least a little.

Harper said the spell's chant one more time silently and clutched the stone. "Did you kill Vinnie or Brendan or both?"

Nick sucked a breath. "How could you ask me something like that?"

"That's not a denial."

Nick locked eyes with her. "I did not kill Vinnie or Brendan or anyone else. I've never killed anyone, Harper, and never would."

Even if she hadn't had Nick under a spell, Harper would have believed him. "Then we need to figure out what's happening." Harper's cellphone rang and she saw that it was Hattie. She wanted to send the call to voicemail, but something told her to pick it up. "It's Hattie so I have to take this," she said to Nick and then stood from the table.

"Give me a second and then I'll be able to talk," Harper said to Hattie as she answered. She walked through the dining area and out the front door. Once she got to the sidewalk, she told her aunt to go ahead.

"Harper," Hattie said nearly breathless, "you're not going to believe this, Fr. McNeely found the necklace."

"What do you mean Fr. McNeely found it?" Harper had no idea why the priest would be rummaging around Hattie's house.

"You don't understand. He found it in a box in the auditorium over at St. Joseph's parish." Hattie spoke to someone on the other end of the phone and then got back on the line. "I don't know what you're doing or where you are, but you need to come to the auditorium right now." Hattie hung up before Harper could say no.

She clutched the phone in her hand and then she punched in a familiar number. It rang three times and Dan picked up. "I'm so sorry," she said, her voice rushed. "I need to get home to see Hattie. I was supposed to have a meeting with one of the freelance writers in fifteen minutes. Can you meet with her?"

"Sure, that's not a problem," Dan said. "Is everything okay?"

Harper looked to her left and then to her right. She cupped her hand over the phone and whispered, "Hattie found the necklace."

Dan whooped loudly. "I can't believe it! That's amazing, Harper. What are you going to do with it?"

"I don't know yet. I need to meet Hattie and have a look at it. We'll turn it over to the police, of course."

"You could use it as bait to draw out the killer."

Leave it to Dan to think of the most dangerous thing they could do. He came up with the craziest schemes but was rarely a part of them. "I think you like to see me in danger," she laughed.

"I can't lose my business partner. I have faith in you."

Harper could see him sitting at his desk smiling. She knew he wanted to ask her to let him see it. "Do you want me to call you when I confirm it's real so you can take a look?"

"I thought you'd never ask."

"Confirm what's real?" Nick said from behind her.

Harper bit her lip and turned to face him. "It's Dan about a meeting at work."

Nick didn't move. He stayed right there watching her.

Harper needed to get out of there without raising Nick's suspicions. She cleared her throat. "Dan, Nick's here and I need to finish meeting with him. I'll call you after I speak to the freelancer."

Dan laughed. "I'll call you when I'm on my way to Hattie's."

"Sounds good."

Nick stood there rocking on the balls of his feet and had his hands in his pockets. When she hung up, he said, "You said it was Hattie who called you."

"It was and then Dan called right after." She moved past him to head back into the restaurant. "I can't believe you left my purse on my chair. We need to pay the bill."

"I paid the bill," Nick said, following in after her.

"I could have paid for mine." Harper got to the table and pulled the strap of her purse off the chair and looked inside. Her wallet was still there.

"I can buy you lunch, Harper. That's not a problem." He stared her down. "What are you doing now?"

Harper raised her head to him. "You just heard me tell Dan I have a meeting for work. That's where I'm headed." She headed out of the restaurant and Nick followed right behind.

"When can I see you again?" he asked when they were back on the sidewalk.

Harper wanted to say never and tell him to go back to Manhattan. She needed to play nice for a while longer. "Give what I said some thought and call me when you realize I'm telling you the truth. I'm sure then we can help each other out of this mess."

Nick pulled her into an awkward hug. Harper had her fists balled up in front of her nudging herself out of his embrace but he didn't let go. "I know you care about me even if you won't admit it. You have too much pride."

Harper grimaced and shoved him backward until she was free of him. "Whatever you want to think. Just call me when you come to your senses." Before he could say anything else, she crossed the road and walked in the direction of her car. She turned back once and Nick was still standing in the same spot, watching her. Harper would be looking over her shoulder all the way to Hattie's to make sure he didn't follow.

Chapter Twenty-Eight

H attie stared down into the cardboard box at the necklace that sat atop costume jewelry and a collection of men's hats from bygone eras. She still couldn't believe that Fr. McNeely had the necklace all this time.

After Fr. McNeely said that he might have the necklace, Hattie had rushed him out of her house and followed him to the auditorium next to the church. The space was used for youth group activities, children's plays, and other youth-focused events. The back part of the building held a basketball court used by local Catholic schools and community basketball leagues. The building had the faint smell of peanut butter and jelly sandwiches, Play-Doh, and a weird funk Hattie couldn't distinguish. It smelled like a grade school, or at least, every grade school Hattie had been in. It wasn't horrible but not entirely pleasant either.

Fr. McNeely had opened up the auditorium for Hattie and then guided her to the stairs that sat left of the stage. They went around to the back of the stage to a row of small dressing rooms. Fr. McNeely had entered one of the rooms and flipped on the light. Along the back wall were rows of cardboard boxes. He had pulled off a box that sat atop two others and pulled back the flaps and pointed.

Hattie had peered down into it and couldn't believe her eyes. She also hadn't been able to make sense of it. She immediately called Harper and then stood there staring into the box.

That's how Harper found her, guarding the necklace like it might jump out of the box at any moment and run away. "Is it the necklace? Are you sure?" Harper asked out of breath and flustered.

All Hattie could do was point. "Those hats are your Uncle Beau's. A few months back I gave the parish some old clothes, hats, and costume jewelry that had been sitting in the attic for ages. The kids have school plays and I heard one of the women at the shop talking about how they needed some used clothes for costumes. That's when I remembered all this stuff that I had boxed up. Jackson helped me carry it over here."

"You didn't go through the boxes again before you donated them?" Fr. McNeely asked.

Hattie shook her head. "There was no need. I knew what had been in them. There wasn't that much in the attic. We loaded ten boxes into the car, drove it over, and then carried them in here. I never once opened them."

"How did you find it?" Harper asked, turning to Fr. McNeely.

"I feel so foolish now but one of the seventh-grade girls wore the necklace in the last play. Some of the parents questioned if it was real, but as you can see," he said, pointing to it, "it's hard to believe an emerald that big would be real."

Hattie had to admit he had a point. The quality of the gems was so clear that they didn't look real. If she had stumbled upon it, she might have thought the same. "It's been sitting in this box since then?"

Fr. McNeely nodded. "The theater director didn't want it to be ruined. She had kept it on her desk, but she just moved offices and told me she put it in the box for safekeeping. She rarely let the children have access to it – only for special performances. She moved offices a few days ago. That's why it was on my mind when Hattie told me the story about the necklace."

Harper leaned over the box and picked it up. She held it across her two hands. "It's heavier than I thought it would be, then again, that emerald is enormous. I've never seen anything like this. Photos don't do it justice."

Hattie thought of the curse and wondered if Harper should even be touching it. "Fr. McNeely, has anything bad happened at the auditorium in the last few months?" Hattie figured she had donated the items about four months ago.

"What do you mean?"

Harper looked at him. "The necklace is cursed or that's how the story goes. The last owner's life went downhill so fast after owning it that he cooked up an insurance fraud scheme to get rid of it. He told me he couldn't find a buyer. Everyone that could afford and might want a necklace like this wouldn't touch it for fear of the curse."

The priest's eyes opened wide. "We had to move the theater director's desk down to an office closer to the front door because she broke her leg in an accident during a play rehearsal a few weeks after the school play that I mentioned. It was after that play that she started keeping the necklace on her desk. Her husband also lost his job recently." He looked to Hattie. "You don't believe it's cursed, do you?"

"I don't know what to believe, Father. I know you don't believe in such things, but I don't think I'd be taking any chances." Hattie turned to Harper. "What do we do with this now?"

Harper gently set the necklace down on a nearby table. "Fr. McNeely, did you find any diamonds in your search of these boxes?"

"I didn't search them and not all of them have been opened."

"We need to do that now, and we'll need help."

Harper made a quick call to Dan, who arrived nearly immediately. He admitted he had canceled the freelancer meeting and drove to Hattie's house. Harper let him see the necklace and then immediately put him to work. For the next hour, they searched the boxes one by one, pulling out all the contents and going through shirt and pants pockets, but no diamonds were found.

Hattie folded the last pair of pants and dropped them back in the box. "If they were here, they are long gone."

"They could still be at the house," Harper said. "We have no idea if the person who left these in your house kept them together."

"That's true," Hattie admitted, feeling overwhelmed again. "Let's take this back to the house and search. I'm feeling like if the necklace is there, the diamonds will also reveal themselves."

Fr. McNeely smiled at Hattie. "You can always say a prayer to St. Anthony."

Hattie reached over and squeezed his hand. "I've been praying every night that the necklace would be found so looks like he came through so far."

"He always comes through. Let's say the prayer together right now. A little added oomph can't hurt." Together Hattie and Fr. McNeely said the prayer with Harper and Dan looking on. When they were done, Hattie hugged him and told him she'd be in touch.

"Make sure to update me. I can't wait to hear the rest of the story." Fr. McNeely smiled like a child who had been let in on a secret.

Harper thanked him over and over again. "I don't believe there is any reward for the necklace, but if there is, we will donate it to the church. Hattie and I will also donate to thank you for your help."

"The children will appreciate that. We are so grateful to anyone who helps support our parish," Fr. McNeely said. "I'm just glad I could be of help."

As they walked out of the auditorium and headed for home, Harper carried the necklace awkwardly in her hands like she wasn't sure what she should do with it. "I can't shove this in my pocket. I don't want anything to happen to it."

Hattie looked around making sure they were alone as they crossed the dirt path from the parish grounds to Hattie's backyard. The last thing she wanted was to have finally found the necklace and then have it stolen again.

"How did lunch go with Nick?" Dan asked.

"I described the person who had stolen the necklace and hid it in your house. He is Marco's cousin, Richie De Luca. Marco had to have known where the necklace was hidden this whole time. I assume Richie hid it upstairs in the attic and figured it would be good for safekeeping until they retrieved it later."

They reached the house and Hattie opened the back door for Harper, who stepped up slowly into the house. She walked through the back porch and then placed the necklace on the dining table.

"Why would Marco hide the necklace down here and then claim it was stolen from him? That doesn't make a lot of sense," Dan said, sitting down.

Hattie shook her head. "I'm going to have to check my cards to see if I can pick up anything because it's confusing me."

"It doesn't make any sense," Harper agreed. "I tried to get Nick to talk to me about why Marco would set him up like that. I wasn't even able to convince Nick that my vision was real. They thought they would hide the necklace in a place where it wouldn't be found."

Dan pointed to her. "What is it, Harper? I know that look."

Harper rubbed at her forehead. "In my vision, Marco didn't seem to have any idea where the necklace was. He even mentioned sending someone else down here to help Nick search for it. Why would he go to the trouble?"

"Unless it wasn't Marco," Hattie said.

Harper raised her head. "Who would it be then?"

"I don't know. I'll have to look at the cards and see if I can get more information."

Harper ran her finger over the emerald. "I don't understand how Fr. McNeely played into this. Did the spell tell you that the necklace was over there?"

"Oh my," Hattie said dramatically, realizing she never told Harper about the earlier events of the day. "Didn't you see the holes in the backyard as we passed by? I figured Jackson would have told you."

"Holes? Like someone digging?" Harper asked and Hattie confirmed. "I didn't see them and I haven't spoken to Jackson all day. What happened?"

Hattie explained about James Wiggins coming to the shop and about the man and woman digging for the necklace in Hattie's yard. She watched Harper's face fall as she told her.

Harper interrupted. "Nick was late for lunch and he was disheveled – his shirttails were out and his hands looked like they had been digging in the dirt. I wonder if it was him."

"I showed Fr. McNeely a photo of Nick. He said it wasn't him. Beau said the woman called the man Sam, like the guy who was in your office."

"You think it was Cora?" Dan asked.

Hattie nodded. "James confirmed it was Cora." Turning to Harper, she asked, "Did you find out anything about Brendan?"

"Nick said that I knew him. I don't remember meeting him. Nick said he worked with him at the financial firm and was involved with Marco, too."

Hattie tapped at the table. "It seems all roads lead back to Marco."

Harper looked up toward the ceiling. "We need to check the attic."

"What's in the attic?" Jackson asked, walking into the house and smiling at Harper. "I went to your office, but it seems neither of you is working today."

Harper pointed to the necklace on the table. "Hattie found it," she said and recounted the last couple of hours. "I need to check the attic for the diamonds."

"Let's go. I'll help you."

Chapter Twenty-Nine

Once Dan left to go back to the office, Harper and Jackson headed upstairs. The door to the attic was right outside Harper's bedroom door. She hadn't been in the attic since she first moved into Hattie's house and stored a few boxes up there.

She felt along the wall. "I know there is a light switch somewhere."

Jackson reached across her shoulder. "It's right here. I found it the last time Hattie sent me up here."

"Thanks," Harper said not sure what else to say to him. There had been so much tension the last time they spoke that she didn't want to make things worse. Jackson acted as if nothing had happened, but Harper couldn't forget the look of disappointment and anger on his face when he found out she had used a spell on Sam.

"You don't have to help if you have something better to do," Harper said, climbing the stairs.

"No place I'd rather be than with you."

Harper wasn't sure if he was being real or sarcastic and she was afraid to turn around and look. She stepped up onto the landing. The place was surprisingly clean. Hattie had a few racks of clothes in one corner and a handful of boxes. There was an old chair and then Harper's boxes on the other side. "I guess Hattie cleaned this place out when she donated those other boxes."

Jackson stood next to her with his hands on his hips assessing the space. "I'll take Hattie's boxes and you take yours. Then we can go through all the pockets of those clothes."

Harper thought that was a good idea. "Do you know if there are any secret hiding places up here? Any floorboards come up or spots in the wall open up? Old houses have those sometimes."

He turned to her. "You'd have to ask Hattie, I'm not sure."

Harper nodded and started to walk past him to her boxes, but Jackson reached out and grabbed her arm. She didn't turn to face him and made Jackson move in front of her.

"What?" she said, a hint of annoyance in her voice.

"Don't you think we should talk?"

"I don't have much to say." Harper didn't realize how much anger she had bubbling up inside. She wasn't sure if it was from the situation or if she was truly angry with Jackson. It seemed a bit irrational. She stood her ground. "I was embarrassed enough having to tell Det. Granger what happened with Sam, you didn't need to act the way you did."

"I know. I was wrong," Jackson said. "This has been a learning process for me, too. It seems every few months you develop another power. Sometimes it's so overwhelming for me that I forget you're the one living it. You've had to take on so much over the last few years. I couldn't do it if I were you. I'd go to sleep at night wondering if tomorrow I'd wake up and be able to fly."

Harper raised her eyes to him. "Flying would be pretty cool, though."

Jackson cracked a smile. "Flying would be cool, but you know what I'm saying. It's hard for me to keep up. Then to hear that you nearly killed a man with a spell. I was more worried for you than anything."

"You didn't seem worried. You were angry and disappointed in me." Harper shrugged. "I wondered if you were embarrassed, too."

"Never, Harper. I'm never embarrassed." Jackson reached up and stroked his finger under her chin. "I wasn't angry. I was shocked that you'd try a spell. Last I heard, you had no interest in doing spells. Then when I heard that, I was completely taken aback. I wasn't angry or disappointed in you."

Harper explained that Hattie had been encouraging her to learn the spells in their family's grimoire. "She said there was no real harm to Sam, that he was overreacting to the spell. I don't know why, but he is trying to cause trouble for me."

"That much is obvious. Have you figured out who Brendan was?"

Harper explained what Nick had told her at lunch. "If Nick says I met him, then I'm sure I did. I don't remember him. Then again, I don't remember many people Nick worked with. The ones I remember, I didn't like any of them."

Jackson wrapped her in a hug. "Even if you knew him, it doesn't mean you killed him. I'm sure Det. Granger doesn't suspect you."

Harper leaned her head against Jackson's chest. "Let's hope it doesn't get to that. I'll have to tell Det. Granger that I have met Brendan and at least explain what Nick said."

"Did you find out anything else at lunch?"

Harper pulled out of Jackson's arms. "Let's search and then we can talk. We never got a chance to talk last night. I want to get this out of the way before we decide what to do with the necklace."

"I assumed you'd call Det. Granger."

"I will, but it was stolen to commit insurance fraud. Then it seems it was taken from Nick by someone related to Marco. It's not like there is a clear line of ownership. I don't want to keep it here though. I believe it's cursed now."

"You don't normally believe in such things."

Harper laughed. "My mind has expanded."

The two of them got down to searching. Harper sat on the floor and pried open the taped flaps on the first box. She hadn't taken much with her from Manhattan – some of her favorite books, a few personal items, and awards she had won for the magazine. She also had some jewelry that was her mother's but she had that in her bedroom. Harper pulled out the first book and then the rest of the books in the box. A mix of autobiographies and fiction, there weren't any diamonds among the books. She went to the next box and then another. Still nothing.

Harper glanced over at Jackson who was going through Hattie's things. He didn't seem to be having much luck either. Refocusing on the box in front of her, Harper pulled out some clothing she had saved. Designer dresses and shirts and her favorite pair of Manolo Blahnik gray ankle boots. She held one boot in her hand. "Can you believe I used to spend over a thousand dollars on shoes and didn't even think twice about it?"

Jackson looked over at her and pointed to her feet. "I much prefer your Converse."

Harper laughed. She set the boot back next to its twin and continued her search through the boxes. Nothing other than the things she packed from Manhattan. She pushed herself up from the floor and brushed off the back of her pants. "I'm going to start looking through the pockets of the clothes."

"I'm not finding anything here," Jackson said, closing the lid on the last box. "I'll help you."

They searched down the rows of clothing. Harper reached into each pocket and then ran her hand down the garments to make sure nothing had been sewn into the seams. She didn't feel anything unusual. She raised her head over the rack of clothing and looked at Jackson, who shook his head indicating he hadn't found anything either.

"Maybe they didn't stash the diamonds here," he said, coming around the rack to Harper. "What did you see in your vision?"

"He wasn't carrying anything in his hands so I can't be sure. He might have stashed the diamonds someplace else in the house."

They left the attic together and once they hit the landing, Harper turned and shut the door, making sure it was closed firmly. A cold draft from the attic often made its way to her bedroom and caused her room to be colder than the rest of the house.

As they made their way to the first floor, Harper said, "We are going to have to call Det. Granger."

Jackson pulled his phone from his pants pocket. "Do you want me to call?"

Harper nodded. She wasn't sure what she'd say to him anyway. "What do you think they will do with the necklace given that it's stolen property?"

"I suspect they will need to return it to the rightful owner."

"George Lennox," Harper said absently. She couldn't imagine that he'd want it back when he'd gone to such lengths to get rid of it. Then she thought of the insurance money that he was paid. She reached her hand out and touched Jackson's arm. "What happens to the insurance money he was paid when it was stolen? Does he have to return it?"

Jackson stopped on the steps. "In that case, if an insurance claim was paid, then the insurance company would own the necklace."

"I'm sure George will be fine with that unless they figure out it was a fraudulent claim and then he's in big trouble. I can't worry about that though," Harper said and they walked the rest of the way to the bottom.

Jackson placed a call to Det. Granger as he and Harper went into the kitchen to see Hattie. Harper found her sitting at the table staring down at the necklace.

She raised her head to her niece. "I don't want to keep this in the house any longer than we have to." Her face had paled and Hattie's hand trembled.

Harper rushed over to her. "What's the matter? Did something happen?"

"Can't you feel it?" Hattie asked, pushing the necklace away from her.

Harper had no idea what her aunt was talking about. "What is it?"

"The energy shift that's occurred since we brought that into the house." Hattie stood from the table. "You didn't feel it as you carried it over here?"

"Hattie, was there a spirit here? I've only seen you this upset when you're visited by a negative spirit."

Hattie clutched her chest with her hand. "She came to me, Harper, and told me she had cursed the necklace." Hattie squeezed her eyes shut. "She was hideous."

"Princess Olga?" Harper asked, confused by what her aunt was saying.

Hattie shook her head. "This has nothing to do with her. A witch cursed the necklace. She was one of us. A man she loved gave the necklace as a gift to another and she cursed it. The curse must have bounced back on her, too, because her skin..."

"What about her skin?"

Hattie's eyes had a vacant stare about them. "Her skin was peeling off, her eyes were sunken, and every tooth had rotted out of her head."

"The witches code," Harper said more to herself than her aunt.

"That's right. She broke the code and is paying for it in death."

Harper took Hattie by the hand and guided her into the living room. "Is there a way to lift the curse?"

"I don't know," Hattie said, shaking her head. "The witch's spirit remains over the necklace. She goes wherever it goes. She only gave me the warning because we are witches. She's even angrier because the spell came back on her."

Hattie sat down in her favorite chair and looked up at Harper with fear in her eyes. "She's out for revenge and won't stop until she gets it. As long as that necklace is in the house, she will be, too."

Chapter Thirty

Night had fallen by the time Det. Granger arrived. Harper had made Hattie a warm cup of tea and walked her upstairs to take a nap. Harper had to promise she wouldn't bring the necklace any farther into the house than the kitchen.

Before climbing into bed, Hattie reached up to Harper and whispered in her ear. "If we destroy the necklace, we can destroy the spirit of the witch."

Harper wasn't sure how they'd be able to destroy the necklace since the insurance company owned it now. It's not like they had millions of dollars to buy it from them only to destroy it. Harper assured Hattie that they would figure it out, but it was probably best to rest up for now while she handled things with Det. Granger.

"I'm here if you need anything," Hattie called after her as she walked down the stairs.

Harper walked into the kitchen just as Det. Granger came in. "Jackson said to come right over."

Harper wasn't sure how to be around him now that he had been so angry with her the night before. There was a thick air of tension between them. She pointed to the table. "Hattie found the necklace today but still no luck on the diamonds."

Det. Granger could barely meet her eyes. He went over to the table and stared down at it. "Where is Hattie?" he said, angling his head in her direction.

"She's upstairs." Harper got closer to him as he reached out his hand to touch the emerald. "I wouldn't touch that if I were you. There is a curse, and Hattie said the spirit of the witch who cursed it is always around. She was such a distressing sight for Hattie, she's in bed now resting."

Det. Granger slowly pulled his hand back and glanced at Harper. "Seriously?"

"Jackson and I were up in the attic searching for the diamonds. When we came back downstairs, I found Hattie quite distressed. She was almost transfixed on the necklace." Harper sat down at the table. "I rarely see Hattie afraid. I think we should take it seriously."

Det. Granger stepped back from the necklace and finally looked down at Harper. "It's awkward between us, right?"

Harper nodded. "I'm not sure what to say. I've never seen you get angry like that with me. I know what I did was stupid. It wasn't intentional."

"I overreacted."

Harper raised her head and locked eyes with him. "It turns out I do know Brendan Miller. I asked Nick today if he was familiar with him. He told me Brendan worked with him and was connected to Marco De Luca. I don't recall meeting him. I certainly wasn't involved with him, but according to Nick, I have met him."

Det. Granger said evenly, "We have Brendan's time of death. It was mid-day so I assume you were at the office. I'll have to confirm with Dan."

"Feel free," Harper said, annoyed that he even had to do that much. "Do you have any other suspects?"

Det. Granger chuckled. "Harper, you're not a suspect."

"You've known me for close to two years. You should know by now that I'd never intentionally hurt anyone unless they were causing my family harm and then it would be in self-defense."

"Harper," he said, his voice soft. "Sam said you nearly killed him at your office. Then you had a connection to Brendan. I didn't think you had anything to do with the murder, but I had to ask. Sam wanted to make a report that you had assaulted him. I stopped him from doing that."

"I shouldn't have tried the spell without more knowledge about it," Harper admitted. "Sam shouldn't have come into my office and threatened me though. I used a truth spell. Hattie said that his reaction was based on him trying to lie and that a spell like that would never cause death. I think you probably should focus on him."

"We are checking into Sam among other people." Det. Granger remained quiet for a moment. He sat down at the table right next to Harper. "This spell and ghost stuff gives me the creeps," he admitted. "I've been trying to deal with it because of how I feel about Sarah and Hattie and you, but it doesn't mean it's easy for me. I didn't grow up with this. I grew up in a conservative religious household where this kind of thing is thought of as evil."

Harper had denied her gifts for the majority of her life. It was only after moving in with Hattie that she was open to exploring them. "It creeps me out a little if I'm being honest. I'm adjusting to having these gifts. I didn't even know that I could perform a spell. I've seen Hattie do it and most of the time, I figured it was fluff. I thought the person believed in the spell so they were changing their behavior or something to make the spell come true – like a placebo effect. Doing that spell on Sam was the first time I understood the power I have."

He didn't say anything and Harper wanted to lighten the mood. She smiled up at him. "You and Jackson should form a support group for boyfriends of the supernatural."

Det. Granger laughed, showing off a row of straight white teeth. "I hope you both are okay."

"We talked and we're fine." Harper pointed to the necklace. "What are we going to do about that?"

"Tell me again how it came to be in your possession."

Harper sat back in the chair and explained her vision to Det. Granger and how the necklace came to be with the priest. When she was done, she said, "Because George Lennox committed insurance fraud and the insurance company paid out the claim on it, the rightful owner is most likely the insurance company."

Det. Granger had a look of confusion on his face. "Let me see if I got this right. George Lennox got the De Lucas to take the necklace, and it was Nick who helped plan the fake robbery. George collected the insurance money and Nick kept the necklace at your residence in New York. Then Richie, Marco's cousin, stole the necklace and left it in Hattie's attic, unbeknownst to any of you. It then ended up in a donated box of items at the church. In the meantime, someone stages this ridiculous hunt for the necklace because Nick told people you stole it."

"That about sums it up. As strange a tale as it is."

"Where do the diamonds come into play?"

"They were part of Princess Olga's collection that George bought. He dumped everything on Nick, probably not sure if the diamonds were cursed too."

Det. Granger looked up at the ceiling as if processing the info. When he looked back to Harper a moment later, he asked, "Can we safely assume that Marco had no idea that Richie stole the necklace and diamonds?"

Harper didn't trust anything about Marco. "I would assume so, but I don't think we can rule it out one way or the other."

"Why would Marco risk losing the jewelry? Even if he wanted to set you up for something, it's too risky of a move."

"I agree with that."

"Do you think Nick and Richie are working together?" Det. Granger asked but didn't wait for Harper to answer. "Hear me out. What if Nick and Richie wanted to sell the necklace so he faked that it had been stolen. Richie kept it hidden at Hattie's, where no one would have ever thought to look. Nick was here before you all got back from New Orleans. He could have searched Hattie's house, found them gone, and panicked. Maybe he goes back to New York and tells Marco he doesn't have the necklace and blames you to cover for him and Richie. Then Marco, who even you said doesn't trust Nick, concocts this whole scheme to get the necklace and diamonds back."

"It's as good as any other theory," Harper said and meant it. "Marco didn't have to send other mobsters to look for the necklace though. He has men he trusts, like Brendan, who he could have sent down here. Why bring in others? He risks having the necklace and diamonds stolen from him if they're found."

Det. Granger seemed to consider it. "Could Marco have another reason for bringing these people here?"

"Like killing them?" Harper couldn't discount it. "Men are being murdered while Marco sits in New York with a good alibi."

"Why would Marco kill Brendan after he sent him down here?"

"Maybe it was Brendan who killed the others, and when he tried to kill a third, he was overpowered."

Det. Granger reached out and patted her hand. "Are you sure you don't want to be a detective?"

"Absolutely not! It annoys me when things don't make any sense." Harper pinned her gaze on the necklace. "What are you going to do with it?"

Det. Granger sat back and thought for several moments. "I think we should use it to our advantage. No one but you, Jackson, Hattie, and Fr. McNeely know it was found, correct?"

"Dan does too but he wouldn't tell anyone. Do you think we can use it to lure the killer?"

"I'm not sure yet," Det. Granger said, looking at the necklace. "Have you touched it and tried to see if you can get a vision?"

"I carried it over here, but I didn't try to get a vision. I don't think Hattie would have wanted me to do that. She didn't like me touching it at all."

Det. Granger pursed his lips. "Want to try now?"

Harper could hear Hattie's voice screaming *no, no, no* in her head, but she tuned it out. "I might as well give it a shot before you take it into evidence." Harper reached across the table and slid the necklace over to where she sat. "Jackson is in the living room if you need him for anything. Shake me if I seem too panicked."

Harper took the necklace in her hands and closed her eyes. She evened out her breath and waited for the vision to come. When it did, she let it pull her under as she watched the scene unfold around her. At first, she felt like the vision took her too far back in time. Harper tried to hit the forward button in her mind and tap into something more recent, but her vision remained focused.

What she saw shook her to her core. Harper tried to back out of the vision, but it held on tighter than anything she had experienced before. She saw the witch, young and beautiful, cursing the necklace.

Jackson's voice, yelling from the living room, dragged her out of her vision. She dropped the necklace, letting the delicate item clang on the table. "What?" she said breathlessly.

Det. Granger stood next to her, pointing to the living room. "Jackson fell. He tripped over one of the dogs when he heard you whimpering. He tried to check on you."

Harper jumped from her seat and rushed toward the living room. Once she was in the hallway that led out of the kitchen, she saw him sitting on the floor holding his ankle. His face contorted in pain and both dogs stood protectively over him. Harper knew it was the curse.

Jackson raised his head to her. "You're going to have to drive me to the emergency room. I think it's broken."

Chapter Thirty-One

Hattie arrived at her shop the next morning still distraught about the events of the evening before. Harper hadn't admitted trying to get a vision from the necklace, but Hattie knew she had. The witch had warned her when Hattie was in her bed. By the time Hattie got herself out of bed and to the top of the stairs, Jackson was already yelling for help. She couldn't get to him in time, and for that, Hattie couldn't forgive herself.

Det. Granger had helped Harper get Jackson to the car and they left for the hospital. Hattie warned Det. Granger about touching the necklace and encouraged him to find a safe neutral place for it at the police station. She warned him about spending too much time with it. In police custody, Hattie had no idea who the witch would target next.

Hattie shrugged off her coat and hung it on the coat rack in the corner of the shop not far from the door. Sarah was already behind the counter. "Have you heard from your brother this morning?" Hattie asked from across the room.

Sarah raised her head from the display case. "I heard from Harper. She said Jackson was still sleeping. They gave him some pain medication at the hospital. He's in a cast and on crutches. It's going to drive him mad having to rest for so long."

Hattie hadn't been awake when Harper and Jackson had arrived home from the hospital. They spent the night at his place. Hattie hadn't called this morning for fear of waking them. She made her way to the counter and grabbed the coffee. Tea was far too tame for the kind of morning she was having. "Is it a bad break?"

"It's bad enough, but at least it won't require surgery. Harper said the doctor was perplexed how he could have broken it so badly tripping over the dog."

Hattie whispered in her ear. "It's the curse. Have you seen the spirit of a witch this morning?"

"No. Should I have?" Sarah asked with a tinge of fear in her voice.

"She's attached to the necklace." Hattie took a sip of her coffee knowing she'd have to explain to Sarah what had happened. She waved Sarah over to the side of the counter farthest away from the earshot of any customers. In a hushed voice, Hattie explained about finding the necklace with the priest and the appearance of the witch's spirit when they brought the necklace back to the house.

Hattie's voice caught with emotion when she explained the witch. "She was hideous. She's been eaten away by her own jealousy and revenge. She never told me her name, but she said the man she loved gave the necklace to another woman. The witch cursed their love and the necklace out of jealousy and spite. Now, she haunts the necklace and curses its owner, especially if the people are in a happy relationship."

Sarah's eyes got as big as saucers. "Do you think this is why Jackson and Harper are having issues with their exes? Did the witch lure them down here to cause strife?"

"I hadn't thought of that," Hattie admitted. She wasn't sure of the answer. It could be plausible, but Harper and Hattie hadn't even known they were in possession of the necklace. "Do you think I should try to call the witch to speak to her?"

"Tell me about her." Sarah checked the shop to make sure no customers were waiting and then she leaned back on the counter to listen to Hattie.

Hattie gripped the coffee cup in her hand so hard her knuckles turned white. "When she first appeared to me, she was young, blonde, and very pretty. As soon as I focused my eyes on her, she turned into a wretched old hag. Her skin peeled off, her eyes sunk deep into her head and she looked about two hundred years old. The spell she used came back on her. As I said, her jealousy and revenge tore her apart from the inside."

"What era is she from?" Sarah asked.

Hattie recalled the image of the young woman and how she was dressed. "I'd say maybe 1930s or 40s, which would be right in line with the timing because Princess Olga perished in 1918. I know the rumor has been that she cursed the necklace because her family was murdered but that's not what the witch told me."

"The witch told you she cursed it because her love gave it to another woman?" Sarah asked, confirming with Hattie, who nodded. "Then I think you need to speak to the witch and see what other kinds of trouble she's been stirring up. The only spirit to visit me this morning was Charlie. He told me to tell you he's not making much headway on the murders. There are no suspects."

"Did Det. Granger tell you the same?"

"He has no idea what's going on." Sarah had to stop talking and help a customer at the counter.

Hattie wasn't sure what to make of it, but as distressing as it was last night to see the witch, she was going to have to call her again. "I'm going back to my reading room and see if I can connect with her."

Sarah turned her head toward Hattie. "Call me if you need anything."

Hattie made her way through the shop, stopping briefly to say hello to some of her regular customers. It had been a while since she'd seen the group of older ladies who stopped in each day. Hattie seemed to miss them each afternoon because she was tucked away in her reading room with an endless line of customers who had scheduled readings and wanted spells. By the time she finished, the ladies had already left the shop. It was good to catch up with them today, if only for a moment.

Hattie parted the curtain and walked down the hall to her reading room. Before her hand even touched the doorknob, she felt the dark presence of the witch fall over her. "I know you're here," she said sternly. "You better show yourself to me. I came back here to speak with you."

The spirit of the witch appeared right next to Hattie. She hissed, "You do not call me. I will not be summoned like some common spirit. I am the one in control."

Hattie took a deep breath. She knew the only way to handle a dark spirit was with force and confidence. The witch could do damage to the living though. Hattie saw that with Jackson last night, but still, she couldn't tread lightly.

Hattie turned her head. "I need to speak with you and you showed up. Does it matter which one of us summoned the other? Let's not squabble over details."

The witch clicked her tongue. "You're different than you were last night. Stronger."

Hattie opened the door to her reading room and flicked on the light. "I'm an old woman and I was tired last night. Not to mention you caught me off guard. Why don't you transform yourself back to the pretty young woman you once were and have a chat with me?"

The witch stood on the edge of the doorway. "Are you afraid of looking at me like this? This is how I died."

Hattie sat down in her chair and adjusted her skirt. "You can look however you're most comfortable," she said, hoping her voice sounded like she meant it. "We need to talk regardless of how you look. I figured look good, feel good. I thought it might improve your mood."

"You think my mood improves?" the witch cackled.

"Don't you get tired of being so hateful and hurting people all the time? It's been years since you died. It's time to move on, don't you think?"

The witch rose off the ground and peered down at Hattie with a menacing scowl. All Hattie could do was shrug. "Okay, I guess you like what you have going on then. Never mind, just trying to help." Hattie waited for the witch to float back down to the ground. "You can sit if you'd like."

"What do you want?" the witch asked.

"I need your help. I figured if you've been watching the necklace, you might have a clue to what's going on." That was technically true, but Hattie also wanted to figure out how to get rid of the witch. The only way she knew how to do that was to talk to her. "Also, what can I call you? I'd like to know your name."

"You may call me Delia." The witch stood in place for a moment and then gave in and sat on the couch across from Hattie. As she did, she transformed herself back into a young woman. "Why aren't you afraid of me?"

Hattie motioned with her hands. "I'm an old woman and mean you no harm. We are the same – witches. I figured we might be able to help each other. The better question is why do you want me to be afraid of you?"

That brought a smile to the witch's face. "All people should fear me. I can do much damage to the living like you saw last night."

"Speaking of that," Hattie started, resting her arm on the side of the chair. "Jackson is a good man and there was no reason to injure him. He hasn't done anything to you."

"Not to me, but he left his wife for another woman. For that, he deserves what he got. You are lucky I didn't do more."

Hattie shook her head. "You have it all wrong. Jackson left his wife a long time ago because she cheated on him. It was long after they divorced that Jackson met Harper and they got involved."

Delia looked momentarily confused by this news. "How do you know that?"

"Jackson lived here for months before he even met Harper," Hattie said with force. "His wife Cora was the one who made sure her marriage ended. Now, she is here causing trouble trying to get him back."

"My mistake then, but not my problem." Delia sat back and appraised Hattie. "As per your other question. Yes, I always watch the necklace. I know what's happening here. I know who murdered those men. It amuses me that so many people are out for revenge."

"Is that what this is about? Revenge?" Hattie asked, sitting on the edge of her chair.

"Yes," Delia said with a sick smile. "There is much more to come."

Chapter Thirty-Two

Harper blamed herself for what happened to Jackson. If she hadn't tried to tap into a vision, he wouldn't have gotten hurt. Harper sat in his living room working on her laptop. She had explained to Dan what happened to Jackson and that she'd be working from home today. She was not leaving Jackson's side until she knew he was well enough to get around on his crutches.

The break had been bad enough that the emergency room doctor had called in an orthopedic specialist, but after he looked at x-rays, he determined Jackson wouldn't need surgery. The doctor set the break, put his ankle and foot in a cast, and prescribed pain medications. Jackson had tried to have a brave face for Harper as he hobbled out of the hospital on crutches, but she wasn't buying it. He had taken the pain pills and fallen asleep in the downstairs spare bedroom after they arrived home. He had woken long enough that morning to give Harper his insurance card for his prescription and eat a piece of toast and drink a glass of orange juice. Then he went right back to bed.

Harper went to the pharmacy and had the prescription filled. By the time she arrived back at the house, Jackson's face had been contorted in pain. She could tell by the way he couldn't sit still that he was uncomfortable. He promised her that he'd be okay, smiling through gritted teeth.

Harper had given him more pain medication and sent him off to bed.

Thankfully, Jackson slept most of the day while she worked. The vision from the night before had stayed with her all day, invading her thoughts while she tried to focus. It was only after hours of processing what she had witnessed that it began to make sense.

The witch had been romantically involved with a man who had intended to give her the necklace, but he had met someone else. He had left the witch right when she thought he might propose. Harper wasn't sure how the witch managed it, but she had gotten her hands on the necklace.

In the vision, Harper watched as the witch put a curse on the necklace using herbs and candle magic, and stones. The energy the witch had summoned was dark and filled with rage and hate. She poured all her grief and sorrow over lost love and hatred for her ex's new love into the spell. Harper had never experienced something so powerful before. It terrified her that so much negative energy could be summoned.

Harper hadn't been sure where she had been while she watched the witch work. Stone walls surrounded them and the floor beneath was nothing more than the Earth. Harper figured it was a cave of some sort, but she had been brought out of the vision too quickly to be sure. The air had been so slick it was electric, making the hair on her head lift on its own and fan out around her head. Even her skin prickled. The most terrifying part had been the end of the spell when the witch was knocked off her feet by the force. It was then Harper had been jolted to the present.

She had no idea how the witch got the necklace back to the man, but Harper assumed she did. Harper assumed the necklace was given to his new love and the curse carried on from one owner to the next.

Harper tried to push it from her mind and focus on work. She pulled up a freelancer's article and started editing. She only made it four paragraphs in when a knock on the door drew her attention. Harper set her laptop to the side and got up to get the door, hoping that it hadn't woken Jackson. She pulled the door open and found Det. Granger waiting there.

"Is he doing okay?" Det. Granger asked as Harper held the door open for him.

Harper explained about the break and that Jackson was resting. "The doctor isn't sure how tripping over the dog could lead to such a bad break, but it will heal. He's sleeping now."

"I came to speak to you. I called your office and Dan said you were here." Det. Granger entered the living room behind Harper and sat down on the end of the couch.

Harper moved her laptop to the coffee table and sat down next to him. "I'm not going to try to get another vision if that's why you're here. I learned my lesson the first time."

Det. Granger shook his head. "That's not it. I feel bad I encouraged you. I wanted to run a name by you. Bobby Kemp. Ring any bells for you?"

"I can't recall anyone by that name. Should I know him?"

"No, but you knew Brendan and had contact with Sam so I wondered if you've had any contact with him, too." Det. Granger pulled up a photo on his phone and showed it to Harper. "He's the guy I found on the trail near the river. He'd been shot most likely with the same gun as the others."

That was now three confirmed dead bodies – Vinnie Ruggiero, Brendan Miller, and now Bobby Kemp. "Are they all from out of state?"

"Every one of them. Bobby is from Chicago."

"Have you determined how many are here in Little Rock searching for the necklace?" Harper was starting to lose track of the people she had come across.

"Including Nick and Cora, I have seven of them – three of them are dead."

"Who is left?"

Det. Granger tucked his phone back in his pocket. "Besides Nick, Cora, and Sam, there's James Wiggins, who Hattie said she met. I don't know of anyone else right now. We can't be sure who is here."

Harper wasn't even sure what to ask him. It was like searching for a needle in a haystack. "Is there any way to check the hotels and see who has checked in from out of state?" She realized that was probably a dumb idea the moment she said it.

Det. Granger shook his head. "Even if the hotels would give us that info without a search warrant, which they won't, there are far too many hotels to cover. What do I ask for? Every Italian sounding male?" he asked with a laugh.

"Right. I assume ballistics have been checked and none of that matches anything you have in the system." Harper knew just enough to sound like she knew what she was doing. She didn't really. It was all things she picked up along the way.

Det. Granger eyed her. "Nothing matches. Although, as I said, we believe the same gun was used in all the crimes. That bit of info doesn't go anywhere but here though."

Harper exhaled a breath. "This seems to be our toughest case yet."

"Our?" Det. Granger asked, stifling a laugh. "There is no 'our' in homicide investigations. More than half of the info I share with you and Hattie could get me fired. You just have a unique perspective sometimes that helps me solve cases."

Harper knew what he meant. "I know you consider us your secret weapons," she said, teasing him. "I think all I can say is this whole thing started because of Marco De Luca. His cousin is the one who stole it from Nick and brought it here."

Det. Granger sat back on the couch and stared off into space. He stayed like that for several moments. Harper remained quiet while he was lost in thought. Finally, he snapped his fingers. "Would you be willing to set up a sting call with Marco? You can tell him you might know more about the location of the necklace, but he has to share information with you. You can see what you can get out of him."

Harper scrunched up her face in doubt. "I'm the one who caused his father to be taken down by the FBI. I don't think he'll trust me."

"Right, you're a mob informant. I forgot," Det. Granger teased. "I think it's worth a try though. He doesn't need to trust you. You're good at angering people so make him mad and maybe he will slip up."

"I'm good at making people angry? I didn't realize that was my skill," she said laughing. Harper wondered though if she could try the truth spell. She had no idea if it would work with someone who wasn't right in front of her. "Do you want me to do it down at the station?"

Det. Granger stood. "Let me get some equipment and we can use your cellphone here. Just block the number and make the call. Do you have his number?"

Harper hadn't thought of that one tiny detail. "I'd need to get it from Nick. I think he'll be suspicious, but I can attempt it."

"I'll search and see if I can find it." With that Det. Granger headed for the door.

Harper called him back. "Have you heard much from Cora? She's been suspiciously quiet."

Det. Granger turned back to face Harper. "As I said before, I didn't have anything to hold her the day I questioned her. She didn't tell me anything useful. I don't think she killed Vinnie, but I suspect she might know who did."

Harper tried to temper her emotions. "That wasn't reason enough to hold her?"

"I wish I could have, but that's not the way it works. I couldn't charge her with anything so I had to let her go. I don't think bullying the information out of her was going to work anyway. I certainly tried to be strong with her and that only shut her down more."

Harper didn't like that one bit. It was bad enough that Nick was out there roaming around. "Hattie heard it was Cora and Sam who dug up her yard. That's really what led us to find the necklace."

"If Hattie wants to call me and make a report of the damage done to her yard, I'll gladly take it."

"I don't think Hattie will do that." Harper wished her aunt would.

"Do we know why Cora is mixed up in this?"

Harper hated admitting this, but she didn't see an option. "I had lunch with Nick yesterday and he admitted he called Cora and got her to come down here. Cora wants Jackson back and Nick wants me back. It sounded to me like they were working together to break up Jackson and me. He promised her money from the necklace and that was all she needed to hear."

"You two have matching trouble." Det. Granger stepped down from the porch to the walkway. He waved as he left and called, "Tell Jackson I hope he starts feeling better."

"I will." Harper waved him off and then closed and locked the door. She knew she should sit down and get back to work, but she had a craving for Hattie's chocolate chip muffins and figured Jackson would appreciate something sweet when he woke up. Harper grabbed her jacket from the back of the kitchen chair, found Jackson's keys hanging on the hook, and left the house, locking the door behind her.

As Harper started her walk to Hattie's shop, something in her gut told her that this trip might be more beneficial than a simple snack.

Chapter Thirty-Three

"What does that mean?" Hattie asked with fear in her voice. Delia had told her that there would be more revenge to come, and Hattie wasn't sure if the witch meant from her or the murders that had been happening.

"It means what it means. There are still people who have to pay."

Hattie leaned forward and tried to control her emotions. "Are you talking about the men who were murdered or my family? I told you already that Jackson didn't hurt his ex-wife. It was the other way around."

"What about your niece?" the witch asked with a smug look on her face.

"What about her?" Hattie asked with anger.

"She's the reason all of this is happening."

"Harper didn't steal your necklace." Hattie explained to the witch how George Lennox had it and then how it was Nick who took it and how it was stolen from him.

Delia smiled. "I told you I watch the necklace carefully. I know all of that. I didn't say Harper stole the necklace, but she is the reason all of this started. You think my jealousy is bad. You have no idea how bad it can be for some people – the lengths they're willing to go."

"Cora? Nick?" Hattie asked. "Are they the ones killing people?"

Delia wouldn't say anymore. She stood from the couch. "I've told you enough. There's no fun if I give away all the secrets I know." Delia's spirit floated to the door. "That detective took the necklace last night. Do you think I should do something to him? Does he deserve punishment?"

Hattie pushed herself off the chair with force and got right up in Delia's face. The energy from her radiated heat. "You will not harm one hair on him. Det. Granger is a good man, better than most. You leave him alone. Understand me?"

Delia cackled. "It's not like you can stop me."

Hattie narrowed her eyes. "I've stopped worse than you, and I'll do it again if I have to."

Delia turned on Hattie and reached out her hand, shoving it right into Hattie's chest. Hattie clutched at the spot in pain and her heartbeat pounded in her ears. Hattie reached into her pocket for her tiger's eye stone and said a protection chant over and over again until the spirit of the witch disappeared before her eyes. The pain eased off and her breathing returned to normal, but Hattie knew she hadn't seen the last of the witch.

Hattie made her way down the hall and into the main area of the shop. Sarah stood behind the counter waiting on a customer. Hattie rushed over to her and waited patiently while she finished.

After Sarah handed the customer her change, Hattie grabbed her by the arm and turned her around. "You need to call Det. Granger right now and warn him the witch might come after him."

"What?" Sarah asked confused. "Why would the witch go after him? He doesn't own the necklace?"

"That's what I told her, but that doesn't seem to matter. She threatened to go after him. The witch's name is Delia and I got the impression she hates all happy people. She went after Jackson for no reason. She has Harper in her crosshairs and now she's threatening Det. Granger. You have to warn him."

"Okay, calm down." Sarah patted Hattie's arm. "If you watch the register for a moment, I'll go in back and call him instead of texting. He might take it more seriously that way."

Hattie stood there staring out at her customers wondering how she could protect those she loved most. The safety of her shop and home felt like it had been invaded. A few customers came in and Hattie went through the motions of getting them tea, coffee, and treats. Her mind wasn't engaged with them though. She ran through spell after spell in her mind that she could use to stop the witch. Protection spells worked fine most of the time, but they were a little more complex when one witch needed protection from another.

No spirit should ever be as strong as Delia unless there was evil attached. Hattie had fought evil in New Orleans, but even they had been mortals at one time with no magical powers. This was entirely different. This was the spirit of a powerful witch who seemed to be wielding magical powers even in her afterlife.

Hattie reached for her phone and called a number she had only recently added to her contacts. Father Ignatius Cormier, who wanted to be called Iggy. He was a retired exorcist priest who had traveled the globe expelling demons back to the underworld. He was one of the quirkiest people Hattie had ever met. He swilled whiskey like a barroom drunk and paid no attention to the formalities of the Catholic religion. She had warmed to him over time and was grateful for the help he had provided them in New Orleans.

There was something though, an edge about him, that kept Hattie from fully trusting him. It was maybe just that he had seen and dispelled so much evil in his life that he carried a bit of the energy with him. Hattie wasn't sure how old he was – maybe eighty or so. Older than her by a good margin.

Hattie placed the call and the phone barely rang when Iggy answered it. "Father...er, Iggy, this is Hattie."

Iggy laughed. "I figured I'd never hear from you again. Thought we had scared you off for good."

"I'm in a bit of a pickle," she started and then told him the entire tale. Thankfully, midway through the conversation Sarah was back and could handle customers' requests. Iggy seemed fully engaged in her tale and asked questions throughout. It was at the end that Hattie asked her most important question. "Since I cannot destroy the necklace, how do I destroy the witch?"

"I have just the solution for you," Iggy said with a bit of pride in his voice. "Grab a pen and I'll tell you what to do."

After the call, Hattie had confidence she hadn't had before. Iggy's suggestion had made perfect sense and she wasn't sure why she hadn't thought of it sooner. Hattie needed a few supplies she was sure she had in the shop and then she'd be on her way to at least getting rid of the witch.

"You seem a little better," Sarah said when she finished with a customer.

"I have a plan to deal with the witch." Hattie started to walk toward her backroom workshop, but Sarah called her back.

"I spoke to Tyson. Of course, he didn't take it seriously, but he asked me a question I couldn't answer."

"What is that?"

"He was quite hesitant to believe anything about a spirit of a witch hurting those living, but he wanted to know if that were true, could she be the one murdering people."

Hattie hadn't thought of that. Delia had been strong enough to break Jackson's ankle. "I don't know. She's cursed people to become ill and hurt. The men died from gunshot wounds. I can't see the witch having the energy to hold and fire a gun. I don't believe she could cause outright death. That's not to say she couldn't make a tree limb fall on someone's head and they die as a result. A gun is different though."

Sarah clicked her tongue. "Is it possible she is influencing someone to kill?"

"Now, that may be possible. We have no way of knowing that though and I'm not going to summon her again." Hattie leaned into Sarah and whispered in her ear, "Not until I'm ready to get rid of her."

Hattie couldn't disclose what she was going to do. Part of the power of the spell was keeping the energy to herself, for now at least. She went to her back workroom and began collecting the items for the spell. Luckily, Hattie carried it all, even some of the most obscure ingredients. She pulled a bit of this and that from her shelf and placed it into a green silk bag.

As Hattie finished putting the last of the items in the bag, Sarah popped her head into the room. "There's someone here for a reading, but I'm not sure you want to give it."

Hattie hated hearing those words. "Is it that woman from a few weeks ago who won't leave the married man alone? I told her fifty times if I told her once I wasn't going to help her."

Sarah shook her head and frowned. "It would be easier if it was her. It's Cora."

Hattie grumbled, "I get rid of one witch and replace her with another." She raised her eyes to Sarah who smirked. "That's probably not very nice. I'm all out of positive energy today. Send her back, and I'll do what I can."

Sarah left and Hattie tied up the spell bag and left it on her worktable. She wiped off her hands on a towel to rid her fingers of the remaining loose herbs. Hattie met Cora in the hallway and pointed out the reading room. "Head in there and I'll be right in."

Cora did as she was told while Hattie stood in the hallway, taking a deep breath and trying to get herself in the headspace to give the woman a reading. She felt like throwing her out of the shop on her behind. Hattie shook the energy free and entered the room.

"What can I help you with, Cora?" Hattie said as she pulled her tarot cards from the shelf.

Cora sat forward on the couch with her hands resting on her knees. "I'm surprised you'd agree to see me considering you're Harper's aunt, but I didn't know who else to ask for help."

Hattie sat down in her chair, adjusted her skirt, and locked eyes with Cora. "Before we get to that, explain to me what gives you the right to do what you did to my yard."

Cora shifted her eyes away. "It wasn't my idea. The guy I was with did it and he attacked the other man that was there. That's why I'm here. I think he's going to try to kill me."

Hattie raised her eyebrows. "He's killed someone else?"

"Several people we have spoken to are dead now. He's said things that made me think it might be him that's been killing people."

Hattie tried to zero in on the energy because she worried that she was being manipulated. "Has this man tried to hurt you?"

"Not yet, but he's threatened me." Cora sat back on the couch. "Can you give me a reading to see what my future holds?"

Hattie didn't need to read the cards to know what this path would bring her. "Who is the man you're speaking about?" Hattie assumed it was Sam, but she needed to hear it from Cora.

"I can't tell you."

Hattie stood. "Then you can leave my shop."

Cora didn't move, but she shifted her head to look up at Hattie. "Sam Franza."

Chapter Thirty-Four

Harper tilted her head back and let the sun shine on her face. The air had a nip to it and she was glad she had pulled on a sweater. Being outside perked her right up. She walked from Jackson's house in the direction of Hattie's shop and had made it a few blocks when she saw a man off in the distance. He had a familiar look about him, but Harper couldn't quite pinpoint how she knew him. It could have been someone new in the neighborhood she had seen once or twice.

As they got closer, Harper realized that wasn't it. He was someone she had seen in New York. More than that, he was someone she had seen in her building when she lived with her father. "Excuse me," she called as she approached the man. "I'm so sorry to bother you. I know you from New York. Did you just move here?"

The man stepped back a little, searching Harper's face. He didn't seem to recognize her. That made sense to Harper. She was quite young when she had seen him, but he looked the same only slightly older. "I don't think I know you," he said and tried to walk past her.

Harper wasn't sure why she was so insistent on knowing. She blocked his path. "Please, this will drive me a bit nutty for the rest of the day if I can't figure it out." She rattled off the address of her father's penthouse in Manhattan. "I'm Harper Ryan. My father is Maxwell Ryan. I'm sure I've seen you in the building."

"I don't think so." He kept walking and quickened his pace a little.

Harper was fast on his heels. "What's your name? Maybe that will help me."

"James," he said over his shoulder and continued to scurry past her.

The name didn't mean anything to her at first. She looked him over again and it came to her at once. "James Wiggins?" Harper asked, catching up to him and walking in step.

"Why are you following me?" he asked with annoyance.

"I'm not sure, to be honest," Harper said, laughing. "I don't normally follow people. I rarely see anyone from Manhattan here in Little Rock. Are you James Wiggins?"

"Yes, yes, I am." James stopped and turned to her. "I might have been in that building. I have many clients all over the country."

The moment he said that it connected for Harper. "You know George Lennox."

"What if I do?" James put his hands on his hips.

"George heard about the missing necklace and sent you to find it, didn't he?" Harper shot in the dark and even saying it didn't feel right to her.

"It wasn't George. He doesn't have anything to do with me being here."

"Do you know George because you were trying to buy the necklace from him before?" Harper asked. She didn't think so because George had such a hard time selling it, but she needed to ask anyway. She wasn't even sure why this mattered. Something in her gut told her to keep at it.

James looked to the sky and blew out a breath. "You're persistent on things that aren't any of your business."

"This is most certainly my business when you're here looking for a necklace that people think I stole and have hidden."

James laughed. "I know you didn't steal the necklace."

"How do you know that?"

James looked away.

Harper raised her eyebrows. "Marco sent you?"

"No." James brushed past Harper and didn't stop this time. Even when she tried to ask him a question, he wouldn't respond.

Harper had no idea where he was going in their neighborhood so she stood there and watched him. He didn't head toward Hattie's house though. He went down a block and turned right in the opposite direction. Harper stood there for a moment longer making sure he didn't double back. When it was clear James was gone, she resumed her walk.

She only made it a few feet when her phone chimed. Thinking it was Jackson, she reached for it. It was Nick and she couldn't walk and text so she called him instead.

"What's going on?" she asked as he answered.

"Where are you?"

"I'm walking to Hattie's shop. Why?" Harper had a sarcastic tone in her voice. She needed to stop because she remembered she needed Marco's phone number from him.

"You told me to give you a call when I believed you." Nick blew out a breath. "Marco called me. Brendan is dead. I didn't even know he was down here."

"Do you know James Wiggins?"

Nick paused a moment too long. "I know the name but never met the man," he said finally. "Is he dead, too?"

"No. I just met him on the street. He's been to Hattie's shop." Harper wasn't sure how much to share with him. "I've seen him in New York before. How do you know him?"

"It's a long story. I need to meet you."

"You can meet me at Hattie's shop. I'm on my way there now."

Nick grunted. "I can't do that. The last time I was in there a ghost or spirit or her magic knocked me off my chair to the ground. I don't trust her."

Harper had forgotten. "That's where I'm headed now. Take it or leave it. I'll make sure you're not attacked." Nick hesitated so long Harper wasn't sure he was still engaged in the call. "You there, Nick?"

"I'll meet you there in ten minutes. I'm only going into the shop once you're there."

Harper hung up not sure if bringing him to the shop was a good idea. She didn't want to meet him at Hattie's house and he definitely couldn't meet her back at Jackson's. She didn't have a lot of time to meet with him so this was probably the best option available.

Harper walked the few blocks to the shop. As she entered, she waved to Sarah who was behind the counter. "Where's Hattie?"

Sarah leaned over the counter. "She is giving Cora a reading." Harper scrunched up her face like she smelled something bad and Sarah laughed. "That's how I felt when she walked in here."

"I can't say anything. I just told Nick to meet me here." Harper went behind the counter and fixed herself a cup of coffee and grabbed a chocolate chip muffin. "Could you please box up a few treats for Jackson and take my money before Hattie comes out and refuses it?"

"How is Jackson?" Sarah said, taking the money Harper had in her hand.

"He's miserable and in pain but sleeping right now. The pain pills seem to help. I figured it might be nice if he woke up to some treats from Hattie's."

Sarah grabbed some of Jackson's favorites and put them in a to-go box. She set it on the counter. "This is why you're good for Jackson. Cora would be standing over him right now telling him she needed him to wash her car or would be upset that he wasn't doing things for her. Instead, here you are letting the poor man sleep and then waking him up with chocolate. Never doubt you are the right woman for him, Harper."

Harper was a little overcome with emotion and didn't know what to say. With no siblings of her own, she loved that Sarah had become like family. "I appreciate that more than you know, especially now with Cora here. I'm not handling it well."

Sarah shook her head. "No one handles Cora well. Don't beat yourself up." She pointed toward the door and Harper turned her head to see Nick walking into the shop. "If he gives you any trouble, let me know and I'll call Charlie again. That's how we got rid of him the last time."

"I'll keep that in mind," Harper said winking at Sarah. She walked over to Nick and guided him to a table. "If you want coffee or a snack, feel free to order."

"I'm good," Nick said as he pulled out the chair and sat down. When Harper sat across from him, he asked, "Let me get this out of the way first. Is there any chance you'd be willing to take me back?"

Harper wasn't sure how many times she needed to say no. "If this is why you're here, it's pointless. It's never going to happen. I'm happy here in a way that I've never been happy anywhere else. We aren't a good fit." She could have thrown all his wrongdoing in his face again, but it served no purpose. They both knew what he did.

Nick held his hands up in defeat. "I accept that then. I needed to make sure."

"What did you want to talk about?"

Nick sat back and kicked his legs out in front of himself under the table. "I've been thinking about what you said and I don't think it's Marco doing this."

"I don't understand. I believe it was Marco who sent that email to get all these people here to search for the necklace. If not him, then who?"

Nick blew out a breath. "Marco is genuinely freaked out that the necklace is missing. He wouldn't send anyone he didn't know to try to find it – let alone his enemies. I should have never blamed you for stealing it. That was a mistake. Marco is the one that asked me if I thought you could have taken it when you moved, and I panicked and said yes."

"It was Marco's idea that I might have had it?" Harper wasn't sure why that made more sense to her but it did.

Nick nodded. "If Marco hadn't brought you up, it would have never occurred to me to say anything about you. When he did and then I agreed, it was an excuse to come down here. After I agreed with him, he was positive it was here."

"You think someone else told him I stole the necklace then."

Nick nodded. "That's what I got thinking about last night. I think that's why he sent Brendan down here. I don't think he trusted that I could find it. I think Brendan got here before me."

"Who do you think pointed Marco in my direction?"

"Carmine," Nick said with confidence. "It's the only thing that makes sense. He was livid that he was sent to prison. He talked about getting you back for that. I think he had Richie steal the necklace and frame you for it. It also makes me look incompetent to Marco, which would please Carmine to no end. He hated how things went down and that my ex-wife got wind of the affair with his daughter and that you ratted us out."

It made sense to Harper. It was the first thing that had made sense since all of this started. "Could he pull that off from prison?"

Nick leaned over the table and looked Harper right in the eyes. "He's had people killed since he went to prison. He could easily pull this off."

Chapter Thirty-Five

Hattie tried her best to convince Cora that Jackson was never coming back to her. At first, Hattie had delivered the information as gently as possible, but when Cora insisted Hattie was only saying that because she was Harper's aunt, she used more force. Finally, after throwing the cards down three times in a spread and coming back with the same answer over and over again, Cora seemed resigned. She asked Hattie to move on to other topics – like her safety. Hattie had wanted to start there, but Cora had insisted she start with Jackson.

Hattie shuffled the cards once again and began placing the cards in a spread. She turned them over one by one. The number of sword cards that were present indicated Cora wasn't safe. She had gotten herself involved with some dangerous men and had little way out.

Hattie pointed at the cards. "There are two men here and one woman. You said that you were involved with a man – Sam. I'm seeing more than that here."

Cora peered down at the cards. "Could that be Harper? I'm sure she'd hurt me if she had the chance."

"It's not Harper," Hattie said with force. "Is there another woman you've had contact with since you arrived in Little Rock?" Before Cora could respond, Hattie amended. "A woman who is tied up with this necklace situation. Does Sam have a girlfriend?"

"Not that I know of. I'm not sure who the woman is you're seeing."

"Who is the other man then? He's a dark-haired man with a temper."

"I've only had interaction with Sam and Nick. Maybe you're seeing Nick."

Hattie thought it might be but that wasn't the feeling she was getting. Hattie shuffled the cards again and asked a direct yes or no question. The answer was a firm no. This other man in the reading was not Nick.

"There is someone else, Cora. I can't help you unless you're honest with me."

"I'm being honest," she screeched. "I don't know who it is you're seeing. You could be wrong."

Hattie took a deep breath. Clients always did this when they didn't want to disclose information or didn't want to own up to what Hattie saw. "Have you and Sam had any luck finding the necklace or the diamonds?"

"Why would you ask that? What do you see?"

"I'm seeing that you found something and I wasn't sure if this was past or present."

"We haven't found anything." Cora crossed her arms. "You still didn't answer my question – am I safe here?"

Hattie sat back in her chair. "I did answer you. You're not safe, Cora. It's not safe for you to be around this man and woman that I'm seeing in the cards. You won't tell me who they are, but I know you've already met them. No matter your denials, I see it. They don't care about you and will use you as a pawn if they have to. Sam is not a good man. He's dangerous so don't cross him. You'd be better off if you packed your things and went home."

Cora didn't say anything for a few moments and then dropped a bomb. "I gave up my apartment."

"What do you mean you gave it up?"

"I figured Jackson and I would get back together so I sold my furniture and put other things in storage. I got out of my lease. I have nowhere to go."

Hattie felt all the air go out of the room. "You can't stay here."

Cora's face registered surprise. "Why not?"

"What do you have here?"

"Jackson," Cora said defiantly.

Hattie could see that the woman was not going to give up so easily. "What would you do for work here?"

"I don't work in Virginia. Jackson pays my bills."

Hattie expelled a breath. "You can't live the rest of your life like that."

"I don't see why not."

There was no reasoning with the woman and Hattie didn't know what else to do. "Let me pull some cards and see how things will turn out for you if you stay." Hattie had never prayed so hard in her life that the cards would be terrible. Not that it would dissuade Cora, but at least Hattie might have a glimpse into how bad it might be for the rest of them.

Hattie shuffled the cards again and placed them in a spread. The cards were worse than she could have imagined. "There is no easy way to tell you this, but it would not be good for you to stay here. It's time to make your own way in the world."

When Cora didn't budge, Hattie pointed at the cards. "There is nothing but misery and unhappiness for you here. Arguments and heartache. You are never getting Jackson back and you will drive a wedge between you. Eventually, the kindness he shows you will be gone and so will the money."

Cora held on defiantly. "He will never cut me off."

"He will. I see it right here." Hattie pointed to one particular card. "You're going to push him too far and he will snap. Everyone has a breaking point, and if you tell him you're moving here, that will be it. You'll be lucky if he ever speaks to you again."

Cora's expression faltered and she uncrossed her arms. She lowered her head and looked at the cards. "That bad?"

"That bad," Hattie said seriously. "He moved here for a fresh start just like you need to find. I know divorce is hard, and it's a radical change to how life has been, but you have to find your way in the world on your own. Let me put some more cards down to see what life will be like for you if you find the strength to move on."

Hattie shuffled the cards again and placed them down one by one. Cora had a bright future if she let go of the past. "See, look here," Hattie said. "There are amazing things for you if you leave and break free from Jackson. There is a new relationship and financial improvements. There is a whole world waiting for you."

"A new relationship?" Cora asked her voice filled with a tinge of hope.

"Yes, it's right here. A man who will love you and be better for you more than Jackson ever could." Hattie wasn't lying about that. It's exactly what she saw in her cards. "For that to happen, Cora, you have to make better decisions. You have to get free of the people here in Little Rock that aren't safe for you to be around."

Cora sat back and didn't say a word for several minutes. Hattie wasn't going to pressure her because she was contemplating something. Hattie hoped it was the truth. A moment later, she wasn't disappointed.

Cora took a breath and exhaled it slowly. All at once, she admitted, "We found the diamonds in your yard under the bird feeder."

That was what Hattie had seen in the cards. "When you say 'we' who do you mean?"

"Sam and me. After Sam ran off that other guy, we started digging and found the diamonds."

"Where are they now?"

"Sam has them. I know where he hid them."

"Why would he tell you that?" Hattie didn't trust he'd tell her the truth.

"In case something happened to him." Cora rubbed at her forehead. "I met Sam at the hotel bar and he seemed nice enough. I told him I was looking for the necklace and diamonds and that I had an in. I told him I knew where Harper lived and worked."

Hattie had suspected that long before Cora said it. "I think we need to call Det. Granger and you can sort this out with him."

"Won't I get in trouble?"

"I think you'll be in less trouble if you go to the police directly." Hattie stood but Cora wasn't moving. "I'm serious. The only way for you to avoid trouble is to be open and honest with Det. Granger. The diamonds were stolen and left in my yard. You and Sam took them off my property. If you're turning in stolen property and helping Det. Granger, I'm sure he will be lenient with you."

Hattie still sensed Cora's hesitancy and reached for the woman's hand. "Come with me into the shop and we can call Det. Granger together. I trust him so you should as well."

Cora let herself be led out of the reading room, through the hallway, and into the shop. Hattie stopped short when she saw Harper sitting at a table speaking to Nick.

Hattie pointed to a table far from Nick and Harper on the other side of the room. "Sit there while I grab the phone." She wanted to grab Harper and tell her what was going on, but the last thing Hattie wanted to do was spook Cora into changing her mind. She walked over to Sarah and grabbed the cellphone she had left on the counter.

"Have you heard from Det. Granger recently?" she asked Sarah.

"A little while ago. He was in a meeting but will probably be done now. Why?"

As quietly as she could, Hattie whispered, "Cora knows where the diamonds are and we need Det. Granger here before she changes her mind about telling him."

It was then that Charlie appeared. "What's happening? I heard you say something about the diamonds being found. It's Sam, right?"

"How did you know that?"

"I had been watching Cora. I watched her and Sam walk into the hotel together after they were in your yard. I figured they were up to something, but I couldn't see what was in Sam's hand. It looked like a small black bag. He stashed it in the safe in Cora's room but didn't tell her the code to unlock it. The code is 2792."

Hattie smiled, and if she could have hugged him, she would have. "You are heaven sent. Please go watch the safe and let us know immediately if Sam comes back."

Hattie placed the call to Det. Granger. When he answered, she filled him in on what was happening including the fact that Charlie got him the code for the safe. "You better hurry though. We don't know how long Sam will keep the diamonds there."

"Keep Cora occupied while I go to her hotel room. I don't want her tipping him off. After I secure the diamonds, I'll be up to interview her."

Chapter Thirty-Six

I t was hard to pay attention to what Nick was saying while Harper watched Hattie out of the corner of her eye. She couldn't hear what Hattie was saying to Sarah or who she spoke to on the phone, but she acted keyed up like something big was happening.

Hattie hung up the phone and then filled a tray with tea and coffee and some treats and took them over to Cora. Harper wasn't happy that Cora was still hanging around the shop, but there wasn't much she could do about it. Harper glanced at her watch. Jackson would probably be awake by now. She had hoped to be back by the time that happened.

"Are you paying attention to me?" Nick asked, drawing Harper's attention back to him.

"Sorry, I'm wondering what Cora is doing here with Hattie."

Nick ran a hand through his hair. "I'm sorry I brought her here. I don't know of a nice way to say this, but she is kind of unstable."

Harper raised her eyebrows. "I can't disagree with you. You have enough skeletons in your closet though that you shouldn't be calling out someone else on theirs. How did you even know about Cora?"

Red rose up Nick's neck to his face. "I hired a private investigator. I thought we might have a chance again. When I found out you were seeing Jackson, I dug into his past and found Cora. She wanted him back as much as I wanted you back. It seemed perfect."

Harper sighed. "A perfectly good way of bringing more drama into our lives." Harper paused and considered the best way to ask. In the end, she went for it. "Nick, I need Marco's phone number. If Carmine is doing this I need to talk to Marco and see what I can find out."

"That's not a good idea. He's not going to talk to you."

"I'm not going to debate this with you. I need the number." Harper held firm and she wasn't going to let Nick get out of this. "I have ways of making him talk if I need to. It might help you be in the clear. We are both in danger and Marco might be our only way out. If Carmine is doing this behind Marco's back, he's going to want to know."

Nick had a skeptical look on his face. "Do you think Marco will believe you?"

"I'll make him believe me."

"I don't know, Harper. This might cause more trouble."

Harper wasn't going to debate this with him. "Trust me on this. If someone is setting us up then they are setting up Marco, too. The three of us are in this together whether we like it or not." Harper didn't think that was technically true, but at this point, she'd tell Nick anything to get what she needed.

Nick reluctantly picked up his phone and scrolled through his contacts. "I'm sending you his information now."

Harper checked her phone and read the text he sent. "Don't tip him off. That's the only way this is going to work. I don't know what you have planned, but if I were you, I'd lock myself in my hotel room and not come out until the coast is clear."

Nick said he'd heed her warning. "Since you're being so nice, you asked me earlier about James Wiggins. I'm not sure what more I can tell you. He wanted to buy the necklace from George Lennox but didn't want to pay what it was worth. He told George he should get a discount because of the curse. George tried to get him to up the offer, but James wasn't willing. That's the last I saw or heard from James Wiggins. I know that George and James had a long-standing relationship. James had bought other jewelry from George and sold him unique pieces over the years that George gave to his wife. George told me their relationship soured after the back and forth about the necklace."

"You never met him?"

Nick shook his head. "I told you before I never met him. All that interaction between George and James took place before George wanted the necklace stolen. I never met James, only heard about him, and wouldn't recognize him if he were in the shop right now."

Harper believed him. "He told me he knew I didn't steal the necklace."

"How would he know that?" Nick asked confused.

"I don't know that's why I wondered if you knew him. He's close to Carmine."

Nick ran a hand through his hair and rubbed at his forehead, seemingly frustrated. "To be honest, since getting out of prison, Lola has kept me sheltered from a lot of her family stuff. A condition of my parole is to stay on the straight and narrow. Kind of hard to do with the De Luca family. My father gave me my job back at the financial firm. Not as much money and I've been demoted, but it's still work. If it wasn't for the necklace, I'd be closer to getting my life together."

Harper didn't want to hear about Lola. Nick had cheated on her with the woman and even though she didn't harbor any feelings for him, it still stung. Sitting in Hattie's shop having to hear about Lola while Cora sat on the other side of the room was a little too much for her. It would probably be too much for any woman.

She looked at Nick. "I hope you turn your life around. You have a child now and need to be a good father." It was the only thing she could say that she meant. Out of the corner of her eye, Hattie motioned for her to come over. "We should wrap up here. I have to get back. Please don't tell Marco I'll be calling him. The element of surprise is important."

"I'll be back at my hotel laying low for now." Nick stood and tugged his shirt down. "I promise I won't tell Marco that you're calling. You'd probably know if I did anyway."

Nick walked to the door, but before he left, he turned back to look at Harper. "Believe me or not, I am trying to be a better person. It doesn't come as easy for me as it does for you."

As soon as the door shut behind him, Harper made her way over to Hattie and Cora. She couldn't handle another confrontation right now and hoped Cora wasn't there causing trouble.

"Sit down with us," Hattie said, pulling out the chair next to her. "Cora has admitted that it was Sam who stole the diamonds. They were hidden under the bird feeder in the yard."

"You have them now?" Harper asked, her voice rising as she said it.

Cora clasped her hands on the table. "They are back at the hotel. Sam took them and stashed them in the safe in my room. I don't know the combination though."

"I've taken care of that," Hattie said, giving Harper a knowing look.

Harper took that to mean a ghost had obtained the information. "It was good that you came forward with that information. Do you know who murdered those men?"

"I have no idea." Cora looked Harper right in the eyes. "I told Hattie that I got rid of my apartment and that I was going to move here to be with Jackson."

A lump formed in Harper's throat and she didn't have any words. She sat there staring at the woman trying to come up with an appropriate response. She didn't have one though. "I see," she said, although she didn't.

Cora sat up straighter and forced her chest out, holding her head high. "I've decided to let you have Jackson. You seem like you're happy settling for him and I deserve better. Jackson never treated me right. I'd be careful if I were you because he'll tire of you, too."

Harper forced a smile through gritted teeth even though she wanted to tell Cora exactly the kind of man Jackson was and that she was lucky he did so much for her. Harper saw no point in that. Why convince the woman Jackson was great when she was agreeing to do them all a favor and finally go away? "I think you're right, Cora. Jackson and I deserve each other so best let us be. I'm sure there is much better for you out there."

"He will leave you," Cora stressed with a sickening smile.

"I'll have to face that when the time comes." Harper stood. "If that's all, I'm going to take some treats to Jackson so we can mire down in our inadequacies together."

Hattie stifled a laugh. "I'll walk you out."

Harper went behind the counter and grabbed the box of treats Sarah had prepared. She also poured some hot coffee in a to-go cup and fixed it just the way Jackson liked it.

Sarah patted her on the back. "You're a better woman than I am. I would have slugged her."

"Trust me, I wanted to." She laughed and hugged Sarah. "Thank you for being a part of our family. I'm so happy Jackson has such an amazing sister."

"Right back at you. Anabella wants to know when you're coming over to bake cookies with her."

"Tell that sweet daughter of yours to name the night and I'm there."

"She will be thrilled!" Sarah called to Harper's back.

Hattie followed her out the door to the sidewalk. "Jackson doing okay?"

Harper gave Hattie an update about his condition. Because she knew her aunt would ask, she also told her about her meeting with Nick and gave her a warning about James Wiggins. "I don't trust that man. He knows too much and he is someone who is connected to both the De Luca family and George Lennox. I saw him earlier walking in the neighborhood and recognized him from Manhattan. Don't let him in the shop again."

"I didn't trust him from the start." Hattie pulled Harper away from the door. "Det. Granger is at the hotel looking for the diamonds now. He asked me to keep Cora here until he can interview her."

"Hopefully, he will find the diamonds. When you see Det. Granger, tell him I got Marco's number and to call me when he's done and we can make the call."

"What is he going to have you do?" Hattie asked, concerned.

"I'm going to call Marco and see what kind of information I can get out of him."

Hattie reached for Harper as she was walking away. "Before you go, I saw in the cards that Cora had a connection to a man and a woman. She denied it, but I know what I saw. Do you have any idea who that might be?"

Harper shook her head. "I have no idea. There's no telling who the De Lucas involved in this. That's why the faster we can get this solved, the safer we will all be."

Chapter Thirty-Seven

By the time Harper made it back to Jackson's house, she found him sitting in the living room with his leg propped up on the ottoman. He had showered, put on a clean tee-shirt and shorts, and had turned on the television.

Jackson turned his head toward the door when she walked in. "I thought you left me," he teased.

Harper held up the coffee and the box of goodies. "I thought I'd only be gone long enough to grab you some treats and be back before you woke up. Seems like you made some progress today."

Jackson's face lit up with the mention of the word treats. He held his hand out to take the box. "I'm starving! I tried to stand in the kitchen to make myself something, but I'm a bit too awkward with the crutches."

Harper handed him the box and set the coffee cup on a coaster on the table near his chair. "Let me fix you something more substantial. Eggs? French toast? How are you feeling?"

"I can't believe how much this hurts. That pain pill knocks me out. I'd rather be up and in a little pain than knocked out cold. Eggs would hit the spot if you're sure you don't mind making them."

Harper leaned down and kissed him. "I'd be happy to. You need to stay ahead of the pain though. Don't wait until it's unbearable before you take something. I know it makes you sleepy, but even if it's for a few days, rest is better than suffering. This isn't the time to be manly." She said the words and giggled. Jackson was half into a chocolate croissant and chocolate smeared his cheek. He looked anything but tough and manly at the moment.

"You said you were gone longer than planned. What took so long?"

"I'll explain while I cook." Harper went into the kitchen and found a pan and eggs and started preparing things. As she did, she explained to Jackson about seeing James Wiggins on the walk over and then meeting with Nick. She also informed him about Cora and the diamonds.

"I'm surprised she didn't take them and run," Jackson called from his chair.

Harper stood in front of the stove and poured the egg mixture into the pan to make an omelet. "She couldn't. Sam locked them in her hotel safe and didn't give her the combination."

"I hope she was nice to you."

Harper wasn't sure if telling Jackson that Cora had thought about staying was a good idea or not. She debated for a moment and recalled Hattie's warning about secrets. "Cora told me that I could have you after Hattie talked her out of moving here. I guess she gave up her apartment and planned to move back in with you."

Jackson let out a string of curses the likes of which Harper had never heard from him before.

She laughed. "I'm guessing you would have said no to that idea."

"That's probably the nicest way you could have put it. There is no way that is ever going to happen. I'm annoyed that she is still in Little Rock. Did she say when she's going back?"

Harper finished making the omelet and put it on the plate. She grabbed the toast and put some butter on it and set it next to the omelet. She carried it into Jackson in one hand and a fork and napkin in the other. He took the plate while she moved the box of treats out of the way. When he was all set with breakfast, Harper sat on the couch across from him, tucking her legs underneath her.

"Cora didn't say when she was going back. There's not anywhere for her to go back to, assuming she's cleared to leave by Det. Granger. She seems to be up to her eyeballs in this, and that's my ex-husband's fault for bringing her here."

Jackson took a bite of eggs and told her how good it was. "Don't let Cora off the hook. She would have found her way into a dramatic mess on her own. She didn't need help."

"Cora said she doesn't know who killed the three men." Harper leaned back and stretched her arms overhead. "We tried having a conversation two nights ago about who we thought might be suspects, but we got interrupted. What do you think? Any ideas?"

"Who is still alive?"

"That's probably a good way to look at it. Assuming there isn't some random killer out there, we can look at who we know. There are Nick and Cora, but I don't think it's either of them. Sam is high on my suspect list and so is James Wiggins. There are Marco and his cousin Richie, who stole the necklace. Nick said he thinks Carmine is controlling things from prison, looking for a little revenge on Nick and me."

Jackson agreed that was possible. He finished eating and set the plate to the side. "Are you sure you want to rule out Nick?"

Harper considered for a moment. "Nick has done a lot of stupid things, but I don't think he's killing those men. If he was, I'd have picked it up already."

"Fair enough. What has Det. Granger told you so far?"

"He said he's sure the same gun was used in all three murders. I don't know of any connection among Bobby Kemp, Brendan Miller and Vinnie Ruggiero, other than all three of them were here searching for the necklace. It could have been revenge or knocking off their competition. I know Brendan was connected to Marco and the De Luca family and Vinnie told Hattie he was connected to the mob. I can only assume Bobby was, too. I don't know much about him."

"I'd start there. Do a little research on Bobby and see what you can find." Jackson looked at her with a strange look on his face. "You're going to think I've lost it, but why don't you ask Vinnie some questions through Hattie. He may not remember who killed him, but you may be able to figure out if he has any connections to Marco or the others."

Harper smiled. "Even when you're in pain and half-drugged, you've still got some stellar ideas. I'll start some research on Bobby Kemp now." She stood and went to get her laptop from her bag. As she passed by Jackson, he grabbed her hand and pulled her down for a kiss.

"Why don't you take a break first?" he said with an unmistakable huskiness in his voice.

"You're broken and you're thinking about that!" Harper stood back with her hands on her hips. "I don't want to hurt you. You can't even walk."

"Who said anything about walking or standing for that matter. What I had in mind neither are required." He looked up at her with expectation in his eyes. All Harper could do was stand there laughing as he pouted. "I can't believe you'd turn down an injured man."

"I'm not turning you down."

"That's all I needed to hear." Jackson pushed himself up from the chair and grabbed his crutches. "You lead the way and I'll be right behind you."

Harper moved out of his way and put her hand on his back to guide him. "How about you lead the way? I like the view from back here." Together they walked to the spare downstairs bedroom.

Later, when they were both well satisfied and Jackson had fallen into a deep sleep, Harper got up and went back into the living room. She poured herself something to drink and sat down on the couch. She typed the name Bobby Kemp into a search engine and came up with far too much information. She refined the search, adding in where he was from, and came back with some interesting results.

If Harper had the right person, Bobby had been in and out of prison in the Chicago area for the last several years. According to one website, he had been newly released from a three-year state prison sentence for armed robbery.

The same newspaper article mentioned his affiliation with a crime family out of Chicago. Harper dropped a few words into the search and came back with additional articles. One gave more information about the crime family and their connection to New York City and the De Luca family. The article mentioned Bobby by name.

He had been accused of attempting to kill a member of the De Luca family a few years back when he was in Manhattan. There hadn't been enough evidence at the time to hold him so he was released. Harper read a few more articles on the subject. It seemed no one was ever held accountable for the crime.

She knew Brendan had a connection to the De Luca's and now Bobby, too. Harper bet if she dropped Vinnie's name into the search, she'd come back with similar information. It seemed everyone had a connection. Even Sam had mentioned knowing Brendan.

This was becoming more sinister by the second. Harper wasn't sure how long she had sat there reading article after article. Her ringing phone brought her back to the present.

"Did you get Marco's number?" Det. Granger asked.

"I got it from Nick. Do you want to meet me at Jackson's?"

"Give me a few minutes and I'll be there."

Harper closed her laptop and put it on the coffee table. She straightened up the living room and checked on Jackson who was still sleeping. He looked so comfortable that she fought the urge to kiss him. Then she sent a quick text to Hattie asking if she'd be able to speak to Vinnie and sort out his connection to the De Luca's.

Chapter Thirty-Eight

Hattie closed the shop early and walked the distance to her house. Det. Granger had shown up late in the afternoon and took Cora down to the police station for questioning. This was the third time he had to bring Cora in for questioning and the look on his face indicated he was as tired of dealing with her as the rest of them.

He had warned Cora that if she didn't tell him everything she knew that he might very well arrest her for obstruction. Hattie believed him. She assumed that Det. Granger had found the diamonds in the safe, but he never confirmed it.

When she arrived home, Hattie let the dogs out and made her way into the kitchen to make herself something for dinner. Beau surprised her at the dining room table.

"Have you been waiting for me?" she asked, setting her bag down on the counter. "You could have just popped over to the shop if you wanted me."

"I couldn't leave here. The spirit of the witch was in the house."

Hattie sighed. "What was she doing?"

Beau moved over to Hattie. "I found her in Harper's bedroom. I'm not sure what she was doing, but it doesn't look like she moved anything around. She was here last night when Jackson got hurt. She caused it to happen."

"Did you chase her off?" Hattie asked, heading to the stairs.

"She didn't go willingly. It took all the energy I had and even then I needed help." Beau followed right behind her. "We got rid of her for now, but I'm afraid she will come back."

Beau was right. The witch would be back if Hattie didn't do something. At the top of the stairs, Hattie headed right to Harper's bedroom to look for any sign of hexes. She had no idea why this dead witch was so powerful against the living. She assumed it was because so many people put energy into believing the curse that they had made her stronger.

Hattie would have to do the spell tonight. It was getting far too risky now to let the witch continue. To do that though, she'd need the necklace. That was the trickiest part of all.

She opened Harper's door and stepped into the middle of the room. Hattie closed her eyes and let the feeling of the room settle into her. The witch hadn't cursed the space. She hadn't done much at all except look around. The witch was fascinated with Harper's ability to read an object with just her hand. It had been a skill the witch had heard about in her time. The witch wanted to know how to gain Harper's power. That's why she had been in the room – hoping to soak up Harper's power and learn her trick. There was no trick to be learned though. It was an innate skill that Harper possessed.

At least there was no hex. Hattie pulled the tiger's eye stone from her pocket and placed it in the western corner of the room and said a protective chant. That should keep the witch out for a while at least. If Hattie could get the spell done tonight, they'd never have to worry about her again.

Hattie needed to make quick work of it. She pulled her cellphone from her pocket and called Det. Granger. The phone rang three times and he answered.

"Are you spying on me?" he joked.

"What?" Hattie asked, taken aback by his comment.

"I'm kidding. I'm just pulling up across the street. Harper is helping me with something."

Hattie went to Harper's window, pulled back the curtain, and saw Det. Granger's car in Jackson's driveway. "Do you happen to have the necklace with you?"

"I do," he said hesitating.

Hattie had a sinking feeling. "Why did you bring it with you?" When he didn't say anything, Hattie pushed harder. "You had a feeling you should bring it, right? You thought you might get Harper to tap into a vision even though you know we both said she shouldn't."

"I...well...um," Det. Granger stammered.

"It's okay," Hattie reassured. "It wasn't of your doing. The witch is putting ideas into your head and urging you to do something you wouldn't normally do. You need to bring that necklace over to the house right now. Go inside and get Harper and the both of you come over here."

"We will be right over." Det. Granger hung up and Hattie stood at the window, watching as he got out of his car and went to the door. He knocked and Harper opened it. He spoke to her and she glanced over to Hattie's house. She didn't hesitate with his request. She shut the door and the two of them rushed over to the house.

Hattie turned back into the room. "Beau, I need you to gather your family around. Any good spirits in the house, I need you to bring them down to the living room. I know they like to stay out of sight and that's okay. I don't need to see them. I need to use the power of their collective energy."

"We'll be there." Beau disappeared before her eyes.

Hattie left Harper's room and went to her own bedroom. She opened her nightstand drawer and grabbed her quartz crystal. She felt the weight of it in her palm and then closed her fingers around it. Harper yelled to her from the floor below and Hattie headed for the stairs.

Hattie entered the kitchen and found Harper and Det. Granger sitting at the table. "We need to banish this witch for good. Harper, your Uncle Beau saw the witch in your bedroom and I felt the energy of what she was trying to do. None of you are safe until we disconnect her energy from that necklace. She's feeding off the spell she did on it and all the energy from people who believe in the curse."

"What can we help you with?" Harper asked, walking over to her aunt.

Hattie pulled her grimoire out of the cabinet and pointed to her workbag sitting on the counter. "Bring that bag for me, please. Det. Granger, bring the necklace. I can work in the living room."

Hattie made her way into the living room and set up a makeshift altar with one of the tables. She cleared off the lamp and a book she had been reading and positioned the table against the wall next to the fireplace. Hattie pulled items from her workbag and arranged them on the table.

"What are you doing?" Delia said from behind Hattie, her voice screeching in fear. The witch had appeared from nowhere, but Hattie had anticipated this. She had told Hattie she stayed with the necklace.

Hattie ignored her and worked faster to get the materials ready for the spell. She reached her hand back to Det. Granger. "Place the necklace in my hand."

"You can't touch my necklace!" Delia said, getting right up in Hattie's face.

Harper and Det. Granger shared a look, neither able to see the witch. Hattie still didn't respond to her. She lit two candles – one black for sucking up the negative energy and one white for purity. She placed the necklace on the altar and then opened the anointing oil. She dabbed some on her finger and then rubbed it gently over the stones on the necklace. Det. Granger balked, worried she'd damage it, but Hattie assured him it would wipe off after the spell was completed.

Delia's power grew by the minute. Hattie could feel her rage like a cloak around her. She paid no attention to it. Hattie also felt the power of her husband's family nearby and it energized her. She moved through the fog of Delia's negative energy and used the power of those in the room as she rubbed oil over the necklace and then applied the special herb mixture she had made earlier in the day. Once it was all ready, Hattie began the chant that Fr. Ignatius had given her. Hattie closed her eyes and said it over and over again. She could feel Delia's energy spinning around her.

"What are you doing to me?" the witch yelled. "You cannot stop me!"

But that was exactly what Hattie was going to do. She imagined a black cord coming from the necklace to the spirit of the witch. With the words of the chant and in her mind's eye, Hattie envisioned cutting the cord – separating Delia from the necklace once and for all.

The more Hattie focused on cutting the cord, the angrier Delia became. The witch's spirit thrashed around the room, knocking over a vase on a table and smashing the mirror not far from where Hattie stood.

As the mirror shattered and pieces fell to the ground, Harper shrieked. Det. Granger asked Hattie if she was okay. Hattie could not break her focus to respond. It took all of her energy and that of Beau's ancestors to break the tie between the necklace and Delia. Hattie gave the energy one final push and yelled the chant aloud. Delia screamed and shrunk down to almost nothing and evaporated into the floorboards.

Hattie expelled a breath and reached back for the chair. Harper rushed over to her aunt and helped her sit down. Hattie eased herself into the chair and caught her breath. She knew the spell had worked, but her energy was depleted. "Could you make me a cup of tea, please?"

Harper hurried off to the kitchen while Det. Granger sat down across from Hattie. "Are you okay?"

Hattie explained the spell she had done and what was happening around her that neither Det. Granger nor Harper could see. "The witch's name is Delia and she had so much rage in her. It was her energy that broke the vase and mirror."

Det. Granger offered to clean up the mess for her, but Hattie declined. She wasn't sure if the broken pieces contained any energy from Delia and she didn't want anyone else touching it. "The necklace should be fine to take back. Delia no longer has any control over it."

"You broke the curse?"

Hattie nodded. "I'm not sure if I'll need to do another spell to banish Delia. My guess is without the power from the necklace, she won't have the energy or ability to hurt anyone else. I'll have to watch and see. Delia had more power than any spirit I've encountered."

Det. Granger pinched the bridge of his nose. "I don't think I'll ever get used to this."

Hattie smiled. "Me either."

Harper brought in Hattie's tea and set it down on the table beside her. "You probably don't have the energy now, but there was a favor we had to ask you. I texted you before I came over."

"I didn't see the text. What do you need?" Hattie asked, reaching for the tea.

"Could you connect with Vinnie and ask him some questions for me?"

As soon as Harper said his name, Hattie felt his presence. "Even if I wanted to say no, he's already here."

Chapter Thirty-Nine

"Vinnie," Hattie said, turning slightly to look at him. "I know you're here. You might as well step out so I can see you."

He came out from his hiding spot by the living room drapes. "You aren't going to do that voodoo thing to me, are you? You messed up that scary broad."

"Broad?" Hattie said, rolling her eyes at him. "Be respectful or I might."

"Sorry, lady." Vinnie rubbed at his head. "Is this how I'm going to spend my afterlife hanging out with you? No offense, but it's kind of boring here."

"I'd like you to be able to go. Maybe you can answer some questions for me and that might set you free." Hattie pointed to the spot where Vinnie stood. "Harper, Vinnie is right over there. Vinnie, this is my niece Harper and Det. Granger. They have some questions for you."

Harper turned so she was looking in Vinnie's direction. Hattie knew she couldn't see him. She asked, "Vinnie, did you know the De Luca family – Carmine or Marco or maybe Richie?"

It took Vinnie a moment. He stood there with a dumbfounded look on his face. He asked Hattie a few questions, complained that since he died his memory was terrible, and then, like being struck by lightning, it came to him all at once. "I had a run-in with Marco De Luca at a casino in New Jersey. He was down there with his cousin. Can't remember the guy's name. But they were hassling some women on the casino floor and they were asked to leave. They didn't take too kindly to it so I roughed them up a bit and threw them out of the place."

"Did you work for the casino?" Hattie asked.

Vinnie grunted and snickered. "Not in so many words."

Hattie wasn't sure what that meant, but she turned to Harper and Det. Granger and reported what Vinnie said.

"Is that his only interaction?" Harper asked.

Vinnie shook his head. "There were others. They came back a few nights later. A few of the security guys and I took them out back and made sure they knew they weren't welcome anymore."

"How badly did you hurt them?" Hattie asked, annoyed that she had to interact with a spirit like Vinnie.

"Bad enough we never saw them again."

"Would it be fair to say Marco and Richie might want some revenge?"

Vinnie shrugged. "Now that you mention it, probably."

Hattie explained what Vinnie said. "There is a connection."

Det. Granger looked to Harper. "Why do you ask that?"

"Brendan Miller and Bobby Kemp also had connections to the De Luca family." Harper sat down on the couch and Det. Granger sat next to her. "All three had direct connections to the De Lucas and so does James Wiggins and Sam is connected to Brendan somehow."

Det. Granger asked, "You think the De Lucas are behind this?"

"I'm not sure if it's Marco or Richie or maybe even Carmine. I asked Nick today and he said Carmine has had people killed even from prison."

"That's not surprising," Det. Granger said. "With mafia families, a prison sentence doesn't mean much even for the head of the family. Carmine could still retain control. Do you think Marco is involved?"

"I would think he'd have to be."

The pieces of the puzzle weren't adding up for Hattie. "Why would Marco send these men to find a necklace he could find himself? Didn't you say that Richie is the one that stole it from Nick's safe?"

"That's the part that's not making any sense to me. Richie is family so I would assume Marco would know where the necklace has been all along."

Det. Granger sat back. "What if he didn't?"

"What do you mean?"

"Hear me out." Det. Granger sat thinking for a moment and then explained himself. "What if Richie double-crossed Marco. He steals the necklace from Nick's place and brings it down here to frame Harper, making Nick look like he is either conspiring with his ex or making him look stupid in the process. Has there been any rivalry between Marco and Richie in the family?"

Harper bit her lip. "I don't know about that, but Nick said Marco is the one who suggested to him that the necklace might be with me. Richie could have stolen it and then dropped that suggestion to Marco."

Hattie raised her hand like she was asking permission to speak. It drew Harper and Det. Granger's attention. "If Richie was going to do that, why not just come down here himself, find the necklace, and save the day. He knew right where it was."

"What if he didn't though? You donated those boxes, Hattie," Det. Granger said. "Richie could have been here and tried to get it back as Harper said, but it was gone by that point. He might have panicked."

"I remember seeing Richie down here," Vinnie said, drawing Hattie's attention to him.

Hattie turned around to look at him. "When? Recently?"

"Yeah, when I first got down here. I saw him coming out of a bar downtown. I thought of taking another go at him, but I couldn't be bothered. I wanted to find that necklace."

"Do you think it could have been Richie who killed you?"

Vinnie shrugged. "I don't remember who killed me."

"Do you remember anything?" Hattie pointed to a chair in the far corner of the room. "Sit down and try to clear your mind and then let the memories come to you."

Vinnie did as Hattie suggested. It seemed hard for him to relax enough to get into the right headspace. He squirmed and shifted.

"Close your eyes and let your mind go blank," Hattie encouraged. Vinnie didn't seem like the kind of guy who would have enjoyed being alone with his thoughts. Hattie didn't care. He knew more than he was telling them.

Vinnie tried again and this time his spirit relaxed. He seemed to relax so much Hattie worried he might have fallen asleep. She worried he might disappear.

"What do you see, Vinnie?" she asked, encouraging him.

He reached up and touched the back of his head. "My head hurt because that crazy lady at the hotel attacked me. She thought I had already found the necklace but I hadn't. She was all over me. When she hit me in the head, she thought she had killed me. After she left the room, I took off."

Vinnie remained quiet for a moment as if searching for another memory. His eyes flew open. "I went down the street to a bar and had a beer. I got a text to meet someone at Allsopp Park. I didn't know who it was from. but they wanted us to work together. I figured I'd go. Anything to get me closer to finding that necklace."

"What happened when you got there?"

"There was no one there at first. I stood around feeling stupid. As I turned to leave, that's when I saw them. Next thing I knew I was dead."

"Them?" Hattie asked with excitement in her voice. She inched closer to the edge of her seat.

Vinnie reached up and rubbed his head. "That's the first time I remembered that. There were two people – the man who shot me and a person standing off in my periphery."

"Was it another man or a woman?"

"I don't know," Vinnie said, but then he hesitated. "I think it might have been a woman."

Hattie explained what Vinnie said to Harper and Det. Granger.

"How does he know it was a woman?" Harper asked.

Vinnie gestured toward his shoulder. "She had long hair, kind of messy-like. Her voice was loud. She told the man to shoot me. He hesitated when I first turned around, but then she told him to shoot me and he did."

"Do you remember her name or what she looked like?"

"Just the hair and her voice. I don't remember much else." Vinnie's spirit started to fade and he couldn't hold onto his form. He waved as he disappeared.

That's what happened sometimes to new spirits. It takes so much energy to be seen that it's hard for the new ones to interact with the living for too long, even people who are mediums. Hattie explained that Vinnie had left. "He might be back later when he has more energy. He doesn't remember much. This is the second time I've heard about a man and a woman. The first time I saw it in my cards connected to Cora. She wouldn't tell me who they are though."

Harper and Hattie turned to Det. Granger. "Cora didn't tell me anything like that. She's still not being honest with me. I threatened to charge her with obstruction of justice and she broke down in tears."

Harper rolled her eyes. "All dramatics. Did you throw her in a cell?"

"I didn't but probably should have." Det. Granger blew out a breath. "I don't like arresting innocent people, and I believe Cora is innocent. I believe she has gotten herself mixed up in something she doesn't understand. I didn't think arresting her and giving her a criminal record would do much to help the matter."

Hattie didn't disagree with him. She hated that Cora hadn't taken her advice and told the truth. "Some people can't be helped. Det. Granger, I know Cora has brought out a certain sympathy in you, but if it means you solve three murders, you might just have to get tough with her."

He nodded. "I'm prepared to do that. Today wasn't the day though."

Hattie yawned. "After that spell, I'm a bit tired. You two feel free to stay and do what you have to do. Det. Granger, let that necklace sit on the altar for another thirty minutes, and then you can take it. The connection between Delia and the necklace is broken."

Harper raised her eyebrows. "The curse is broken for good?"

"It is. Delia can't do anything about it because she can't do another spell with no physical body. I broke the energetic cord between her and the necklace. Now, she might be back. If so, I'll need to do something else to banish her. Let's hope she goes away quietly."

Chapter Forty

After Hattie went upstairs, Harper pulled out her cellphone and handed it to Det. Granger. "What do you need to do to record?"

Det. Granger pulled out a simple wire and inserted one end into an audio jack on her phone and the other end into a digital recorder. "It's as simple as that. Did you decide what you're going to tell him?"

"I think we should tell him that I found the necklace and the diamonds, and if he wants them back, he will have to meet me." Even when Det. Granger protested, Harper wasn't taking no for an answer. "I'll tell him that before I'm willing to meet, I have to know who is killing people. I need to know his role in all of this. If he won't tell me that, I'll tell him he'll never get the necklace or diamonds back."

"I don't think that's a good idea," Det. Granger said adamantly.

"He's not going to tell me anything otherwise. I have to get him to talk. He's not going to be forthcoming with information."

Det. Granger bobbed his head like he considered what Harper said. "If he's willing to meet you, then what?"

"Then we set up a sting or whatever you call it. You can be there and other officers. Wire me up and send me in."

Det. Granger narrowed his eyes. "Jackson is going to kill me. I need him on my side because I want to marry his sister."

Harper couldn't be happier for Sarah. "I'm so excited for you!"

Det. Granger held his hand up. "Slow down. I'm not proposing yet. Soon though so I need Jackson to like me."

"Jackson likes you. He doesn't even have to know we are setting up Marco. He can barely make it from the bed to the couch. Besides, he knows how persuasive I am. We can tell him that you knew I'd do it without your help so you were protecting me."

Det. Granger smiled broadly. "I believe that. Go ahead and call."

Harper brought Marco up in her contacts and then hit the call button. It rang several times and she was sure the call would go to voicemail. Marco answered as Harper was about to hang up.

"What do you want?"

Harper pulled back unsure of what to say. She had no idea that Marco would know it was her. "Marco, it's Harper. Nick's ex-wife."

"I know who it is. As I said, what do you want?"

She took a breath and went for it. "Why did you send all these people to search for the necklace here?"

"I don't know what you're talking about. I didn't send anyone down there. Nick went on his own and Brendan is down there because Nick is incompetent." The sound of papers shuffling and hushed voices echoed through the phone line. "I'm starting to think Brendan is incompetent, too, because I haven't heard from him. He's not someone you want to cross, Harper."

Marco had no idea Brendan was dead. "When was the last time you heard from Brendan?"

"A few days ago. I'm assuming he hooked up with Nick and is planning to double-cross me."

"Brendan is dead, Marco. The police found his body in the park."

"What?" Marco barked. "That's not possible. What did you do?"

"I didn't do anything. I didn't know he was down here until a detective showed up at my door asking why there were photos of me in Brendan's phone. I didn't even realize that I knew him until I asked

Nick."

Marco let out a string of curses. "Do they know who killed him?"

"Not that I'm aware of. Who is Sam?" Harper was met with silence. "You know that name, don't you? Who is he? He told the detective that I had an affair with Brendan. You and I both know that didn't happen."

"If you're on Sam's bad side, no one can help you." Marco let out a little laugh. "I can't believe Brendan is dead."

"You don't seem to care."

"You don't get too attached to anyone in this business. If he's dead, then he did something to someone."

Harper had no idea how someone could be so callous. "He's not the only one, Marco. Bobby Kemp and Vinnie Ruggiero were murdered as well. Someone is killing people searching for that necklace and I think it's you."

Marco grunted. "You got the wrong guy, sweetheart. I'm sitting here in Manhattan. I haven't been out of the city in at least three months."

"Do you know the names I mentioned?"

"Let's not play games, Harper. You know I do, but I didn't kill them or have them killed. Got it?"

"Maybe it's Carmine then," Harper said with emphasis.

Marco called her an ugly name. "Getting my old man sent to state prison wasn't enough for you. Now you're trying to pin murders on him while he sits in a cell. There's low and then there's low, Harper. No wonder Nick took up with my sister."

She didn't let the insult impact her. "That still doesn't help me understand how these people came to know the necklace was here or why they are dying."

"I have no idea." Marco spoke to someone else and then got back on the line.

"Who told you that I had the necklace?"

"Nick."

"No, Marco," Harper stressed. "Nick told me that you asked him if he thought I might have stolen it. Someone gave you that idea. Who was it?"

Marco ignored the question. "You just said the necklace is down there. Are you telling me you're willing to give it back?"

Harper took a deep breath. "I didn't steal it, Marco, but I know who did. I came across it recently. I have the diamonds, too. If you want them back, you're going to have to come down here yourself and get them from me."

Marco whooped loudly. "That's not happening. You'll give the necklace and the diamonds to Nick. You're lucky I'm letting you live, Harper. Stealing from me usually ends in death."

"I'm not giving them to Nick. I don't trust him." Harper remembered Nick's last conversation with her. He had told her that Marco confirmed that Brendan was dead. Nick had lied because Harper knew the shock in Marco's voice had been real. She didn't understand.

"Harper, are you there? Give them to Nick."

Harper refocused. "Marco, no, Nick is the one who lost them. I have them now, and if you want them back, you'll meet me."

"Where?" Marco asked, frustration and anger in his voice.

"Here in Little Rock."

Marco cursed again and then disconnected the call. Harper pulled the phone back, looked at it, and turned to Det. Granger. "Maybe I pushed too hard."

"You did fine. I think he's telling the truth that he didn't know Brendan is dead. I also believed that he didn't know there were others down here searching for the necklace and diamonds."

"He didn't tell me who suggested to him that I had the necklace. I feel like that's an important part of the puzzle."

Before Det. Granger could respond to her, Harper's cellphone rang, making them both jump in their seats. He pointed. "It's Marco. Answer it."

Harper said hello. "Did we get disconnected?"

"Meet me tomorrow evening at eight. Name the place."

Harper smiled and gave Det. Granger a thumbs up. "Meet me at my Aunt Hattie's shop. I'll text you the address. Make sure to come alone."

"You do the same or you'll regret it." With that, the line went dead.

Harper rested the cellphone on her leg. "We got him to come down here if he isn't here already. Do you think he's already here since he wanted to meet so quickly?"

"I wondered the same thing. He could be flying out tomorrow morning though." Det. Granger inched forward on the couch. "Why Hattie's shop?"

"It's a high traffic area and there is the back room where you can wait. It also can easily be wired for sound if that's what we need."

Det. Granger smiled. "I'm telling you we need to recruit you. You can be my sidekick."

"Aren't I already your sidekick? You don't even have to pay me."

"Fair enough." Det. Granger got up from the couch and headed for the table that had the necklace. "You think this is okay to touch now?"

Harper checked the time on her phone. "I think you're good to go."

"Do you want to hold it again and see if you can pick up anything?"

Harper walked over to the table and peered down at it. She knew Hattie had cleared the curse. Its energy pulsed differently now. But after the previous experience, Harper didn't think it would be a good idea. "I know Hattie said the witch is gone, but I don't want to press my luck."

Det. Granger understood. Before he turned to go, he looked back at Harper. "You need to be careful. I haven't been able to locate Sam and arrest him for the diamond theft. He provided no information about the murders when I interviewed him before. I've not been able to confirm his alibis so he's definitely on the suspect list."

Harper walked Det. Granger to the door, assuring him she'd be fine. "If you don't mind me asking, who else is on the suspect list?"

Det. Granger ran a hand over his head. "It's a short list. Not short because I'm close to the killer, but short because I have no idea."

"That bad?"

"There is little evidence other than the same gun used. The only connection among them is the link to the search for the necklace and tonight you mentioned the connection to the De Luca family."

Harper knew he wasn't going to like what she had to say. "Vinnie told us there was a man and a woman there. That's something to go on."

Det. Granger lowered his head and smirked at her. "You want me to investigate based on the word of a ghost? You know I can't do that."

Harper laughed at his frustration. "It's an idea and it's helped you before. I thought by now you'd be a little more openminded."

He pointed to the living room. "I watched Hattie perform a spell on a necklace I didn't believe was cursed. My mind is cracking open an inch at a time. Just know I'm working on it." He laughed.

"Fair enough," Harper said. "Where is Cora?"

"I put her in protective custody and changed her hotel again. She has security right now until we can catch Sam."

"That's probably a good idea." Harper stepped outside on the porch steps with Det. Granger. "Stop by the office tomorrow if you want to work out a plan for my meeting with Marco. I'm hoping I can get him to confess to cooking up the insurance fraud scheme with George and maybe to the murders."

Det. Granger raised his eyebrows. "You think it's some kind of De Luca family hit?"

Harper shrugged. "I'm not sure what else it could be."

"Let's see how it goes. I'll have to put in a call to the New York Police Department because the insurance fraud happened up there and it's out of my jurisdiction."

Harper had forgotten about that. No matter. She hoped Marco would confess to the murders, or at least, give her some clue to who it was. She figured with Marco being there in person, she'd use the truth spell on him. Now that Hattie had told her she couldn't kill someone using it, she saw no reason not to keep it in her arsenal. She waved goodbye to Det. Granger, locked Hattie's door, and went back across the street to Jackson's house for the night.

Chapter Forty-One

Hattie stepped through the door of her shop at eight-thirty the next morning. She had been anticipating a rush of customers but nothing could prepare her for the mess she walked into. Broken plates and mugs littered the floor and the bowls of gemstones that had been sitting in neat rows across the back of the shop had been overturned, leaving multi-colored piles of stones all over the floor.

As the door closed behind her, Hattie took in the scene. "What happened here?"

Sarah stood in the middle of the shop with a broom and dustpan. "I'm not sure. The door was locked when I got here and nothing in the back was disturbed. We weren't robbed as far as I know."

"The security alarm never went off," Hattie said, walking to the counter and setting her bag down. "I don't think anyone could have broken in. It was probably Delia. Last night, I broke the curse she had on the necklace and she vowed revenge."

Sarah swept some broken glass into the dustpan. "You think this is the worst she will do?"

Hattie had no idea. She didn't think the witch would have done this, but she shouldn't have been surprised. "Let me call her and see if I can make peace. Otherwise, I'm going to have to banish her, and I don't like doing that with the living or the dead."

Hattie went to the shop door, turned the sign to closed, and locked it. "I'm fine closing for a few hours until we can get this cleaned up. You shouldn't have to do that and wait on customers. If you'd like to sit down and wait until I summon Delia, I'll help you with clean-up."

Sarah waved her off. "You go ahead and I'll keep working. Beatrix should be in soon. The two of us should have this place looking back to normal in no time."

Hattie told her how much she appreciated her and then charged to her reading room, calling the witch's name as she went. Hattie found her sitting in her chair in the reading room. "Get out of my chair," Hattie demanded as she flipped on the light.

"Make me." Delia stared at her defiantly.

Hattie sighed. "This is why I wanted to see you. I can certainly make you if I have to. Wouldn't you rather go away on your own and live your spirit life wherever that may be? I had hoped you would have seen the errors of your ways by now. You're back to looking like the beautiful young woman you once were."

Delia held her arms out wide and smiled. "I should probably thank you for that. The spell made me ugly."

"It was the negativity that ate you alive." Hattie took a step closer to her. "Don't you feel any better? Lighter maybe?"

"I feel different, but I'm angry with you."

"My destroyed shop is evidence of that."

Delia winked. "You deserved that. I don't know what to do with myself now that the curse is broken. You ruined my life."

Hattie groaned. "You're dead, my dear, you don't have a life. You have an old curse that you were hanging on to for no reason. You were hurting people who never did anything to you, and it destroyed you in the process." The witch was about to argue, but Hattie held her hand up to silence her. "I understand you were wronged. I get it. We have all been there – loved the wrong person, thought we'd have a life with them and it turned out they were using us or cheating or some other nonsense. I'm truly sorry you had to go through that in your life. I know heartbreak is never easy to heal from but seeking revenge is not the answer."

Delia lowered her eyes to the ground. "What do I do now?"

"Start trying to do some good in the world. You're incredibly powerful, but you've been abusing that power. You have some karma to pay back. Do good and you'll figure it out."

"I don't even know how to be good anymore. It was like the negativity took over."

"It did. The more you mire yourself down in that, the harder it is to see the light." Since the witch seemed to be so forthcoming, Hattie figured she'd use it to her advantage. She sat on the couch, which gave her an entirely new perspective on the room. "You can start doing good by confirming for me who stole the necklace and brought it here to Little Rock."

"Your niece's vision was correct. Richie De Luca stole it and then brought it to your house."

"Do you know why?"

Delia shook her head. "I had no idea what he was doing, but I followed the necklace. You gave it away without even realizing you had it. I didn't curse you because you had no idea it was in your house."

"Kind of you," Hattie said dryly. "You acted the other day like you knew who killed those men. Do you know?"

"No. I lied. I stayed with the necklace."

Hattie had thought that might have been the case, but it was worth asking. "Can I trust you to go away and do some good in the world? A witch never likes having to banish another."

Delia stayed quiet for several moments and Hattie didn't push her. She seemed to be debating what she'd do. Hattie hoped Delia knew she was serious and she'd banish her if forced.

CHAPTER FORTY-ONE

Finally, Delia raised her head. "I'll go peacefully. I think it's time anyway."

"I appreciate that."

Delia rose from Hattie's chair. "You need to be careful, especially your niece. There are people around who mean her harm. I don't know who they are but I can feel the energy."

"Me too." Hattie exhaled a breath. "Take care of yourself," she said as the witch vanished before her eyes. Hattie stood from the couch and left her reading room. As she made her way to the front of the shop, she heard Sarah and Beatrix talking and laughing. She pulled back the red curtain and stepped out, surprised by what she saw. The bowls of gemstones were stacked again on the shelf and had been refilled. The glass had been swept and the shop had returned to normal. Hattie had no idea how they had worked so quickly.

"For the second time today, I'm asking what's going on here?" Hattie said, wonder in her eyes.

Beatrix pointed and smiled. "The bowls righted themselves and the stones rose off the floor and went back into the bowls. It happened on its own, Hattie. I've never seen anything like it."

"The glass too," Sarah said. "It gathered in a pile and then made a trail up the garbage can until the last shred had been disposed of."

A glimmer at the door caught Hattie's eyes. Delia winked and gave a playful wave and then disappeared. "At least I got Delia sorted. One down and many to go." Hattie walked to the shop door, unlocked, and flipped the sign around to say open. She turned back to Sarah. "I need to start with some coffee this morning and maybe a chocolate croissant. It's been a long morning and it's only nine."

Hattie spent the next two hours doing readings for clients and catching up on some spells she had promised a few people. They were all simple enough – helping one woman increase her business sales, giving another woman a boost of confidence, and nudging the energy so one man would have good luck asking for a raise. Hattie liked the straightforward spells.

After the lunch rush, when the shop quieted and Sarah left for the day, Hattie poured herself some coffee and leaned back on the counter savoring each sip. Beatrix waved as she left the shop heading for an afternoon class. Hattie was on her own for the afternoon. She hadn't been in the shop by herself for so long that she couldn't remember the last time. Her business had grown so much that she needed help. Today, though, she'd have to manage.

The bell at the shop door rang and she turned to see who it was and frowned. "I believe I asked you not to come back to the shop," she said loudly enough the only two customers in the shop heard her. They turned toward the door to see who was there.

James Wiggins wasn't deterred. He walked right up to the counter. "I know what you asked of me, but we need to talk now. I'm not leaving until we do."

Chapter Forty-Two

H attie stood ramrod straight and narrowed her eyes at James. "I don't believe I have anything to say to you. According to Harper, she knows you from Manhattan. You lied to me about who you are."

"I did no such thing," he said, pounding his fist on the counter.

Hattie pointed her finger at him. "I'll have none of that in here."

"I know you found the necklace and the diamonds," he said with a menacing stare.

Hattie wasn't sure how best to handle the situation. Her only two customers in the shop glanced nervously at the counter checking to see what was happening. Hattie smiled to assure them all was well and then leaned over the counter. She said in a harsh whisper, "If I found anything, which I'm not confirming I did, it would have been turned over to Det. Granger with the Little Rock Police Department."

"No! No! No! You shouldn't have done that!" James yelled, stamping his feet and balling up his fists.

His fury made Hattie take a step back and call for spiritual help. "You need to calm down. I don't understand why you're so upset. It's not like you were going to be able to keep the necklace anyway."

He pounded on the counter. "I must have that necklace!"

The two women who had been sitting at the table set their cups down and headed for the door. Hattie wanted to stop them and encourage them to stay, but it was probably better they go.

Hattie pointed after them. "See what you're doing? You're scaring away my customers."

"I don't care!"

Hattie reached for her cellphone. "If you don't knock it off, I'm calling Det. Granger."

James shook his head. "I can't have the police involved."

"Then you have two options. Sit down and tell me what's wrong or get out of my shop." She didn't want to entertain him there a moment longer than necessary, but Hattie felt that if she didn't hear him out, he'd be back.

James sat down at a table and Hattie turned her back only long enough to drop some lavender tea in a cup, pour hot water over it, and say magical words as she stirred the liquid around. She carried the cup to the table and set it down in front of him. "Drink that."

James looked down into the cup and then raised it to his lips. "Lavender. You're trying to make me calm."

"If you're not calm, I can't understand what you want." Hattie sat back in the chair and crossed her arms over her chest. "You want the necklace. It seems you've wanted it all along, according to what Harper said. That can't happen. It's not yours to have."

"I must have it," he said softer this time but still the same insistence.

"Why?" Hattie assessed him, trying to pick up psychically what she might have missed before. "No one was going to pay you if you found it. It's stolen property so you weren't going to be able to keep it. What's going on, James?"

James drank more of his tea and then wiped his brow. "I know everyone says that the necklace is cursed but to me it's magical. Whenever I've been in its presence, it enchants me. I can't explain the feeling, but I must have it. From the first moment I saw it, I tried to buy it from George Lennox, but he wouldn't sell it to me. Then he cooked up the insurance fraud scheme and I tried to track it. I tried to get it back. It was always a step ahead of me."

"Did you know it was stolen from Harper's penthouse in Manhattan?"

James nodded. "I didn't think it was stolen but rather moved. I figured Richie De Luca picked it up and brought it to Marco before he brought it to your house. I had been watching your place for a long time but could never find it."

Hattie narrowed her eyes at him. "You've broken into my house and searched for the necklace?"

James swallowed and looked away. "I needed it. It called to me."

"Did you want it bad enough to kill for it?"

James shook his head back and forth so hard Hattie thought he might hurt himself. "I didn't hurt anyone but myself. I've lost clients. I've lost money and my wife. She thinks I've gone mad. The necklace wants me to have it. I'm telling you the truth."

The witch called to him was more like it. Hattie wasn't sure how to explain that to him. She relaxed her posture and leaned forward. "James," she said softly, "it wasn't the necklace that enchanted you. It was the witch attached to it."

"Witch?" he asked his eyebrows raised. "I don't believe in such things."

Hattie laughed. "You believe a necklace called to you but you can't believe it was a witch. Don't be silly, James. A witch cursed the necklace in life and then haunted the necklace in death. She was the one who made all the bad things happen. I don't even think it was the spell she put on it as much as her power causing bad things to happen. You must have been drawn to her energy."

"That can't be." James sat back, confusion on his face. "I heard the necklace calling my name. It drew me to it."

"The witch must have been calling you. Have you always had an interest in the necklace?"

"Yes, from the moment I started in this business. It's one of those rare items in my field. It's like the holy grail of historical jewelry."

"When did you start feeling like it was calling to you?"

James blinked rapidly. "When George Lennox first bought it. He showed it to me and allowed me to touch it. From that moment on, I knew I had to have it. He wouldn't sell it to me though. I thought about stealing it. I've never committed a crime in my life. The call was strong though."

Hattie had seen something like this only once before. She wouldn't call it a possession in the evil sense, but she had to break the tie between James and the necklace in the same way she did with Delia. It would be easier this time. It was more of a cleansing, but there was a caveat if it was going to work. He had to want to let go. Otherwise, Hattie would have to use a stronger spell.

"James, if you could be free of your attachment to the necklace would you choose that?"

His eyes raised and he didn't even hesitate. "Yes, very much so. It's ruined my life. If you're telling me I can't have the necklace anyway then yes, of course. I want to be free of the desire."

"Wait right here. I can take care of this for you." Hattie got up and headed toward the back area of the shop. She glanced over her shoulder to make sure James remained sitting at the table. Hattie worried he might be in shock because he hadn't moved at all.

Hattie hurried to the back and went to her workroom and gathered up all the supplies she needed. She didn't know for sure if James was attached to the necklace or the witch. The spell she would perform would break the connection to both.

Hattie made her way back to the table with a large quartz crystal, some cleaning oils, and a black and a white candle. Luckily, she remembered the words she'd need to say. Hattie made quick work of placing the candles on the table near James, one on each side of him. She handed him the quartz. "You need to hold onto this while I say the spell."

Hattie dipped her finger in the special oil and went to anoint his head with it but he pulled back.

"What are you doing?" he asked, brushing her hand away.

"This is what I need to do to break the connection. It's a special oil blend. Work with me here and don't be difficult."

James squeezed his eyes shut and told her to go ahead. Hattie had no idea what he was being so dramatic about. All she had to do was dab a spot on his forehead and the top of each hand. It's not like she was going to splash it in his face.

When she was done, he opened one eye. "You done?"

Hattie rolled her eyes. "Not yet." She lit the candles and stood in front of him and said the chant she had memorized, envisioning the connection between James and the necklace and the witch severed. She said the words three times calling in the power of the Earth, air, water, and fire, allowing the energy to build and build until it hit a crescendo and James shrieked aloud.

"I feel it!" he cried as he opened his eyes and Hattie looked down at him.

She felt it, too. The energy had shifted and James was free from the tie to the witch and the necklace. Even his energy felt lighter and less intense. "Do you feel better?"

James sprung up from this chair. "I haven't felt this good in years. It's like you lifted a veil from over my eyes. I can see and think clearly. I feel better and not so weighed down." James rubbed at his head. "How do you think it happened?"

"I don't know. Either the witch took an interest in you or you're more susceptible to energy than most people. I can't be sure." Hattie snuffed out the candles and sat back down. "Is there anything you'd like to tell me?"

James glanced over at her. "I'm sorry for digging in your yard and causing you any trouble. I have no idea who is killing people. I swear it wasn't me. I would tell you if I knew."

Hattie believed him because she had watched him transform in front of her eyes after the spell. "What are you going to do now?"

James pulled out his wallet. "I don't think I could ever pay you enough for what you did for me. Please take something though." He held out a wad of cash to Hattie.

She dismissed it. "It was my pleasure to help you." He tried again to get her to take the money, insisting he wanted her to take it. "I'll tell you what. You go down to St. Joseph's Church and see Fr. McNeely and give a donation. Tell him Hattie sent you."

James nodded. "I'll do that right now. Then I'm headed back home to repair things with my wife and rebuild my business." He threw his arms around her and squeezed her tight. "I can't thank you enough. I hope they catch whoever is committing those horrible murders. I feel lucky to get out of here alive."

Hattie smiled and waved to him as he left. She picked up the candles and other supplies and carried them to the back of her shop. It had been a challenging month with everything that had happened on their trip to New Orleans and the return home. Hattie was more than ready for a peaceful few months. She considered putting a spell on herself to ensure that it was.

Hattie arranged things in her workroom and straightened up. As she worked, an idea occurred to her how she might be able to protect Harper. She'd have to give it some thought. Hattie went to the front of the shop, anticipating that the afternoon rush would start at any moment. As she pulled back the red velvet curtain, she was surprised to see Det. Granger standing there.

"I'm glad the shop is quiet," he said, stepping toward her. "I have to wire the place up for sound and video for Harper's meeting with

Marco."

"My shop is yours," Hattie said, opening her arms wide. "In case anything goes wrong tonight, I'm going to cook up a plan of my own."

Det. Granger looked at her with worry written all over his face. "I hope it's nothing too bad."

She winked. "Define too bad."

Chapter Forty-Three

The day had been a flurry of activity for Harper. She and Dan had met with two advertisers, hired another freelance writer, and approved photos for the next edition of *Rock City Life.*

In the late afternoon, Dan walked into Harper's office and sat down. "We've been so busy all day that I didn't even get the chance to ask about Jackson."

Harper moved her laptop slightly to the side so she could rest her arms on the desk and give Dan her full attention. "He's surviving and is in less pain than yesterday. He is going to be housebound for a little bit unless I'm driving. He told me this morning that he was going to take a walk around the neighborhood later if he felt up to it."

"Jackson doesn't seem like the kind of person to stay still too easily."

"He's not. That's going to be the hardest part about this. He can't even wrap his head around the fact that the witch cursing the necklace did this to him. He's chalking it up to old age and the dogs getting in the way."

Dan laughed. "I'd probably do the same. If you need to work from home for a few days, feel free."

Harper shook her head. "It's too much with me there hovering over him all day. He promised to call me if he needs me though." She laughed. "Let's see how well that works out."

"How's everything going otherwise?"

Harper explained to him about Hattie breaking the curse and her call to Marco. "I haven't spoken to Nick since the other day and he seems to be playing nice at the moment anyway. Det. Granger has Cora hidden away and Sam is on the run."

"Do you think Marco is going to show up and confess to all of this?"

Harper shrugged. "It's the best shot we have. Everything ties back to the De Luca family. Carmine is in prison. Richie could be the one behind this all, working for Carmine, but I have no way of finding him. We either get information out of Marco or convince him it's Carmine. I don't see a downside in meeting with him."

Dan lowered his chin and eyed her. "You don't see a downside in meeting with the head of a mob family whose father you sent to prison? I can see lots of downsides, the first being your safety."

It's not that Harper hadn't thought of that. She hated having to deal with the De Lucas, but she didn't see another way. Mobsters were dropping like flies around them and there were still people after the necklace. It was worth the risk and she told Dan that.

"Besides," she said trying to summon up conviction in her voice. "Det. Granger will be there. He is wiring Hattie's place for audio and video today and he'll be right outside in a van listening in."

"I don't think Marco is going to fall for it."

Harper wasn't sure he would either. "If Marco didn't do anything wrong, then he has nothing to worry about. Regardless, it's time to bring this thing to a head – one way or the other. Hattie is exhausted. Have you seen her? She needs a vacation from all of this craziness."

Dan assessed her. "Do you have any suspect in mind? You usually have Det. Granger beat in figuring out his murder cases. Doesn't seem like it this time."

"I'm off my game." She laughed. "I have no idea. It's probably because the whole thing doesn't make any sense. It feels like there are two things at play here. One, finding the necklace and then two, gathering mobsters that have had a beef with the De Lucas."

"Let's not even mention Nick and Cora and the witch cursing the necklace."

"Right!" Harper slapped her hand down on the desk. "I think I have finally convinced Nick that we have no shot at getting back together, and Hattie convinced Cora she needs to be on her way. I don't think either of them killed anyone though. Hattie also got rid of the curse and witch so at least whoever gets the necklace next just has a nice piece of history."

"What about the diamonds?"

"Sam found those in Hattie's backyard. He stashed them with Cora and Det. Granger recovered them. I don't know that they were ever cursed. It's up to the insurance company now what will happen to them. My guess is they will be sold at auction." Harper pointed to her laptop. "The story for *Rock City Life* will be a good one though."

Dan stood. "What time are you leaving to go to Hattie's?"

"I'm not meeting Marco until tonight. I planned to work a full day and then check in on Jackson before the meeting."

Dan looked down at her. "With Jackson out of commission, do you need some backup tonight?"

"There's no way I'm letting you get mixed up in this. Det. Granger has my back."

Dan breathed a sigh of relief and dragged his hand across his brow dramatically. "Good. I wasn't up for it anyway."

"I didn't think you would be. If you're running out to get a late lunch, I'll take a sandwich from the deli downstairs. I haven't eaten since this morning and I don't think I'll get a chance to eat dinner."

"That I can manage." Dan left Harper's office and she got down to work. Nick lying to her the other day about Marco had been bothering her, but she couldn't quite put her finger on what it meant. She was thinking about that when Dan reappeared in her office doorway.

Harper raised her head. Confused by the strained expression on his face, she asked, "Do you need money?"

Suddenly, Dan flew forward and landed in a heap on the floor. A man Harper had only seen in her vision stood in the doorway with Lola De Luca at his side.

Richie pointed the gun at her. "Marco said you have the necklace. Hand it over."

Harper jumped up from her chair. "I don't have it here. I'm meeting Marco tonight and will give it to him then."

Lola, who still had a mane of wild hair and hadn't lost any of the baby weight, shoved Richie out of the way. "Change of plans. By the time Marco gets here, that necklace is going to be long gone."

"What are you talking about?" Harper asked confused.

"You're giving me that necklace. I deserve it more than my no-good brother."

Harper shifted her eyes between them. "You're not working with Marco?"

Lola laughed. "If it were up to Marco, Nick would already be dead. I'm not going to let him destroy my family. He's made a mess of things since you sent my father to prison."

Harper had suspected Carmine had been behind this. That's what Nick lied about. He hadn't heard from Marco that Brendan had been murdered. He must have heard it from Lola. Harper wondered if he suspected Lola was involved.

"What about your daughter, Lola? Where is she with you and Nick down here?"

Lola shook her head. "Don't you worry about Nick's baby. Our family is just fine. You might not be able to keep a man, but I can."

"Why is your father involving you in this? It's not your fight."

Lola cackled. "For a smart woman, you sure are stupid. This has nothing to do with Carmine. This is me and Richie taking over the family business by force. You're coming with us."

Dan gripped the edge of her desk and tried to pull himself into a standing position. "Harper isn't going anywhere with you. She is..." Dan didn't get out the last of his sentence. Richie drove the butt of the gun into the side of Dan's head and he slumped to the floor.

Harper moved around the side of her desk to check on Dan, but Richie shoved her back.

"He's fine." Richie grabbed her by the arm and dragged her toward the doorway.

Harper looked back at Dan in a heap on the floor. "He's bleeding. You might have killed him."

Richie laughed. "Too bad for him then."

Harper ripped her arm free of him and rushed to Dan. She bent down over him and saw the blood pooling on the side of his head. Dan was still breathing at least. "Dan. Dan," she said, nudging him with her hand. He didn't move. It was clear he had been knocked unconscious.

"We need to call for help," Harper said, standing.

Richie grabbed her by the arm again. "You're coming with us. If he dies, he dies. Wouldn't be my first."

Harper's eyes flew open. "It's you who has been killing those people."

Richie didn't confirm or deny it. "Let's go. We're wasting time."

Harper didn't know what option she had. Her phone was on her desk, but when she tried to reach back for it, Lola blocked her.

She pushed Harper. "You don't need anything with you except directions to the necklace. Give us that and we'll let you go."

Harper doubted that, but she let Richie drag her toward the top of the stairs. She didn't have her phone or purse or anything with her. She hoped that once Dan woke up he'd be able to call for help.

As if reading her mind, Richie said, "If you do anything stupid, I'll come back and make sure your friend is dead."

Lola smiled a sick twisted grin. "If you don't do what we ask, I might have to take another man of yours. This time instead of stealing your husband, Richie and I will kill that boyfriend of yours."

"Right after we kill that stupid old aunt." Richie laughed and shoved Harper down the stairs.

Harper gained her balance before she fell and took her time going down the remainder of the stairs, trying to make a plan as they went. She had no idea where they were taking her. Harper didn't have the necklace or the diamonds and had no idea what to do.

Chapter Forty-Four

Harper tried to stall as long as she could. She had also tried to break away from Lola and Richie once they were on the street, but they had snatched her right back – each of them gripping an arm and walking next to her. They had reached an SUV parked along the road and Richie all but threw her in the back with Lola next to her.

"I'm done playing around, Harper. Where is the necklace?" Richie demanded as he climbed into the driver's seat. He looked at her through the rearview mirror while Lola drove a fist into her side for emphasis.

Harper grabbed for her side in pain and resisted the urge to fight back. It wouldn't serve any purpose and probably only lead to her being injured. She caught her breath from the sucker punch. "We have to go to my Aunt Hattie's shop. That's where we hid the necklace and the diamonds."

Harper knew it was a risk. She looked between the seats and glanced at the clock. Hattie would still be in the shop and possibly even have customers. She had no idea if Sarah or Beatrix were there or if Det. Granger had already wired the place for sound. Harper had no idea what else to do though.

"I can tell you how to get there," Harper said.

Lola scoffed at her. "We already know."

They drove out of downtown Little Rock and up Cantrell until they reached the Heights. Richie made the right on Kavanaugh and followed the road until they were in the short block that had Hattie's shop. Harper didn't see Det. Granger's SUV parked near the shop and didn't see Sarah's car either. The lights in the shop were on, but Harper didn't see any customers as they passed by.

"You'll need to find a place to park on the street," Harper instructed, keeping her eyes focused on the shop as they drove by. She caught a glimpse of Hattie standing near the counter. It looked like she was alone. Harper wished there was some way to alert her aunt to leave the shop or call for help. Without a phone, she had few options.

Richie pulled over and cut the engine. He turned around in his seat to look at her. "I'm not kidding when I say, one false move, and I'll kill you. Then I'll kill your aunt and your boyfriend."

Harper believed him. The De Luca family was ruthless. She had witnessed it when she was in Manhattan. "Is Marco on his way down here? If I give you the necklace, I'm not sure what I'm supposed to tell him."

Richie waved the gun at her. "I told him I'd handle it for him." He got out of the SUV, slammed his door shut, and then opened her door.

Harper got out of the SUV with Lola right behind her. They crossed the street together and then walked to Hattie's shop. Her hands shook with fear because she had no plan how to handle this once they got inside. She knew she was putting Hattie at risk, but Harper hoped that the two of them together could come up with a plan.

Richie pulled open the door and placed his hand on Harper's back and shoved her inside. She stumbled as she went through the doorway, drawing Hattie's attention.

"Harper, what's happening?" Hattie asked, her face registering surprise.

Harper swallowed and made her way to the counter. "This is Richie and Lola De Luca. They are here for the necklace and the diamonds."

Harper hoped her expression gave away the fear she felt and indicated to Hattie that they needed a plan.

"I see," Hattie said. Looking over at them, she asked, "Can I get either of you something to drink or a snack?"

"This isn't a Sunday afternoon tea break, lady," Richie said, waving the gun at her. "Get over here and lock that front door and close the blinds. I don't need customers coming in here. Don't try anything stupid either. As I told Harper already, I have no problem killing either of you."

Hattie brushed her hands off on an apron she wore covering her skirt. "No problem. You need to calm down though. I don't think there is any reason to be so uptight. We have what you want and will give it to you."

Harper had no idea why her aunt appeared so calm when her heart felt like it might leap out of her body any moment. Her heartbeat echoed in her ears and thumped in her chest.

Hattie reached out her hand and took Harper's as she came around the corner. "Calm down. Everything is going to be okay."

Harper didn't think her aunt had any idea how bad this was. "Please take this seriously, Aunt Hattie. They knocked Dan unconscious at the office. This is Lola, the woman who had Nick's baby."

"I'm Nick's wife," Lola snarled.

"Nice to meet you," Hattie said, giving her a look that said her words didn't reflect her feelings. Hattie closed the blinds on both windows and then went to the door. She flipped the sign to closed and locked the door.

As she turned back around, Hattie smiled. "Let's get down to business then."

Richie waved the gun at her again. "Where's the necklace?"

"Not here. You and Lola should take a seat. I need to call the person who has it to bring it here. While we wait, I want some information. Sit down." Hattie gestured with her hand, seemingly in command of the entire situation.

Harper went to the table and sat while Richie and Lola looked on like they weren't sure what to do. Hattie went to the table and pulled out the chair next to her. She glanced back up at Lola and Richie.

"You're wasting my time. If you want the necklace, sit down. I have a few questions."

Lola shifted her eyes to Richie and he shrugged. They both joined Harper and Hattie at the table.

"Call the person who has it," Richie instructed.

Hattie pulled her cellphone from her pocket and scrolled through her contacts. She held the phone up to her ear and waited a beat. Then calmly, she said, "Charlie, come by with the necklace and the diamonds now. Bring Delia with you if you get the chance."

Harper's eyes grew wide and Lola caught the look. "What? Who did she just call? Who are Charlie and Delia?"

Hattie gave a wave of her hand. "Tell them, Harper."

As Harper started to speak, the words caught in her throat. "Charlie is the ghost of a private investigator and Delia is the spirit of the dead witch who cursed the necklace."

Lola's mouth hung open and Richie groaned. "You're playing games with me, old lady."

"No games. They have the items you want, but that brings up my first question. Why would you hide the necklace and diamonds at my house?"

Richie looked to Lola, who wasted no time explaining their plan. She spoke with pride. "My family has always underestimated me. It was naturally assumed that Marco would take over for Carmine when he went to prison. My father didn't even think of me. I knew Marco planned to get rid of Nick. I had to stop him and there was only one way – take over the family."

Harper wasn't sure why she hadn't seen that sooner. It was so obvious. "That still doesn't explain why you hid the necklace with us."

"Nick doesn't stop talking about you. I figured I could kill about five birds with one stone. Women are always more efficient than men with multitasking."

"I still don't understand," Harper said, looking to Hattie to see if she did. Hattie shook her head not understanding either.

"You're supposed to be smart, Harper!" Lola groaned. "There were a few guys that had done my family wrong over the years and Marco was too soft to do anything about it. I figured if I lured them here, Richie could bump them off one by one but not before one of them took you out when searching for the necklace. You'd be dead and then my father would see how I could get things done. After a time, we'd retrieve the necklace and diamonds and show my father how incompetent Marco is."

Harper couldn't believe what she was hearing. "You hoped one of the mobsters would kill me?"

"Yeah," Lola said, clicking her tongue. "Now, Richie is going to have to do it for me." She turned to look at Hattie. "And kill the old lady, too."

Hattie looked right at Richie. "You're the one who killed Vinnie and Bobby?"

He smiled. "Brendan, too. Without Brendan, Marco is even more useless. The only one I didn't get to kill was Sam, but I'll take care of him before I go."

"Sam is gone," Hattie said with some satisfaction. "He skipped town and you're not going to have a chance to kill him or me or Harper."

Richie raised his eyebrows. "Why not?"

Before Hattie could answer, Harper asked, "What about Nick? What did he have to do with all of this?"

"Nothing. He doesn't know a thing," Lola said. "Marco sent him down here like some patsy searching for the necklace and diamonds. Marco didn't trust him that's why he sent Brendan after him, which only made our plan even better. It was easy to kill Brendan down here."

Harper still didn't understand something. "Stealing the necklace only made Marco distrust Nick more. Why would you do that to him?"

Lola smiled like a Cheshire cat. "Nicky is so pretty, but he's not that smart. My father hated that Marco trusted Nick at all. I had to set both of them up. Now Carmine will know that I can run this family and Nick can stay in the background. I killed off our enemies, avenged my father's incarceration, and found the necklace and diamonds. It's the perfect fool-proof plan." Lola reached over and gripped Hattie's wrist. "Get me that necklace!"

Richie stood up and started backing away. "What? What's that? What's happening?" he stammered, pointing to the floor near the table.

Hattie pulled her wrist free of Lola and clapped her hands. "Looks like my team has arrived!"

Harper had no idea what was happening around her, but the whole shop was filling up with a thick blueish fog. It covered the floor completely and then crept up the tables and chairs, making everything disappear.

Richie pointed the gun at Hattie. "Make it stop!"

"You want the necklace. Give it time. You'll have it in just a moment." As the fog enveloped them, Hattie reached for Harper across the table and pulled her to her feet. Richie pointed the gun between them unsure of what he should do.

He turned to Lola. "We need to get out of here."

Lola screamed as the fog completely covered her head and she disappeared.

"Let's go!" Hattie yelled, reaching for Harper and pulling her toward the back of the shop.

Richie fired off shots wildly but missed Harper and Hattie as they ran hand in hand through the red velvet curtain and into the back of the shop. The fog hadn't completely covered the backroom the way it had the front of the shop, but it was filling up quickly as it seeped under the curtain.

"Out the backdoor," Hattie said, pointing to the kitchen area and pulling Harper as she made her way.

"What's happening out there?" Harper asked, out of breath from fear and shock.

"The witch owed me a favor. Det. Granger should be showing up any minute. They can't get out of the shop. I put a spell on the lock. Not that they could even find the door. They are locked in."

"Det. Granger was in on this?"

Hattie shoved open the backdoor and dragged Harper into the alleyway behind the shop. "No. I made a plan with Delia earlier and I told Charlie that I'd call him if I needed him. I pretended to make a phone call but all I did was say their names. Charlie will go to Sarah who will get Det. Granger."

Harper felt completely out of the loop. "I thought Det. Granger was wiring the place for audio and video."

"He did. I hit the button he showed me to engage it when you walked in with Richie and Lola."

"How did you know?" Harper asked as they got to the end of the alleyway and took a road back to Kavanaugh in front of the shop.

Hattie smiled. "I may be old, Harper, but I saw it in the cards. You need to let people take care of you once in a while."

Harper didn't care. She threw her arms around her aunt as sirens wailed in the background. Before they reached the front of the shop, Det. Granger had already pulled up and was standing by the door.

"I've got the keys right here," Hattie said, waving them high in the air. "We've caught them and even got them to confess."

Det. Granger looked down at the ground as the fog seeped out of the shop to the sidewalk. "What is all this?"

Hattie laughed. "Don't ask questions you don't want answers to. Just accept our little gift and be grateful."

Chapter Forty-Five

Two nights later, they all gathered in Hattie's shop and she told Sarah and Jackson what had happened with Richie and Lola. Det. Granger looked on as she explained. "You should have seen Harper's face," she said, laughing and smacking her knee. "Harper looked terrified."

"I was terrified!" Harper emphasized. "I didn't want to bring Richie and Lola here because I worried what they might do to you. I knew the necklace and diamonds weren't here, and it was too early for Det. Granger to have arrived. I was worried for your safety." Harper reached over and squeezed her aunt's hand. "I can see you had it all under control."

"That's because I thought your plan to meet Marco was misguided."

"It probably was, but I didn't know what else to do." Harper turned to Det. Granger. "What happens now?"

Hattie had wondered the same. They hadn't had an update since Det. Granger opened the shop door and pulled out a fearful and disoriented Richie and Lola.

Det. Granger took a sip of his coffee and explained. "Thanks to Hattie and Harper we got a recorded confession from both Richie and Lola. We assume they will plead guilty and are both looking at a lifetime in prison. Even though it was Richie who pulled the trigger, Lola conspired on all three murders. I can't imagine she will ever see freedom again."

"How does that make you feel?" Hattie asked Harper.

"Sort of numb." Harper stayed quiet for a moment and then seemed to choose her words carefully. "I never wanted revenge on her. I wanted her and Nick to leave me alone. No child should have to grow up without their mother, but Lola made the choices she did."

Sarah winced. "What will happen with Nick?"

"Nick gave me a statement about the initial insurance fraud scheme with the necklace and is willing to testify against George Lennox so he won't face any jail time in New York," Det. Granger explained. "The cops up there said he served his time for past deeds and is a free man. They appreciated the information he was willing to share about it all."

They all turned to look at Harper. "All I know is that Nick is going back to New York to raise his daughter on his own. We said goodbye last night," she said evenly. "Nick knows there is no hope for reconciliation and he said he's happy to be free of the De Luca family."

"What about Marco?" Jackson asked.

Harper shrugged and pointed to Det. Granger.

"Marco gave me a statement when we picked him up at the airport. He denied knowing anything about the murders. I think he was in shock that his cousin and sister could turn on him like that. I know the New York Police Department will be questioning him about the insurance fraud, but that's out of our jurisdiction. I didn't have a reason to detain him and the NYPD didn't request any assistance with that. Marco left to go back to New York right after. He didn't even want to speak to Lola or Richie. He said he'd make arrangements to bring Brendan's body back to New York and left it at that."

Hattie reached out to Harper. "Does it feel like a chapter closed?"

Harper sighed. "More than it had before. I do feel bad that Nick is now a single parent. I'm not sure he's equipped. I imagine his family will help him though."

Sarah raised her eyebrows and looked over at Jackson. "What about

Cora?"

"I can't say that we left things on as good terms as Nick and Harper, but it went better than I expected. She still thinks I'll come to my senses and go back to her. She won't accept that I've moved on, but at least she left."

"Where is she going?" Hattie asked.

"Don't know. Don't care," Jackson said with an edge of frustration in his voice. "I'll pay the alimony I have to pay, but other than that, I've washed my hands of her and hope my family has as well."

"You don't have to worry about me!" Sarah said. "I'm glad she's gone."

Jackson moved in the chair to get comfortable. "Let's move on to other more important subjects."

Hattie handed Jackson the plate of cookies. "Take another. It will help you heal faster. How's the ankle?"

Jackson grabbed one of the cookies and took a bite. "I'm up and around now. That's progress. I couldn't stand being in the house any longer with Harper looking at me like I might cry at any moment."

Harper smiled at him. "I hated that you got hurt."

"It will heal. In the meantime, I can catch up on rest."

"Retired life must be so exhausting," Det. Granger teased.

Jackson chuckled. "Something like that."

"This all seemed to wrap up nicely then. Even I had my doubts," Hattie said and leaned back in her chair. She looked at Det. Granger and Sarah and then at Jackson and Harper. Both couples looked completely enamored with each other. She resisted the urge to ask where the relationships were headed. Hattie knew they'd both evolve and she was excited for them for the time ahead.

Hattie sat back and enjoyed how happy everyone was until she caught the stern expression on her niece's face as Harper stared out the front window of the shop. "What do you see?" she asked.

"I'm not sure," Harper said, standing. She went to the window and peered out. After a moment, she let out a loud groan. "It's girls I went to high school with, but I have no idea why they'd be here in Little Rock." Harper looked back at the table. "I wouldn't say they bullied me, but they went out of their way to be nasty to me all the time."

"I can't imagine anyone being that way to you," Sarah said.

Hattie raised her eyebrows. "Is it the sinister sisters?" When all eyes turned to Hattie, she explained. "There were three girls who were awful to Harper in high school. No matter what she did, they'd give her a hard time. They would purposefully exclude Harper from weekend plans. Then when Harper would make plans with other friends instead, they'd say Harper thought she was better than everyone. It was like they wanted her to sit home feeling bad she hadn't been invited. No matter what Harper did, they had something to say. If they were mean and Harper remained quiet, they'd say she had an anger issue. If Harper argued back, she was sensitive and didn't have a sense of humor. Harper and I started calling them the sinister sisters for fun."

Harper frowned at the memory. "It's stupid high school things that happened more than twenty years ago, but I figured I would never have to see them again. I avoided them in Manhattan. I think one of them moved away after college. Either way, just strange seeing them here."

As Harper watched them out the window, she balled her fists tightly. As she did, the lights in the shop flickered.

Hattie pointed to her. "You did that, Harper, with your energy. You're going to need to control yourself before you cause a blackout in the whole city."

Jackson laughed. "Oh, here comes trouble."

Harper relaxed her body and left the windows. She went to Jackson and wrapped her arms around him, kissing him gently on the cheek. "I'm over it. It was just weird seeing them together after all this time."

Hattie knew Harper believed what she said, but it wasn't going to be that simple. Hattie could feel it in her bones. Harper's power was growing stronger than ever and a confrontation with the three of them might have some unintended results.

Hattie took a sip of her tea. "Let's hope they are only here for a short time and gone before we know it." Hattie said the words but knew that wouldn't be the case. Jackson was right – here comes trouble.

About the Author

Stacy M. Jones was born and raised in Troy, New York, and currently lives in Little Rock, Arkansas. She is a full-time writer and holds masters' degrees in journalism and in forensic psychology. She currently has three series available for readers: paranormal women's fiction/cozy Harper & Hattie Magical Mystery Series, the hard-boiled Riley Sullivan Mystery Series and the FBI Agent Kate Walsh Thriller Series. To access Stacy's Mystery Readers Club with three free novellas, one for each series, visit StacyMJones.com.

You can connect with me on:
- http://www.stacymjones.com
- https://twitter.com/SMJonesWriter
- https://www.facebook.com/StacyMJonesWriter
- https://www.bookbub.com/profile/stacy-m-jones
- https://www.goodreads.com/StacyMJonesWriter

Subscribe to my newsletter:

✉ http://www.stacymjones.com

Also by Stacy M. Jones

Read Harper & Hattie Book #6 - The Sinister Sisters

Access the Free Mystery Readers' Club Starter Library
Riley Sullivan Mystery Series novella "The 1922 Club Murder"
FBI Agent Kate Walsh Thriller Series novella "The Curators"
Harper & Hattie Mystery Series novella "Harper's Folly"

Sign up for the starter library along with launch-day pricing, special behind-the-scenes access, and extra content. Hit subscribe at http://www.stacymjones.com/

Please leave a review for The Witches Code. Reviews help more readers find my books. Thank you!

Other books by Stacy M. Jones by series and order to date:

FBI Agent Kate Walsh Thriller Series
The Curators
The Founders
Miami Ripper

PI Riley Sullivan Mystery Series
The 1922 Club Murder
Deadly Sins
The Bone Harvest
Missing Time Murders
We Last Saw Jane
Boston Underground

The Night Game

Harper & Hattie Magical Mystery Series
Harper's Folly
Saints & Sinners Ball
Secrets to Tell
Rule of Three
The Forever Curse
The Witches Code
The Sinister Sisters

The Sinister Sisters

When Harper Ryan is confronted with bullies from her past, disaster unfolds – one of them is murdered and the other two are hiding secrets that might be the key to it all. With questions lingering over how Harper found the woman's body, she has no choice but to find the real killer.

Harper must rely on the help of her psychic-medium Aunt Hattie and find a way to control her powers that are shattering lightbulbs and sending objects across the room the more her anger surges.

Throw in the ghost of the victim, two angry local chefs, and the legend of a cookbook worth millions, the two unlikely sleuths have to uncover a web of betrayal and harassment to bring a killer to justice. Will they succeed or will the killer slip through their fingers?

Made in the USA
Las Vegas, NV
28 June 2024

91615015R00163